THAT BLOODY BOOK

A novel by

Tony Flower

An Authors OnLine Book

Text Copyright © Tony Flower 2012

Cover design by Siobhan Smith ©

British Library Cataloguing Publication Data.
A catalogue record for this book is available from the British Library

ISBN 978-0-7552-0706-0

Authors OnLine Ltd
19 The Cinques
Gamlingay, Sandy
Bedfordshire SG19 3NU
England

This book is also available in e-book format, details of which are available at www.authorsonline.co.uk

To Jo, Clare and Sean.

Acknowledgements

I would like to thank the following people, without whom 'That Bloody Book' wouldn't be the fascinating tale that you hold before you:

My good friends Ralph Baker, Richard Packer, Alan Rensch and Mark White – we can now hold a conversation without fear that I'm going to steal your best lines and anecdotes (until the next time!!).

My old mate Paul Bethell, whose positive feedback and encouragement has kept me going till the end. You should share some of the blame for unleashing this monster.

Dave Slade – the inebriated influence behind the stag weekend sequence. Never stop singing Dave.

Claire Steele, whose early advice to this novice writer pointed him in the right direction (I think).

My fellow author Tom Bromley, without whom I wouldn't be happy using the term: 'my fellow author'. Thanks Tom, I hope you agree that, with the help of your input, it's an improvement on the first draft!!

Perfectionist proof reader Phil Clinker.

Old friends, girlfriends, work colleagues, bosses and acquaintances – any resemblances to persons living or dead etc…

The many singers, songwriters and musicians who feature throughout – the world would be a poorer place without your ability to interpret our deepest emotions. You are, of course, also responsible for embarrassing the world's children, by encouraging their mums and dads to dance!!

And finally, to my family – my wonderful wife and amazing children; my late Father whom I still miss; my gracious Mother; and my Brother and Sister. You have all contributed to the character of the man who wrote this book – for better or worse!!

1. Get Down Tonight

Maybe, had the tea leaves foretold of the terrifying adventure ahead instead of just nicking his bike, then Joe Stamford would have been more satisfied with his lot; but then again, maybe not. For then he would have had no story to tell.

The millennium had recently passed without incident; the threat that all the computers would crash on the stroke of midnight 1999 and bring everything to a standstill was unfulfilled. The world still turned and, as far as he could tell, nothing had changed.

He'd always felt uncomfortable in his quest to climb the lower rungs of the career ladder, but, by the age of forty-two, had somehow reached the dizzy heights of Facilities Manager at the Bank's Administrative Office, achieving his promotion through competence at his job, his amenable nature and a reputation for integrity, honesty and diplomacy. All qualities of which he was justly proud, but he soon felt out of his depth when it came to dealing with the moods and idiosyncrasies of Idle Ian, Bullshitting Bob and Femme Fatale Felicity.

He could feel the resentment of the colleagues he used to call his mates, some of whom had been in residence far longer than he and had also applied for the job. It was evident that he'd lost their respect when he overheard one of his charges make the observation that he was a short-arsed, bald-headed old git, a technically accurate description that he'd heard variations of before, but one that he thought didn't require reiteration.

Stuck twixt workers and the upper echelons, the extra few quid in the wage packet seemed scant reward for the inherent hassle and isolation that the role commanded; but escape was elusive, as he realised too late that he'd turned into the very person he used to hold in contempt - a corporate puppet, too scared to speak out or get out for fear of losing status and money.

His once modest ambition faded, he'd reached the stage where he no longer wanted to play the game. Still, the game ground on regardless.

Joe sometimes wished he could travel back in time, back to where he came from, back to basics, to when he could still hold his father's hand, to when he knew who he was, before his world turned sweet and sour, and before he came to inhabit this extraordinary tale. If he knew then what he knew now, would he have done anything differently?

... Joe wistfully recalled the simplicity of his first job, the blistering summer of '76, fresh out of school, naïve and ignorant in the ways of the working world. He took his first faltering steps into adult territory having gained few academic achievements, the school careers officer recommending that he try the local printing and binding factory. A time of relatively low unemployment in complacently Conservative Buckinghamshire saw fresh factory fodder a sought after commodity by local industry; the interview a formality, Joe had no trouble in securing the job. 'You start Monday,' said the nice man from Personnel.

His first impressions, upon entering the imposing Victorian monstrosity of a building, were of the sheer size of the place and of the stifling heat. These were the days before any consideration was given to the comfort of the workforce. The factory appeared to be a living organism, the noisy, black, oily machinery its heart, lungs, guts, the workers its life blood, busily servicing the essential organs.

He was to work on the guillotine, its purpose not as a tool of revolution designed to dispose of the aristocracy, but merely there to trim the edges off bound books prior to their transportation to another machine to be covered. After a brief demonstration, he took his position at the end of the conveyer belt as the knives descended with a thud and cut the books to the required size. His throat dry due to first-day nerves and from the paper dust that filled the stagnant air, he prepared for action as the results of some no doubt brilliant author's labours came hurtling along the conveyer towards him. Clumsily, he grabbed the small pile of books and transferred them to the pallet, as instructed; but, as he turned to repeat the manoeuvre, the second pile of books came crashing to the floor. Chris and Michael, the veteran machine operators, looked on in dismay as Joe scrabbled around to pick them up and, watching their hard-earned productivity bonus disappear, they reluctantly agreed to slow down the machine until he could get up to speed.

By the end of a fatiguing day he had finally managed to master the necessary rhythm and, to the casual observer, the whole process gave the appearance of being choreographed. There's got to be more to life than this, thought a thoroughly exhausted Joe as he clocked out. His first working day over, he vowed never to return.

'How did it go?' enquired Dad, peering over his pile of fish and chips.

'I'm not doing that for a living. I'm not going back,' replied Joe; the longest conversation they'd had for a while. By the end of the meal, however, Dad had somehow persuaded him to stick it out until he could find alternative employment. Dinner had provided some light relief, with Dad shaking the inadequately tightened bottle of HP Sauce all over his white shirt.

Meals were invariably eaten around the Formica-covered kitchen table on stools made by Joe's ever-resourceful father: death traps that would collapse if sat on the wrong way round, leaving the occupant in an embarrassed heap on the floor as laughter resounded. Nothing was ever thrown away in Joe's house and Dad could find a use for every piece of wood or left-over nail and screw; his self-built shed was immaculate, with a place for everything from the largest tool to the smallest washer, and he could fix anything. The house, tastefully decorated throughout in pale green and beige, would never witness the fashion revolution that was 1970s wallpaper.

Joe's dad was a proud man, brought up pre-World War Two on the Victorian values that he'd tried in vain to pass on to Joe and his much older brother and sister. Joe's mum and dad hadn't planned the huge age gap between Joe and his siblings, and he was considered to be a happy accident, never really meant to exist.

He had a grudging respect for his old man and for his generation, those brave men who had fought in the war but would never talk about the gory detail. Derisive comments, made during what Joe thought of as classic war films, were the closest he got to any insight as to what his dad had been through. 'What nonsense, the glorification of war; that's tomato ketchup, not blood. Real war is hell on earth, the loss of thousands of lives just for a few hundred yards of mud.'

After the war, the newly-married Mr and Mrs Stamford had moved from bomb-ravaged London to a quiet market town in the Home Counties at the behest of the Company, just one of many towns expanding rapidly to accommodate the London overspill. From relatively humble beginnings, Dad had worked hard to support his family, to maintain their three-bed semi, and there was to be no argument: he was the breadwinner, this was his responsibility, the undisputed way of the world. Mum was the true rock of the family, keeping house and home together, food always on the table at the right time, the ever-patient mediator in any disputes.

Upon hearing Joe's complaints about his first day at work, Dad had shown little sympathy. 'You don't know you're born. Conditions were far worse when I was young; the Unions fought so you could have a cushy life and do you appreciate it? Do you hell. You should try working down the pit, then you'd know real hardship, lad.'

As far as Joe knew, Dad had never worked down the pit, so

attributed this latest tirade to the fact that he had opinions on most things. Suitably admonished, Joe was back at work on Tuesday.

'Wasn't expecting to see you today,' said Chris. 'We had a small wager that you would be too knackered to get out of bed.'

'Thought he was too good for us more like,' sneered Michael, as if Joe wasn't there. 'He won't last the week.'

Chris and Michael survived the monotony of their jobs with constant, often hilarious banter: the Eric and Ernie of the factory floor, helping everyone to get through the day. When not batting wit back and forth, they would spend their time ruthlessly lampooning the hapless Stan, whose job it was to ensure the continuity of supply of books between the machines. A well-liked but simple soul, Stan could never escape their relentless put downs.

One such exchange saw Chris and Michael discussing the case of a discredited doctor who had recently been the scandalous subject of local headlines after conducting an affair with a patient. Stan appeared part way through their conversation and enquired, 'Dr who?'

Still he couldn't quite hear over the noise of the factory and asked again, 'Which doctor?'

Poor Stan was bemused and baffled by their uncontrollable laughter as he conscientiously pushed his pallet truck away.

Chris, in his early twenties, was free, single and good looking, with *de rigueur* Kevin Keegan perm and angular sideburns, the impressionable Joe in awe of the exaggerated stories of his sexual conquests. Inventing excuses daily to visit the office, Chris was irrevocably smitten with Teresa, the stunning secretary to the Managing Director. Smiling shyly, with hazel eyes beneath an auburn fringe, she was flattered by his attentions, but scared of his reputation.

The ever-staid Michael initially came across as a miserable bastard, but his dry humour was the perfect foil for Chris's never-ending repartee. The senior partner of the guillotine operation, long-serving Union rep and married with four kids, the sum of his parts combined to harbour a healthy cynicism. 'You're doing this for yourself and your family, lad; never forget that. The bosses wouldn't give a shit if you fell over dead into that machine and came out bound and covered.'

To both his and Joe's surprise, Joe did last the week, Friday finally arriving and bringing with it the promise of the impending weekend and a little brown envelope containing his wages. In the scheme of things it wasn't a fortune, but to Joe it meant a degree of independence and freedom from parental ransom.

His only previous income had been from pocket money and a series of paper rounds, from one of which he'd considered himself unreasonably sacked when posting half a dozen newspapers through the same letterbox. Although the dog in the cul-de-sac wasn't large, it had seemed ferocious to Joe and, having made several attempts to cycle to the houses of the intended recipients, he'd decided on the preservation of his ankles and retreated to the next street. Joe had attempted to explain the extenuating circumstances which had contributed to the demise of his previously unblemished record, but the newsagent manager was having none of it and he was unceremoniously shown the door.

But this was real work, this was the Friday of his first real wage packet and, brown envelope burning hole in pocket, he spent the short walk home excitedly considering his new-found spending options.

KC and the Sunshine Band were in town that night, all the way from Miami, Florida, and Joe quickly showered and changed in anticipation of a well-earned evening of soul and funk. He'd tried in vain to enlist the company of some of his mates, but their musical tastes contrasted sharply with his. Most were into what Joe considered to be endless, preposterous posturing - progressive rock and heavy metal. Some of the better-informed ones favoured Mott the Hoople, Roxy and Bowie, but they all treated Joe's love of reggae and soul with undisguised contempt.

His woeful efforts to get a date for the evening had been met with the usual disdainful response. He'd fancied Julie for years at school, but then again so had most of his classmates. Joe and his cohorts were not considered cool, however, and Julie and her friends moved in far more exalted circles. It had taken all of his courage to knock on her door and stutter the well thought out line 'would you like to go out with me on Friday?' It could have been considered shallow when, upon her refusal, he enquired, 'How about your sister?'

There was no way he was going to miss the sensational KC though and he reluctantly made the decision to attend his first gig alone. As he approached the venue, he saw a group of young dudes outside, laughing and enjoying each other's company. Wishing he could join in the banter, he caught a snippet of their conversation as he passed. 'So who's brought the can opener then?'

'Not me. I thought you were bringing it.'

'Give it here,' said the jovial, bearded one, and he forcefully impaled the stubborn Party Seven can upon the railings. The volume of laughter grew louder as one of them lay on his back in an attempt to catch the Vesuvius-like flow of beer.

The club was a modern, white-walled structure with little character inside or out, consisting of a ballroom, cloakroom and two smoke-filled bars, one containing the dartboard exclusive to the regular members. After a few pints of Double Diamond (the joys of real ale a thing of the past and future in the pubs and clubs of English provincial towns), Joe hit the dance floor, determined to blow away his conflicting teenage turmoil. The emotions of the day and brilliance of the band combined in a heady cocktail and Joe danced all night, like he'd never danced before. He wondered at the rhythm section, tighter than the proverbial duck's arse, at the amazing, soaring brass section and instinctively knew that he was in the presence of something special.

Inhibitions eradicated by the beer, he didn't care what he looked like to the on-looking crowd as his unco-ordinated gyrations cleared a large space on the dance floor, the wonderful life-affirming music temporarily exorcising his demons.

What a night! Smiling like an idiot and with his best Ben Sherman soaked in sweat, Joe emerged into the warm night air and made his way happily home, concluding that yes, there certainly was more to life.

2. My Generation

Joe used to be a man of simple needs, happy just spending time with his friends, listening to music, playing football and, whenever possible, attending gigs at the weekend. Still living in the town of his birth (a typical provincial combination of beautiful historical buildings and concrete architectural eyesores) and with no burning desire to move on, his philosophy was - where you are is not as important as who you are with.

The skyline was dominated by a hideous erection populated by the County Council, a blemish on the landscape that could be seen from miles around; he knew of no-one who found it pleasing on the eye. His sensible older brother Tom remembered the town as it was, before history was insensitively bulldozed and turned into a surreal, soulless Clockwork Orange backdrop. 'It's a travesty; why didn't somebody stop them? It will never be the same again.' Ultimately, Joe would come to concur with his brother's sentiments and mourn the passing of the cobbled streets he was too young to know.

At home, Joe could usually be found in his bedroom, his burgeoning record collection played as loud as he could get away with, without pissing off parents and neighbours. He would be forever indebted to his cool older sister Kate, for allowing her annoying child of a little brother to share her space and music throughout the swinging 60's. Kate had been indefinitely grounded, an illicit back-of-scooter day trip to Brighton to witness the infamous bloody battle of the

Mods and Rockers incurring the wrath of Dad. Kate's imprisonment meant more time spent with her best friend Jill, defiantly cranking up the volume in the front room, with a spellbound Joe constantly in attendance, forming his earliest memories.

With a love of Motown, Stax, Roy Orbison, the Stones, the Kinks and a plethora of iconic sixties music indelibly instilled on his psyche, he had even forgiven Kate for dropping him on his head when he was a baby. These sublime audio acorns would grow into a magnificent eclectic oak, with many branches incorporating reggae, soul, punk, new wave and rock, which would become the imperative, awesome soundtrack to his life.

By the time the diminutive Joe had started secondary school he had effectively become an only child, as his beloved brother and sister left home to embark upon family lives of their own. Role models gone, he withdrew to the lonely sanctuary of his room and his music, emerging only at meal times or when *The Likely Lads* were on TV.

Unwritten rules, forcefully wielded by his father, stifled his sense of adventure, nullified the natural risk-taking tendency of youth and delayed the inevitable lessons of his own mistakes. Like most kids of his era, he was poorly prepared for the teenage angst that was to follow: the mystery of girls and the birds and bees a fascinating, confusing, stressful distraction. A combination of a little red book supplied by Dad, old romantic pop songs and films, and the unbelievable conjecture of his peers inadequately formed Joe's sex education.

Apart from vague warnings about homosexuals and getting girls into trouble, there had been no direct advice from Dad; the little red book, of which Joe didn't get beyond the first chapter, a poor substitute for proper parental guidance. The very fact that he and his brother and sister existed presumably meant that Dad knew what went where, but the subject was never raised and questions were discouraged.

In his innocence, he was more than susceptible to the sentimental romance of the classic pop songs and Hollywood movies, conspiring to form a rose-tinted view of relationships that would take years of knock-backs and rejection to dispel. Joe genuinely believed that, if he were to walk down the street often enough, singing Do Wah Diddy Diddy Dum Diddy Do, then true love would inevitably follow.

To Joe, the juxtaposition of puritanical parents and the suggestive sexual speculation of the playground couldn't have been more profound. Ironically, the bizarre theories passed between guffawing boys and giggling girls proved to be closer to the truth, the inherent contradictions in the outlook and aspirations of the sexes evident even at that tender age.

Throughout the endless confusion, though, music was his one constant and Joe increasingly fell under the spell of its passion and its powers to soothe the turmoil of his fledgling adolescent arrogance and vulnerability.

Once, right hand dripping with blood, dizzy with shock, staggering, descending the stairs, better talk to Mum, not Dad. 'What on earth have you done?'

A frenzy induced by the Who's 'Won't Get Fooled Again' had seen an out of control teenage Joe (tennis racket as Gibson guitar, mirror as audience), attempt to imitate the frenetic windmill guitar playing of the mighty Pete Townshend, lampshade smashed to smithereens, shards of glass in hand and tendons close to severance. Music always had the ability to transport him to another place, on this occasion Accident & Emergency.

Fortunately for Joe, he lived in a place and age where his insatiable appetite for live music was amply nourished. The antidote to the sanitised miming of *Top of the Pops*, he knew nothing to compare with the buzz of a live gig and the sight of his heroes in the flesh. He could never sleep afterwards, desperately wishing the natural high to continue and never stop.

The only other pastime that Joe approached with similar intensity was football, the universal game. From tender years he could be found with a ball at his feet, whether in the garden, the playground or in the park after school.

His friend Terry was the proud owner of a misshapen bladder covered with stitched brown leather that would gain weight significantly through water absorption in inclement weather, giving it all the characteristics of a medicine ball. Who knows how many brain cells were irretrievably lost through heading this hefty sphere, the imprint of the laces that held the whole thing together indelibly impressed upon his forehead.

His scabby-kneed buddies and he had frequently been in trouble for hiding in the park beyond closing time to enable them to continue playing, often chased, caught and chastised by Smelly John the park keeper, after scaling the fence as darkness fell.

What Joe lacked in ability he more than made up for in enthusiasm and effort, covering ground and riding tackles until thoroughly exhausted. His hunger for the sport would continue into adolescence and adulthood, the physical exertion releasing the pressure, an outlet for his frustrations. Saturday afternoons and Sunday mornings would invariably find Joe in municipal parks or on village fields, pitting his wits against second division local league opposition, position reflecting his politics, keenly ploughing a furrow up and down the left wing.

To this day he will tell of a goal worthy of Pele. Latching on to a heartfelt clearance from their no nonsense centre back Sam, one touch to control, weaving gracefully between statuesque defence, edge of the area, outside of the left foot, goalkeeper stranded, ball curled majestically into the top corner. 'Would have been a contender for goal of the season if caught by the *Match of the Day* cameras'; but tragically, his moment of true genius was witnessed only by a man and his canine.

3. Do You Remember the First Time?

Love life thus far barely worthy of the name, Joe constantly deceived himself about perceived chances missed; but, despite an active mind in the fantasy department, he could never have imagined the bizarre way in which he would finally be dispossessed of his unwanted virtue.

His perspective on late seventies/early eighties Britain was that of a place of polar opposites; there was no middle ground. He despised Margaret Thatcher and her followers and considered them to be selfish social climbers concerned only with their own advancement, without a thought for others or the wider implications of their greed.

Joe's feet were planted firmly on the left, the solidarity of the Miner's Strike, Rock against Racism, the Anti-Nazi League and the Campaign for Nuclear Disarmament. From a working class, Labour-voting family, Joe liked to think of himself as radical, even further to the left than his old man.

He had been there in '78 on the six-mile RAR and ANL march from Trafalgar Square to the East End, proudly confronting the evil of the National Front. Culminating in a magnificent concert featuring the rallying calls of the Clash, Buzzcocks and Steel Pulse, the day had been a great success, Joe feeling rare optimism among kindred spirits.

Membership of CND completed the set of his provocatively worn badges, precursors of many a political argument with acquaintances and work colleagues of conflicting persuasions. He enjoyed the often heated banter, thoroughly convinced he had right on his side.

It was during one such quarrel that he announced, to much hilarity, his intention to attend a CND peace camp festival at Greenham Common. The camp had been set up as a protest against the decision of the British government to allow American Cruise missiles to be based there and, although exclusively populated by women, concessions were made to allow male visitors in some areas. On festival day, however, all supporters were invited.

'You won't get your leg over, you know, they're all bleeding lesbians,' stated Ted, playing to his usual right wing audience at Joe's expense.

'If you're lucky they might let you watch,' said Pete, with his trademark leer.

Joe argued against and thrived upon comments such as these; they made him feel different and served only to reinforce his theories and allegiances.

As it happened, he did get his leg over, although Joe would have described the unexpected liaison in more romantic terms. A truly momentous, but fleeting experience, it all happened in a blur and was over within the hour.

Thunderstorm, soaking wet, her kind offer of shelter, the overpowering aroma of canvas, incense and patchouli, his first and last joint, huddled together for warmth, spur of the moment, one thing leading to another, her piercing blue eyes, her fake dreadlocks whipping his chest, the distinctive birthmark on her bum in the shape of the United Kingdom. Joe felt both elated in the aftermath and nauseous from a mixture of lager and marijuana. Her finger to his lips, she wouldn't even reveal her name. 'Just enjoy the moment,' she said tenderly.

After staggering, still high, for what felt like hours through the mud, it seemed like a good idea at the time to attempt to climb the perimeter fence. The effect of the ganja and the knowledge that he'd finally done it combined to give him delusions of grandeur and he felt like he could conquer the world. What the hell were these Yankees doing on English soil with their missiles, making us a prime nuclear target for the Russians?

Like the stir crazy character of Ives in *The Great Escape*, he manically approached the fence and, without fear of the consequences, began to climb. Ignoring the pain in his hands from gripping the wire, he made erratic progress, nearly reaching the top, with a small crowd and a barking dog cheering him on, before he noticed the armed guard on the other side.

'Don't shoot, I come in peace,' shouted Joe, forgetting how high he was and raising his hands in the air. A frantic grab for the fence as he started to fall and his sleeve caught fast on the barbed wire, the guard grinning in amusement and shaking his head. By now a large, boisterous audience had accumulated, clapping and cheering as the fire brigade unhooked and helped him down. Taking a bow, he was roughly pushed into the back of the waiting police car and driven away.

No-one noticed the well-built hippy at the back of the crowd, observing the proceedings with curiosity. An angry scar traversed his cheek from the corner of his mouth to the lobe of his left ear. If they had taken the time to look, they would have seen that his wig was a little askew, that his kaftan was immaculate and his sandals brand new, as if recently purchased for a fancy dress party.

Spending a fitful night in the cells at Her Majesty's Pleasure before being awoken and interrogated by a seen-it-all-before detective, Joe felt decidedly dishevelled and embarrassed.

'We found this on your person, sir. Can you confirm that it is yours?' stated Officer Dibble, holding up the remnants of yesterday's spliff.

'Not mine, Officer, it must be a plant,' replied Joe, head throbbing.

'I'm sure it used to be a plant, sir, but it has been adapted for recreational use. Can you tell us where you got it?'

'Can't remember,' said Joe with a wry smile, as he started to recall the events of the previous day. Even if he had known her name, he wasn't a grass.

'You will be required to report for your court appearance in two months' time. I suggest you go home, sir, and try to live a normal life; you don't look like you belong here,' said Officer Dibble, showing him the door.

Although Joe's commitment to left-wing causes was never in doubt, he was essentially just a day tripper. He didn't have the courage to leave his comfortable existence and follow his heart. He was back at work the next day and told no-one of what had happened. They wouldn't have believed him anyway.

4. What Lack of Love Has Done

Frustrated and depressed at a continuing lack of success in relationships, Joe discussed his discontent and loss of confidence over a beer with Rockin' Robin.

'We are not who we think we are; we are what others perceive us to be,' Joe stated. He was sure someone famous had once uttered these wise words, but couldn't recall who.

'You're a bit of a wanker sometimes, but I perceive you to be a decent bloke,' replied Robin. He'd always had the ability to keep Joe's feet planted firmly on the ground by tempering any compliment with an affectionate insult.

Beer lubricating the cogs of discussion, the subject matter bounced wildly between football, music, films, relationships and politics. Robin had empathy with Joe's views on many topics, but found him too intense and opinionated when it came to politics. By this time Joe had become a Labour Party member, the natural progression from his youthful idealism. His stance aligned with the likes of Tony Benn and Michael Foot; he was dismayed and disillusioned as Margaret Thatcher rode roughshod and ruthless over all he believed in.

Robin had long been a good friend and confidant to Joe; their connections, a mutual love of music, socialising in general and taking the piss out of each other, they were inseparable, pint glass in hand, elbow on bar, a jest forever on their lips. Like most people,

Robin was much taller, cooler, more hirsute and confident than Joe. Although just a few years older, he'd been round the block a few times and was far more streetwise and experienced in the ways of the world. Robin was also there for him when at his lowest ebb, there whenever he needed someone to talk to, there when the wheels came off.

A number of work-related contributory factors had preceded Joe's breakdown, but it was Sandy that pushed him over the precipice. With little grasp on reality, he'd fallen helplessly for her obvious charms and, when he wasn't in her company, she was in his thoughts, day and night.

They had met at a party and Sandy, a waitress at Valentino's, the upmarket Italian in town, was the friend of an acquaintance's girlfriend. If he could have created a vision it would have been Sandy: her long blonde hair, blue eyes, inviting smile and perfect legs awakened longings never before felt in such intensity. Inevitably surrounded by would-be suitors, Joe would have to wait patiently for his chance.

He told her that she could be a model, not as a tactic lacking in originality designed to win her affections, but because it was true. She replied by recounting a somewhat discouraging recent experience. A well-dressed customer at Valentino's, purporting to be the proprietor of a modelling agency, had handed her his card and smiled, 'No pressure, love, just give me a call if you want to talk about a free trial photo shoot.'

Enlisting the moral support of Stacey, her fellow waitress, they had eventually located the seedy back street studio, entered warily and climbed the rickety stairs to the second floor. As the photographer had put her at ease, Sandy felt relaxed. She'd dressed for the occasion in her tightest jeans and a simple white t-shirt. Click. 'You're a natural,' he'd said. Click. 'Are you sure you've not done this before?' Click.

At the end of the session the man she'd met at Valentino's admired the results and selected the best pictures. 'These are good, you have potential,' he'd stated, looking her up and down as if deep in thought. 'We make movies here too; it pays well if you're interested.'

'What kind of movies?' she'd replied, shifting uneasily in her chair as the penny dropped.

'We just film you having fun; if your friend wants to join in we pay treble,' he'd said, glancing at Stacey with a lustful grin. 'Sandy and Stacey, you could be stars.'

'Er, we'll think about it and let you know,' Sandy had replied, blushing. Making their excuses, they'd escaped, running as fast as their heels would allow, laughing uncontrollably as they entered the coffee bar, attracting stares of approval and disapproval from the early evening punters. Sandy's modelling career was over before it began.

Although this was the post-punk era, Joe's feelings for Sandy had reawakened his unashamed weakness for late fifties/early sixties teenage love songs, Billy Fury's 'Halfway to Paradise' being particularly pertinent to his predicament. In this sentimental world, Joe's doe-eyed obsession and pursuit should have melted Sandy's heart and, convinced that he was in love, he planned meticulously to ensure that their social circles collided whenever possible. Eventually, his dogged perseverance wore down her resistance and with unbridled enthusiasm she sighed, 'Oh, OK, then,' and agreed to meet him for a drink.

Trendy wine bars were not Joe's natural habitat, but in an effort to impress he'd suggested the Grape Vine. For once he felt good, basking in her radiance, enjoying the envious glances of the usual clientele. He could tell what they were thinking: 'What the hell is *she* doing with him?'

And that was all, one date, ruthlessly unrequited, over before it had begun; he would never get to know the real Sandy. At the end of the evening Joe had clumsily expressed his undying love and Sandy, feeling both embarrassed and sympathetic, had said, 'Sorry, I don't feel that way; we can only ever be friends.' These were the words that passed her lips, but her expression had said it all: 'You must be joking!!'

With yet another broken heart inadvertently added to her collection, Sandy had insisted on making her own way home.

Devastated and disconsolate, Joe returned to his permanently empty house and hopelessly consumed a bottle of whiskey whilst weeping incessantly to Tom Waits' 'Blue Valentines', predictably washed down in the early hours by Bruce Springsteen's 'Sandy'. He didn't normally drink spirits or drink alone, but felt the occasion warranted this despondent gesture.

How could she be so cruel? His heart shattered by one sentence so casually uttered. In his fantasy world he'd planned their future: they would walk on a Caribbean beach as the sun went down, they would watch the fishing boats disappear over the horizon as the sun rose, her long hair cascading over his shoulder in their own paradise; they would be together forever.

The Sandy of Joe's dreams, however, wasn't real. He'd created a mythical persona to fit a life that he longed for, a life and lover that didn't and never would exist. Why would one so perfect even look twice at a pathetic wretch like him?

A broken man, the years of accumulated rejection and disdain mixed with the whiskey in a lethal cocktail. Romance was dead; from now on his heart would be cold, as impenetrable and uncaring as of those who had cast him aside without a thought.

The rebound was severe as Joe became hardened, suppressing his pain. He had but one aim: shallow, casual sex, and he cared little who with. For years he'd watched men who projected an aura of insensitive bravado succeed where he'd failed; he would change his tactics and to hell with the consequences.

Robin attempted to make the dejected, angry man see sense. 'Pull yourself together. You're acting as if you're going through a divorce; you only went out once, for God's sake.'

'I'd prefer if it was a divorce,' replied Joe, inconsolable; 'at least our relationship would have been consummated.'

'There was no relationship, you prat; she didn't want to know, remember? Here's some good advice that my old man gave me - if you fall off the horse, get straight back on and try again. Go and find someone who's interested and maybe try some lower fences next time. You were out of your league; Sandy could have anyone she wants.'

Rebecca was in the wrong place at the wrong time, the unwitting victim of Joe's new-found cynicism; she didn't deserve his insincerity. As mixed up, battered and bruised by previous experiences as he, she was searching for love and compassion, but found only insensitivity and despair.

The weekly singles night at the edge-of-town estate community centre drew together the lonely and dispossessed: divorcees, widows, widowers, the socially inept and unlucky, some looking for love, some just for companionship and, on that fateful night, the desperate Rebecca and Joe. Rebecca was not the kind of girl that he normally went for, but behind the hardened-to-the-world façade there was a mischievous glint in her eye that, in his fragile and desperate state, attracted Joe. Walking her home, he was invited in for coffee and the inevitable followed, as sure as night follows day.

A disastrous collision of volatile worlds, this desperate liaison would last a mere four months. They rarely ventured out or socialised, a mutual depression their only company. He met her family only once, her domineering, scary father and vicious-looking skinhead brother viewing him with threatening, justified suspicion.

Most of their time was spent at Rebecca's flat, among the empty bottles, discarded pizza boxes and a kitchen sink full with neglected washing-up. The broken washing machine resulted in an overflowing laundry basket and a stale, musty smell prevailed, despite Joe's insistence on open windows. The resultant draughts meant more time than was healthy spent in the soft and warm territory of her bed, their only common ground.

Gradually, he remorsefully began to see the error of his ways. This wasn't the real Joe. He wasn't really this uncaring bastard, indifferent to the feelings of others, taking what he wanted without pity. He must end this now, before they got in too deep.

Usually at the receiving end, a new and uncomfortable experience, he'd never dumped anyone before. 'I'm sorry, I want to end it, I don't think we have a future,' he stammered, not knowing what her reaction would be. He was ill prepared for what followed.

'Your timing's immaculate,' she sobbed. 'I did the test this morning. You're going to be a dad.'

'Ah, that changes things,' he replied in shock.

'How does it change things? Do you want to stay now? Do you think I still want you now you've told me you don't love me?' she shouted, beating his chest with her fists.

'I'll help; tell me what you want me to do,' he said, feeling pathetic, guilty and responsible.

'I want you to fuck off. I don't need your help,' she screamed, tears in full flow as she opened the door. 'I'll manage on my own. Now get out, leave me alone and don't come back.'

The door, and any tenuous bond they had, slammed firmly shut behind him. Stunned and head spinning, Joe headed for Robin's and knocked loudly on his door.

'What the hell do you want at this time of night?' said a weary looking Robin, ready for bed. 'You look like shit; what in the name of God has happened?'

Joe didn't expect or deserve sympathy. 'You dickhead, haven't you heard of contraception?' chided Robin in disbelief.

'Never had much use for it before. I always found that being an ugly bastard did the trick,' answered Joe resentfully. He knew he'd been reckless and irresponsible, but that's how he had felt at the time. Besides, it takes two to tango, he told himself; he wasn't the only one who hadn't taken precautions.

Despite his willingness to accept responsibility, Rebecca wouldn't answer her door or his calls. He wanted to talk; apart from anything else, there were practicalities to discuss. Months passed; eventually a quiet, sad voice at the end of the phone.

'How are you?' he asked, genuinely concerned.

'I've had a miscarriage, you're off the hook,' she replied. He knew that she'd been drinking heavily and wondered if that had contributed.

'I'm so sorry,' he whimpered, as she hung up.

He wasn't able to grieve for their lost child. He didn't feel he had the right to.

Poor company and miserable, his friends tried in vain to cheer him up, but a melancholy mood prevailed as he said his goodbyes at the end of the evening.

'We're going for a curry,' said Fat Frank; 'come and join us.'

'No thanks, I'm not in the mood,' replied Joe. 'I've spoilt your evening enough already; you don't want to look at my sad face.'

He had always felt safe on the streets of his home town and, despite increasing reports of muggings and casual violence, thought nothing of embarking on the late night twenty minute walk home. He knew he should stick to the main roads, but Lowbridge Road formed a significant shortcut; besides, winter was in his bones, his bladder was full to bursting and he wanted to get home as quickly as possible.

Glancing over his shoulder at the two men a hundred yards behind, he wasn't too concerned; they were just like he, returning home after an evening out. Lifting his collar against the cold, he quickened his pace, but the two men must have been walking even faster. As their footsteps came closer he moved aside to let them pass. A shattering blow knocked him to the ground. What had hit him? Was it a fist, or a blunt instrument? His hand to the back of his head, he felt the blood seeping from what felt like a large wound.

'What do you want?' he said, looking up fearfully. 'I only have a few quid on me. If you're that desperate, take it and leave me alone.'

'We don't want your money, scum' scorned the larger of the two men, as the first boot struck. Their faces covered, they looked terrifying, a ruthless hatred in their eyes. Protecting his head with his arms, Joe had never felt such pain as the first of his ribs smashed and his stomach exploded with the agony. The brutal onslaught continued for what seemed like forever as Joe pleaded for mercy. 'Please, please stop,' he cried, as he felt the world slipping away.

Waking up, head and body throbbing, everything blurred and white, light shining in his half-closed eyes, a hazy figure in a white coat before him. Where was he?

'You've taken quite a beating,' said the doctor. 'You have three cracked ribs, a cut to the head and severe bruising, but luckily there doesn't appear to be any internal injuries. We'll keep you in tonight for observation. Are you up to talking to the police?'

As he spoke to the young officer it all started to come back to him. 'They jumped me from behind,' he said. 'I didn't stand a chance; they didn't want my money, though.'

'If they didn't take anything, sir, do you know what their motive may have been?'

'Not a clue,' replied Joe, wincing from the pain in his ribs. 'I guess it's just some people's idea of a good night out.'

'They left you for dead, sir. Can you give me descriptions of the perpetrators?'

He paused, thinking. 'Sorry, it was too dark,' he lied.

Just before losing consciousness, he'd resigned himself to a deserved beating and possibly worse. In the glow of the street light he had recognised the tattoo. S-P-U-R writ roughly across Neanderthal knuckles, the final S concealed in the clenched fist. Rebecca's brother.

"Esteemed Plastic Surgeon Dr Kirsty Connor - The Best in Her Field" the towering man had read in the medical journal before making his appointment at the plush private hospital. Now, sitting in the corner of the waiting room, he felt ashamed of his apprehension as he observed the once pretty little girl with severe burns, laughing and joking with her parents. His effort at a lopsided smile immediately halted her laughter and the girl cowered fearfully against her father.

The man looked away and with relief was called for his consultation.

Soon at ease in the assured presence of the expert Dr Connor, he relaxed as she ran through the procedure. He took a deep breath as she gently stroked her finger along his scar. It had been years since he'd felt the warm, gentle hand of a woman on his face, his disfigurement and the unpredictability of his job rendering relationships difficult to kindle and maintain. Her feathery touch invoked nothing but sorrow and emptiness.

'We could do a pretty good job on this,' she reassured him; 'would have been easier if I'd been able to work on it immediately after the incident, but nevertheless you'd be almost as good as new.'

'I'll have a think about it and let you know,' he said. 'Thank you for your time.'

He knew he couldn't go through with it. Despite his employers' promise to pay for the operation, he'd grown accustomed to his scar. It was an integral part of him and the way in which he'd received it had contributed significantly to his character. He walked purposefully from the hospital and returned alone to his clandestine world.

5. Even the Losers

It was a long time before Joe was able to face the unfathomable world of romance again, body and spirit bruised and beaten, until a fateful meeting reignited the flame, soothed the pain. Ironically, Joe found true love when he didn't care any more; the pedestal upon which he'd previously placed his objects of desire well and truly collapsed, along with his self-esteem and fragile optimism.

Just as he'd resigned himself to a life of bachelorhood, a chance meeting on the 19.27 from Marylebone changed his life forever. Louise lit up the carriage and Joe noticed her as soon as he boarded the crowded train, taking the only seat available opposite her. His life could so easily have taken a very different track. He'd reached the train with just half a minute to spare, breathing heavily and perspiring profusely. Louise barely looked up from her newspaper as Joe wedged himself apologetically between two expensive, resentful pinstriped suits.

He didn't mind these occasional work visits to London, they provided brief respite from the stifling daily routine, but was glad he didn't have to do it every day. He'd often congratulated himself on not accepting a previous opportunity to enter the rat race. It would have meant a twenty per cent pay rise plus benefits, but he'd opted for work/life balance long before the phrase had become fashionable. Whenever he did venture to the capital he felt vindicated as he looked at the grey, inexpressive faces of the regular commuters, enduring at least a twelve-hour shift once their uncomfortable journey to and from the office had been added to their extended working day.

In his rush to catch the train there had been insufficient time to purchase a paper, so Joe contented himself with surreptitiously glancing at the sports page on the back of Louise's, the predominant story being Brian Clough's retirement as Nottingham Forest manager after eighteen years in charge. A sad end to a brilliant career, Joe thought, ending as it did in relegation.

As they left the city, Joe reflected on the uniformity of the suburbs and, as he often did on long train journeys, invented fictional lives for the people around him. Both the pinstriped suits worked in the city: the one to his left, reading a report on his Bank's share portfolio, would continue to work late into the night and catch the early train back to the city in the morning. His wife was having an affair because Emily and Joshua were now at boarding school and her husband was never there.

The immaculately power-dressed, confident looking lady across the aisle was in Fashion and her boyfriend would be a rugby-playing hunk with a career in Insurance. They both liked to say that they worked hard and played hard.

Gradually the carriage became less crowded as these strangers to whom Joe had attributed assumed stereotypical lives disembarked into the evening drizzle. Eventually, just he and Louise remained in the immediate vicinity. She had a permanently mysterious and deep expression and, much as he tried, Joe couldn't make up her life story. Deep brown eyes like pools of Bourneville and dark hair with flowing curls that rested naturally on her shoulders, she reminded Joe a little of Linda Ronstadt on the cover of 'Hasten Down the Wind'. He'd recently been scornfully questioned by friends about his ownership of this piece of bland, lightweight country rock and had simply shown them the cover. What more was there to say?

If Louise hadn't dropped her lipstick after unnecessarily

embellishing those luscious lips, their ships would probably have passed in the night and he would have returned unfulfilled and none the wiser to his drab existence. As he retrieved it from beneath his seat and handed it back, her smile of thanks immediately had Joe hooked, floundering like a fish out of water. He must think of something to say; she's gorgeous, he can't just say nothing.

'Going far?' he blurted out, realising immediately that, even taking into account a lifetime of crap chat up lines, this wasn't one of his finest.

'All the way,' she replied, suppressing a snigger and blushing as she realised what she had just said.

'I assume you mean to the end of the line. Me too,' said Joe, laughing.

After introductions and a mutually embarrassed hand shake, to his amazement the conversation flowed. Talking (and mostly listening) to Louise seemed to be the most natural thing in the world. She had taken the day off from her job as manager of a local hairdressing salon to visit her younger sister in Kensington. Her sister was recovering from yet another broken heart and Louise was there, as always, to offer moral support and prevent her from consuming the entire contents of her well-stocked wine rack in one day. They had stopped at a bottle and a half each and Joe realised that she was still slightly inebriated, the explanation dawning as to why she was even talking to him in the first place.

It transpired that they lived little more than half a mile apart and that they had attended the same school, albeit she six years later than he. How had fate so cruelly kept their paths from crossing when they lived so close and had so much in common?

The drizzle had evolved to torrential rain as, too soon, the train reached their destination, the final stop on the line. Joe had arranged to meet some friends in town for a few beers, but impulsively suggested to Louise that they share the only taxi in the rank and, to his surprise, she accepted.

'Can I see you again?' enquired Joe nervously, as the taxi pulled up outside Louise's house. The response seemingly took minutes as she hesitated, deep in thought, then: 'OK, how about Friday?' – that radiant smile once again lighting up the cab as they exchanged numbers.

Joe couldn't believe his luck and, far too excited to return to his empty home, asked the driver to drop him in town, where he joined his relentlessly curious friends. For once he didn't mind the ensuing piss taking and enquiries as to the name of her guide dog; he was on cloud nine and not coming down just yet.

He later asked why she had agreed to share a taxi and a date with him. Hadn't her mum told her not to talk to strangers? 'You were so sweet,' she replied. 'I knew from the start that you were safe to be with.'

Joe had been called sweet many times in his life and usually hated it, knowing from painful experience that sweet didn't get the girls – they preferred danger and unpredictability. Louise, though, had suffered a series of abusive relationships and was thoroughly sick of tolerating men who treated her like shit. She was looking for sweet and, for once, sweet was a good thing to be.

A mutual love of Indian food determined the venue for their first date and, as it was a regular haunt for Joe, the Balti Palace treated them like prince and princess. Initial nerves dispelled by a half decent bottle of red, their easy conversation continued from where they'd finished on the train. By the end of the evening Joe was in no doubt: it was love, and this time it was the real thing.

Despite the thankfully unfulfilled threats of dismemberment from Louise's thug of an ex, Hulk Henry ('Don't worry, he only hits girls,' Louise had reassured him), the next two years were the happiest of Joe's so far modest existence, their combined disposable income sufficient to fund regular nights out and some blissful holidays.

They both loved the romance of Italy: swimming in Lake Garda by day; the wonderful restaurant overlooking the lake by night, where they shared spaghetti like the lovelorn spaniels in *Lady and the Tramp*; and the never-to-be-forgotten day trip to majestic Venice, to which they swore one day to return.

Then to New England, USA, where they spent uncomplicated hours walking on the golden sands of the unspoilt beaches of Cape Cod; the choppy boat trip to Martha's Vineyard, with Louise throwing up vociferously over the side throughout; and the obligatory visit to the site of the first Pilgrim landings.

They took cable cars to stunning mountain views in Austria, Joe overcoming his fear of heights in the process; then back on terra firma they cycled joyfully round the flat bits and picnicked on a row boat in the middle of the deserted lake, surrounded by snow-topped mountains.

It was here, between mouthfuls of apple strudel and sips of dry white cooled in the lake, that Louise accepted Joe's clumsy proposal, nearly capsizing the boat in his painful attempt to go down on one knee. She was contented with this ostensibly unremarkable man, their long, lingering love a stark contrast to the testosterone-fuelled, insensitive lunges of her former relationships.

Ignoring his married friends' pleas of 'don't do it, you fool, it all changes once you're hitched', plans were made for the following May. The wedding, initially intended to be a small affair, grew into a behemoth of enormous proportions. 'If you invite Barbara and Jim, you've got to invite Bob and Sue,' she said, as they rang up another grand on the bill.

When the big day finally arrived, Louise inevitably looked stunning as she glided gracefully down the aisle, and Joe spent the day in a happy daze, smiling and wholeheartedly agreeing with the innumerable people who told him that he was a lucky bastard. Louise's father and best man Robin both agreed that it was about bloody time and Joe survived the speeches relatively unscathed, despite Robin's amusing summing up of Joe's hitherto disastrous love life.

The day passed too quickly and, as well as their close circle, a plethora of rarely seen relatives and friends wished them luck as they embarked upon the rocky, unpredictable voyage of marriage. They waved excitedly as the car drove them to the start of their future together, a future that not even the most vivid of imaginations could have predicted.

6. A Beautiful Morning

No two ways about it, the eventual arrival of Louise and Joe's wonderful, miracle first born proved to be a life-changing experience. Previously, Joe had always yawned disdainfully as radiant new parents expounded upon the delights of parenthood; but he now emphatically understood. Unconsciously, he would become one of them, boring anyone who would listen, about the colour of the poo in baby's first nappy, how tight baby could grip his finger, the sounds baby made when happy, hungry or tired.

Delirious, tears of joy rolling down his face, oblivious to the dawn chorus outside, he phoned drowsy family and friends to proudly impart the amazing news: 'It's a girl!!'

A difficult birth, Emma had taken forever to deign to enter the world, demonstrating a stubborn reluctance that would later become a character trait. Head slightly misshapen from the intrusion of the ventouse (no doubt a significant advancement in medical science, but to Joe it seemed a sink plunger could have performed the same function), she emerged pink and screaming into the early hours.

'Don't worry, in a few days the head will regain its normal shape,' said the midwife, smiling as she presented him with a miniature mother-in-law, the resemblance uncanny and decidedly unsettling. These thoughts were short lived though, as the realisation dawned that this tiny new life was totally dependent and for the first time in his life he felt useful.

Suddenly, everything was in perspective, all his trivial trials and tribulations consigned to the past. His reason for existence pre-ordained and obvious: he was put on this earth to love and protect Emma; nothing else mattered.

There followed days of walking on air, an inane grin a permanent feature as he hung baby clothes on the washing line, put the finishing touches to the nursery, learnt how to change nappies and held their beautiful daughter. Head held high, insisting on pushing the buggy, conversation consisting of Emma and little else, for a while the world was a perfect place, full of promise and possibility; no-one could take away this moment.

Inadequate paternity leave complete, Joe reluctantly returned to work with his thoughts constantly elsewhere. After living on adrenaline for the first three months, inevitably the exhaustion gradually crept up on him. Heavenly angel though she undoubtedly was, sleep appeared to be an alien concept to Emma and, however much Louise and Joe attempted to share the nocturnal burden, it was never enough. Four hours was a good night and a zombie-like Joe was neither use nor ornament in the office.

He felt bad about his previous admonishments of Late Larry. So named not, despite appearances, because he was dead, but due to his penchant for regularly turning up late for work, suitcases under his eyes and dishevelled. He had four young children, all under the age of seven, and sleep was a rare luxury. 'You know what it's like now,' laughed a surprisingly magnanimous Larry, as Joe rolled in late again with shirt buttons misaligned and tie crooked.

Although nothing could have prepared them for the reality, the weekly antenatal classes run by the National Childbirth Trust had offered some practical advice and the opportunity to mix in circles previously unknown. This NCT group was a disparate band comprising, along with Louise and Joe, bank manager Jane, company director Paul, IT manager Trevor, doctor Angela, landscape gardener Melvin and saxophonist Sinead. They had little in common, apart from their impending parenthood, and, the reason they had been put together, their advancing years. Despite occupying varied positions on the social ladder, they would form a valuable support group, most of them remaining friends as their children grew.

The ice was broken and social preconceptions challenged at the first session when, upon exchanging information on work places, Paul enquired of Angela, 'How long have you been a nurse?'

'Actually, I'm a doctor,' replied Angela, smiling at his embarrassment.

Angela and Trevor were expecting twins, the happy result of IVF treatment after many heartbroken years of trying. Midway through the class, the expectant dads were presented with a challenge, a lesson in multi-tasking. Handed surrogate infants in the form of dolls, they were duly despatched to the kitchen to make tea whilst holding their babies; Trevor, perplexed and clumsy, carrying two. After much consideration, he concluded, 'This is impossible', placing one on the draining board as he filled the kettle.

Whether down to their mutual apprehension and lack of confidence in parenting skills, or to the fact that they were all easy going, Joe found himself warming to his new-found friends. Under normal circumstances they would never have met; they were alien worlds colliding, but with a common goal: the best possible start in life for their children.

After eighteen months, life and sleep for Joe and Louise returned to some kind of routine, not so much domestic bliss but at least domestic normality; until, one Saturday, Louise casually announced over breakfast, 'I think I'm pregnant.'

'How, when?' exclaimed Joe, choking on his cornflakes. Since Emma's arrival, passions had been, at best, rationed.

'Must have been on your birthday,' she replied; 'that hotel in Bournemouth. Happy birthday, dear.'

He recalled the day in question. Depositing Emma with Louise's parents, they had snatched some rare time together and escaped to the seaside, spending the entire weekend worrying about the welfare of their precious baby.

'Your mum and dad brought you up and you turned out OK,' Joe had reassured her; 'at least they didn't let your sister drop you on your head.'

Much as they tried, they couldn't sleep knowing that Emma was a hundred miles away. Holding each other for comfort, a rare intimacy, not passionate but cosy, a consolation of their love, they both knew in that moment that they would be there for each other until the end.

After the initial shock had subsided, the thought of a little brother or sister for Emma grew to be an attractive proposition, the not so distant memories of exhaustion subsequent to their first born taking on a positive slant. 'There can't be two like Emma; we'll know how to handle it this time,' said a thrilled Joe.

Everything about millennium baby Jamie was different; although caesarean born and three weeks early, he was immediately contented, sleeping for eight hours a night. 'You'll have to wake him up to feed him,' advised the health visitor, 'he's losing weight.'

Waking a sleeping baby went against all their instincts, but the proud parents did as instructed and soon Jamie was thriving. Joe was over the moon, a son to teach the finer points of the game and to take to the match. His childhood planned from day one, Jamie would never have the chance to be a ballet dancer.

Joe's home life was complete: a beautiful wife, a daughter and now a son. How could it get any better?

7. We've Gotta Get Out of This Place

'More is required,' Joe heard, not for the first time, as he listened to the pontifications of the Suit and Tie across the desk. The one-to-one, they called it, or 121 in corporate speak, the name for the six-monthly pointless ritual of performance measurement. To him it felt like a hundred to one, as those were the odds against receiving any support or empathy. The performance review or appraisal was not a new experience for Joe but, in these times of austerity, it was evident that the emphasis had shifted and that a social malaise now existed that amounted to little less than corporate bullying and intimidation (though he found it hard to be intimidated by a man who relaxed by listening to Cliff Richard, a discovery he'd made during the icebreaker at a recent team-building event).

From the Suit and Tie's perspective it must have been obvious that all Joe's motivation and enthusiasm were long gone and, if it hadn't been for that millstone of a mortgage, Joe would have been out of there years ago. The millennium now six long years past, he'd been routinely going through the motions for the duration. Joe knew that he'd been there way too long and his morale was non-existent; but, in the prevailing climate, there was nowhere to go ... he just had to be grateful he had a job that paid the bills. He'd worked his way up to a decent salary plus bonuses and benefits, the golden handcuffs that ensured he would wait to be pushed into a pot of gold, rather than jump into an empty abyss.

Outside of the office Joe was a contented man and he considered himself blessed, with his beautiful wife, two wonderful kids and, as much as a family man can, a decent social life. Maintaining *status quo* and living standard were his only motivations for enduring the depressing and repressive atmosphere that work had become.

When he considered his early track record with the opposite sex he was amazed at his good fortune. Prior to Louise, his lack of height, hair, charisma and self-confidence had combined to leave him companionless and lonely, their jubilant nuptials and subsequent bundles of joy occurring comparatively late in life. As the children grew, the fiscal responsibility weighed heavy; they were dependent on his income and he traded any thoughts of jumping ship with daydreams of that lottery win.

Two contrasting lives, comfortable contentment at home and soul-destroying boredom at work, older and more cynical, how had his life's journey brought him to this place? Was he even the same person as his younger self? He could see few similarities, apart from a continuing toothless, seething anger at fascism, injustice and politicians in general.

In his view, Margaret Thatcher, along with a pandering press, had effectively made the Labour Party unelectable; until, that is, Tony Blair had recreated himself and the party in her image, New Labour, Thatcher in a red tie. Resigning his membership in futile protest, he became a defeated political orphan, frustrated by the lack of real choice.

Joe felt like he had drifted on the sometimes calm, sometimes choppy waters of life, the circumstances in which he now found himself the result of the whims of the tide, rather than of any conscious decisions he had made.

How would the youthful Joe have viewed his current position? He would have been ruthless in his assessment. He would have said that he had prostituted himself at work, his idealistic values eroded as he licked up the crumbs from beneath the giant's table, taking any position offered for financial reward. He would have found the whole company ethos sordid and would have loathed himself for pandering to this bastion of capitalism, the ultimate institution of avarice. Although just a tiny cog in a huge machine, he was contributing to this all-encompassing piracy, humbly accepting the wages of greed, his socialist principles betrayed.

Was he being too hard on himself? Surely he had brought some compassion and a sense of fairness to the department. He knew, though, that his workmates thought of him as spineless and unfit to manage. He couldn't talk to Dad about how he felt; he knew what the response would be and rightly so: 'Stop whinging, you've got a good, well paid job, far easier than I had; just get on with it.'

Robin had been his usual realistic self. 'Don't beat yourself up. You care too much about what other people think. They don't give a toss about you; just do your job, go home and forget about it. I've had enough of this conversation, you miserable bastard; can we talk about football?'

Work/life balance? Joe had no desire to balance his work and life. He wanted these two incompatible, contradictory components completely separate. Why should this tainted, pointless job impinge upon his ideal home?

Much as he tried to keep them apart, the frustrations of work began to spill over in the shape of a constant irritability, trivial arguments with Louise, shouting at the kids for no reason. He couldn't forgive himself, but couldn't stop. His children were the most important thing in his life, his purpose, their happiness his one objective. They weren't to blame; why was he taking it out on them?

Emma and Jamie used to worship him. They both loved their dad, in awe even when he was simply tying his shoelaces. Now they were beginning to be wary, keeping a safe distance, unsure of which Joe had come home that night. Louise too was becoming distant, understandably protective, keeping Emma and Jamie out of his way when the mist descended. On an emotional spiral, his feelings of remorse and guilt contributed to his already dark moods; there didn't seem to be a way out, until one devastating day when the sensitive Jamie shocked him from his self-pitying downward path.

He'd threatened to leave home once before. They'd caught him in the hallway, coat on, fastening his shoes, with his *Jungle Book* rucksack on his back containing a few randomly selected items of clothing, a toothbrush (no toothpaste) and his favourite teddy bear.

'I'm going to live with Grandma,' he'd said with determination. 'I don't like it when you keep shouting.' Persuaded to stay by the promise of pizza for dinner, he went to bed happy and they thought the matter was closed.

This time, though, he really was gone, missing for half an hour. A hysterical Louise had phoned Joe at work and he'd rushed home with little consideration for speed limits. She'd contacted her parents, his parents, and all the neighbours, family and friends she could think of, but no-one had seen him.

'Where were you?' Joe had asked unhelpfully.

'I was hanging out the washing. Jamie was watching TV with Emma,' she replied. 'Don't blame me for this. It's your mood swings that have upset him.'

'OK, OK, the important thing is that we find him. You call the police and I'll go out looking; call me if he turns up anywhere.' He held Louise tightly. 'Don't worry, I'll find him.'

Frantically, he drove to all the likely and unlikely places, the park with his favourite slide, the shops where they brought a newspaper and sweets every Saturday, to the houses of any friends or acquaintances known to them or the children.

Now Joe understood why his own father had restricted his movements as a child, why he'd forbidden him to cycle to that reggae festival in Birmingham in his teens. It was out of love and the desire to protect him from his own naivety and from the dangers of the world.

After an hour that seemed like a day and getting more desperate by the minute, there was Jamie, this tiny figure sitting on a doorstep, head in hands. 'Daddy!' he cried, as Joe rushed towards him, sobbing with relief.

'It's OK, son, everything's going to be all right,' he said, shaking as he picked him up. As Jamie's little arms tightened round his neck, he vowed never to let him go and never to shout at or scold him again.

'I was waiting for Tommy to come home; he's not in,' said Jamie, recovering quickly from his ordeal. His school friend Tommy's house must have been over a mile away. How had he got here? Joe was surprised that he knew the way; they'd only visited twice.

'I used the crossing on the busy road, Daddy,' he said proudly.

Reflecting upon another hard lesson learned, Joe called home with the best news he'd ever imparted.

Emma had been in tears worrying about her little brother and Louise looked totally drained as Joe walked through the door, carrying the sleeping Jamie. A family hug, he saw a tear in the eye of the smiling policewoman; they were close again and he was determined to keep it that way.

Help was at hand. Soon the main cause of his discontent would be gone, the work/life scales tipped firmly towards life. The writing was on the wall, the rumours rampant, his fate sealed. Due to the cutbacks, the Bank were looking to reduce the levels of management and Joe was a prime target.

A restructure, they called it, but in reality an excuse to reduce numbers, to save money on salaries, pensions, benefits. Service would suffer, but the upper echelons seemed to care little, and even less about the welfare of the previously loyal employees who they were to release into the big, bad world. The mechanisations of the selection process were lengthy, cumbersome and extensive, the constant speculation causing frustration and anger among the workforce.

'Just tell us which of us are going and let us get on with our lives,' implored Joe; 'the not knowing is worse than the possible outcome.'

'We have to follow the due process,' replied Harriet from HR. 'We'll keep you informed at every stage.' Missives few and far between, they were in the dark until the final decisions were announced.

When it finally hit, the redundancy came as no surprise and Joe approached it with resignation and relief. He'd well and truly had enough and was fortunate that his length of service and some Union negotiation meant a decent pay-out. He was confident that he would find alternative employment in time, but his immediate intention was to enjoy a short break.

'Why, if it is the job that is redundant and not the person, am I training others to perform my duties when I'm gone?' asked a pedantic Joe.

'You want to go, don't you?' replied the Suit and Tie. 'Once these guys know what they're doing, you can walk off into the sunset. I envy you, you know; you can make a fresh start, do something you enjoy, escape from this hell hole.'

These comments came as a big surprise to Joe; he had no idea the Suit and Tie felt this way, and now he saw him in a different light.

As he cleared his desk, looking around at the place where he'd spent a large percentage of his existence, he felt a short-lived tinge of sadness. He'd done the rounds and said his goodbyes. Some of his colleagues were also escaping. 'What will you do?' he enquired of the generously endowed Cheryl.

'Thought I'd try topless ironing,' she replied in jest, 'there's many a lonely bachelor would employ me.'

'Topless ironing,' repeated Joe. 'I could do that. I could claim sex discrimination when no-one hired me.'

As he handed over his desk keys, company phone and security card, he firmly shook the hand of his long-suffering boss. 'Good luck, Joe, and thanks for everything. You've been a reliable bloke to have around and the font of all knowledge in Facilities. Let me know if you ever need a reference.'

'Thanks, Peter,' he replied, wondering where all this praise had been when he needed it. 'I'm sure you'll survive without me. ...'

In an office far away, another man was losing his job, a job to which he'd dedicated his life, a job he loved and for which he'd sacrificed all chance of a normal life. As he left the austere surroundings and stepped on to the street, a cacophony of traffic filled his head with confusion and pedestrians ignored him as they passed. How could the world be going about its business as if nothing had happened? The scar on his left cheek took on a fiercer shade of red and his right eye twitched as it always did in times of stress. In a cloud of bitterness, he vowed revenge on all who had crossed him, a list already forming in his mind.

8. Every Day I Write the Book

… 'More is required,' Joe said to himself as, at last, he made his break for freedom. The shackles crashed to the ground and, for the first time in years, he felt a spring in his step. Feelings of liberty and fear fighting for supremacy in his disbelieving mind, he kept walking before they had second thoughts.

Every working day for the last twenty-six years he'd spent in that homogenous, open-plan, glass-clad building and he found it difficult to comprehend that he'd just exited those doors for the last time. The breeze in his face, he sauntered down the street with barely a glance over his shoulder. His dream was to become a writer, a wordsmith, a noble profession, something he knew he could be good at, but hadn't previously had the guts to use in anger. You're on your own now, pal, he thought, as he headed for the horizon in search of a story.

Marie Jones was a very attractive lady in her early thirties and was single by choice, relationships on the back burner while she purposefully pursued her qualifications and career. She had worked hard for this opportunity in Business Banking and, dressed in a brand new matching pinstriped skirt and jacket purchased specifically with this occasion in mind, was both excited and nervous about her first lone meeting with a client.

'Your new phone,' said her boss, handing her something scratched and grubby that looked anything but new; 'you'll need this now as you'll be spending more time on the road meeting clients.'

Her boss had trusted her to get this loan deal right, a good one to start with, he thought, it was a foregone conclusion, most of the leg work had been done and it was simply a question of signing the paperwork.

That morning, however, there had been a serious accident on the motorway and the horrendous traffic was seriously threatening to spoil her day. By a convoluted route and using numerous detours, Marie had made the meeting with minutes to spare, flustered and unprepared. Apologising profusely for her lack of punctuality, she sat down and removed the folder containing the contract from her pristine briefcase. As the meeting progressed, she recovered and began to relax. She was generally a confident person and knew what she had to do. 'This is going well,' she thought, as she presented the terms of the agreement.

Suddenly, without warning, the confrontational sound of the Clash's 'London Calling' emerged at full volume from her handbag. Jumping and looking less than impressed, the potential client, previously hooked and almost landed, returned to terra firma and declared, 'We'll be in touch once we've decided. Thank you for your time.'

Unfortunately, part of the reward for Marie's promotion had been the inheritance of Joe's old phone, with its distinctive personalised ring tone that she hadn't got round to changing. In her rush, she'd neglected to switch it to silent. Had he been a fly on the wall, Joe would have found some amusement in his legacy.

At first his new-found freedom felt just like being on holiday: summer was in full bloom, Emma and Jamie were off school and, for the first time in years, he was having fun, spending precious time with his family, only this time without the dour prospect of having to return to the office.

After some weeks of chilling out, however, the guilt and shame began to creep up on him. Joe had never been unemployed before and his upbringing had instilled in him a work ethic that was proving to be an irritant. Hadn't he earned a career break? Why shouldn't he enjoy this moment of relaxation?

He didn't like to admit it, but in some respects he was actually missing the daily banter and the sense of purpose that his job had given him. Pointless and trivial though it had been, his work had at least given him a role to play. Although temporarily financially comfortable from a generous redundancy payment, there was a festering stigma to unemployment that was constantly nagging at the back of his mind. He told himself on countless occasions that he was making his contribution to the smooth running of the home, the school runs, cooking, cleaning, etc, but he had been raised in an era when it was the husband's responsibility to bring in the dosh, a responsibility in which he was patently failing.

'You're never happy, are you?' teased Louise. 'Take your time and find something you want to do; you don't need to earn as much, there's only a few years left on the mortgage.'

Louise, now the sole breadwinner, was being her usual pragmatic, non-judgemental and charitable self and put no pressure on him to get back on the treadmill. Comments from Dad about being a kept man, though, had done nothing to alleviate his self-reproach and the fortnightly ritual of signing on didn't help, the patient people at the Job Centre insisting that he take his job search seriously.

An element of 'I told you so' in his attitude to the credit crunch and subsequent recession, he felt no pleasure in the vindication of his opinions on unfettered capitalism and greed and the inevitable, terrible consequences that were coming to fruition around the world. In common with the majority of the population, he too was to be a victim of the lack of regulation in the financial sector. He knew, of course, that the fat cats would retain their luxury and continue to practise their tainted trade uninhibited.

Relatively unambitious in his criteria, he still found that every position applied for had multiple applicants, most of whom younger and, on paper, better qualified than he. Interviews were few and far between, negotiating the seemingly arbitrary selection process of employment agencies, an achievement in itself. Did experience count for nothing? He was perfectly capable of the tasks advertised in most of these jobs. What was he doing wrong?

At first selective in the kind of employment sought, he gradually learnt to be less fussy, but with the same discouraging results. If he received a response at all, it would be a standard e-mail or letter – "thank you for applying for the role of dogsbody; unfortunately, due to the high number and quality of applicants, we will not be offering you an interview on this occasion. We wish you luck in your job search."

A job description on an agency website appeared to be the perfect match for his expertise, such as it was, but still the swift rebuff came. "Thank you for forwarding your Curriculum Vitae to Scam Personnel. Unfortunately, your experience doesn't meet all of our clients' requirements in this instance."

Frustrated and in serious grumpy old man mode, he phoned. 'Could I have some feedback on how my CV differs from the clients' requirements, please? The job description is an exact match; it's what I used to do. Have you shown it to your client?'

'The client hasn't seen it, sir. We are employed to vet the applications,' patronised the girl on the phone. 'There have been over a hundred applicants.'

'And may I ask what qualifications you have for playing God with people's lives?' replied Joe. 'Might I suggest that you take longer than ten minutes before replying in future; it would at least give the *impression* that you have looked at the CV and given it some thought. You people make me sick. You're just parasites feeding off the misery of the unemployed.'

He wouldn't be hearing from that particular agency again.

A rare interview saw Joe suited and booted, attempting to secure the position of Brewery Assistant and Drayman at the local micro-brewery. Now this was a job into which he could put his heart and soul. Having sampled their wares on numerous occasions, he would have no problem in advocating the product and he would be thorough and dedicated in his duties. All very admirable, but they were looking for someone who gave the impression that they could lift a barrel, rather than drink one.

Another opportunity looked attractive: a franchise for a children's cookery school. Joe was a good cook and had enjoyed successfully instilling the joys of the culinary arts into Emma and Jamie. This was the very job for him. The shocking pink website had sold the concept well until he came across the almost incidental strapline at the bottom of the page – 'promoting women in franchise'. A phone call determined that there were currently no vacancies locally.

He wondered what the reaction would be if he were to set up a blue website that promoted *men* in franchise. He had always been a vociferous believer in equal rights and, though his experience was insignificant in comparison to the right to vote, for instance, he felt he'd just had a Nuevo Cuisine taste of inequality.

Not wishing to return to the mundaneness of his previous existence, he continued to apply for jobs that interested him, but also, in order to keep up his job centre quota and to secure some kind of income, for any role within his realm of experience and ability. All to no avail and the months multiplied relentlessly without reward.

Infinite advice for the disenfranchised was freely available on the web - creating the perfect CV, maximising time and efficiency in your job search, successful interview technique, networking, etc. But, despite diligently studying these lessons in the art of bullshit, nerves always prevailed and Joe never did himself justice in interview.

'What will you bring to the table that is special, how dedicated will you be, why should we choose you?' asked the smart thirty something high flyer, fluent in smarm.

'I don't proclaim to be anything special,' replied Joe. 'What you'll get is a conscientious, honest day's work. I am reliable and flexible.'

He tried to muster some enthusiasm and to pitch himself as dependable, trustworthy, someone who got the job done, but in an employer's market they always wanted more. His philosophy on employment was simple: fair exchange of labour for a reasonable living wage; he asked no more or less, but in these days of austerity that wasn't enough for potential employers. He wanted to say, 'You are buying my time, a substantial proportion of my life, you are not entitled to my soul. I wish to work to live, not live to work. I will do a good job, but I will not dedicate my entire existence to you.'

Maybe these negative thoughts were transmitted in his demeanour during interview. Perhaps he didn't look or sound ambitious and hungry enough, his meagre acting skills inadequate to fool anyone. He felt tired and helpless as the innumerable rejection mails accumulated in his inbox, there to taunt him every time he logged on.

Throughout this involuntary hiatus, Joe withdrew daily to work on the book that he dreamed would one day make him famous, alleviate his financial concerns and regenerate his self-esteem.

Previously, he'd only ventured into short articles, a music column for the Bank magazine, a review of the season for Jamie's football team presentation programme; but could he write an entire book? Were there sufficient words in his vocabulary and ideas to sustain a novel?

'Wherever possible, write from experience,' his old English teacher had advised. The late Mr Benson had been inspirational, the only one who'd cared, the only one who'd instilled a passion in Joe for anything at school. He'd introduced him to the genius of Steinbeck, Harper Lee's masterpiece *To Kill a Mockingbird*, the colourful Broadway characters of Damon Runyon, and had even awoken an interest in history through George McDonald Fraser's hilarious, politically incorrect, but historically accurate, *Flashman* books. Joe would be forever in his debt, his life enriched.

As he began to type, Joe considered his advice. Surely it wasn't intended to be taken literally? If so, then every book would be an autobiography. Besides, who the hell would want to read about *his* life? His take on what Mr Benson had been trying to convey was to use your own perception and knowledge, use any information you have attained, use your very being and your deepest feelings for inspiration.

Snippets, seeds amassed from his prior hidden literary dabbling, began to shoot to form the sapling of a story. He was enjoying the challenge; the endless possibilities in the combination of words; the bizarre and normal situations, one leading to another, through which the lead actor stumbled.

His aim was to portray the main character as human, deeply flawed, capable of love and devotion, but also of hatred and deceit; of loyalty and dedication, but also of fickle betrayal; of blissful happiness, but also plunging the depths of despair. Would he emerge as hero or villain, or would he reflect reality and be a combination of the two?

The supporting cast would be moulded from a conglomeration of characteristics borrowed from people he'd known, but with the names changed to protect the innocent. The story would be loosely based upon his life and times, set in his era, but somewhat exaggerated for dramatic effect.

As the tale unfolded, the book developed into an obsession, every waking hour spent in front of the PC transforming his thoughts into words, a small notepad by his bed to capture any nocturnal inspiration.

'Pretend I'm at work,' he'd said when Louise questioned his unhealthy compulsion and the amount of time he was wasting.

'You need to get a proper job and start bringing some money into the house,' she'd replied, changing her tune from her earlier tolerance and finally losing patience with his intransigence. 'We can't live on the redundancy money forever.'

'Don't you think I'm trying?' he proclaimed. 'Look how many jobs I'm applying for each week. It's not my fault if no-one will give me a chance.'

'If you put as much effort into job hunting as you do into that bloody book, you might stand a better chance,' she argued.

'Brilliant,' he smiled, clapping his hands together, 'that's it, that's the title, "That Bloody Book". I like it.'

Louise groaned. 'And how many words have you written now?'

'Sixty-two thousand nine hundred and seventeen,' he said proudly. 'All perfectly good words; not sure if they're in the right order, but good words nonetheless.'

'Do you really think it will be good enough for publication?' she sighed.

'How will you know if you won't even read it?' he retorted.

Louise had steadfastly refused to look at his efforts. 'I'll read it when it's finished,' she'd said, not thinking for a moment that it ever would be. Joe had an irritating habit of seldom completing a task and the house was full of half-completed DIY projects in which he'd lost interest as he moved on to his next fad.

Knowing it was partly written from experience, she was insecure, afraid that it would reveal too much. She didn't want to know how he felt about his previous relationships, how he felt now, about thoughts best supressed.

Her uninformed comments, though, further fuelled his self-doubt. Was it good enough? Was there sufficient depth in the characterisations? Would anyone want to read this thinly veiled exercise in self-analysis? Returning to his flawed script, he rewrote much of it, adding to the descriptive text, fleshing out the main protagonists, determined to make it work.

He was unsure about the chapter in which the hero expounded vociferously upon his political and philosophical ideals, remarkably similar to Joe's as it happened, but these things had to be said. They were integral to the very fabric of the character and story.

He sent his work in progress to acclaimed left wing author Alistair Ball, who, for a small fee, offered the service of working with unpublished authors in an advisory or editorial capacity.

'How much?' exclaimed Louise.

'Four hundred quid,' repeated Joe, taking a step back.

'What! We can't afford four hundred quid.'

'Just look upon it as an investment,' he replied, taking another step back and bumping into the fridge.

'Aagghh!' she screamed, as she stomped out of the room.

At a methodically arranged desk many miles away, a man had hacked into Alistair Ball's computer. He traced his scar with his index finger as he contemplated Joe's words with interest.

9. This is The Day

Eleven months, seventy-three thousand seven hundred and eighty-eight words later and 'That Bloody Book' was, amazingly, complete. Joe was finally happy with the outcome, the constant tweaking and honing worthwhile. A work he could be proud of, he'd presented it to a number of people whose opinions he respected and their comments had been predominantly positive, the small matter of publication his next hurdle.

Somebody must be interested, he thought as he trawled the thousands of Publisher and Publishing Advice websites – "The vast majority of manuscripts submitted by new authors to traditional publishing houses are rejected," he read with concern; "the truth is that very few first time authors have their work accepted and most are *never* published." The article went on to tell how the likes of Byron, Hemingway and Kipling, among others, had actually paid for the privilege of converting their first work to print after banging their heads against a wall of Philistine publishers. What chance had the rookie Joe got if such brilliance was initially ignored? Consoling himself with the thought that, if Jeffrey Archer can sell books then it can't be that difficult, he resumed his internet search.

Hardened to endless, thoughtless rejection letters by his continued job search, he commenced hawking his wares around purveyors of fine literature, avoiding the ones that didn't accept unsolicited manuscripts. He was sufficiently confident in his own modest collection of words to persevere and, after months of polite but negative responses, eventually his patience was rewarded.

Expecting yet another thanks, but no thanks, he'd opened the e-mail from Embryo Publishing, a relatively new company that specialised in work by first time, mainly young authors. With amazement he read that they actually wanted to meet him.

Petra Hunter, one of the partners in Embryo, had been intrigued by the unusual title of Joe's manuscript and, before she knew it, had eagerly consumed half the book. Although Joe wasn't exactly a fit for their usual finger-on-the-pulse market, it had a page-turning quality and she read on fascinated to its unorthodox conclusion.

Petra's parents were ardent dog lovers and, during her idyllic childhood, the house was always full of canine waifs and strays. She was in her mid-teens before they casually informed her that she'd been named after one of the *Blue Peter* dogs. Her brother Shep was equally unhappy with his unfortunate moniker.

'The main character reminds me of my dad,' she'd said to her sceptical colleagues at the weekly manuscript selection meeting; 'he was a self-pitying, miserable git, but with a great dry sense of humour and full of love. I really think a lot of people will relate to the imperfections, the contradictions, the hope, the despair in this book.'

Petra's father had recently passed away, the unbearable consequence of a short terminal illness, and, as she had absorbed Joe's creation, the tears came from nowhere. She recalled how her dad had always been there for her, making her laugh when she was down, a shoulder to cry on. This ostensibly unremarkable book had somehow extracted all her supressed emotions, her deep sorrow, her anger at him for leaving so soon, her gratitude that she'd known such a wonderful, imperfect man. She was living proof that daughters can forgive a lot where their dads are concerned, oblivious to their faults. A man would have to be a bunny murdering, poodle poking, homicidal maniac before a girl would relinquish her love for her father.

The loss of her beloved dad and the break-up of her marriage the previous year had left her bereft, so she had thrown herself into her work to avoid thinking about the pain. She achingly missed both the men in her life, although she had no regrets about divorcing her macho husband, whose disturbing penchant for playing with guns and obsession with PlayStation war games had finally tried her patience once too often. When her ultimatum of me or the games was ignored, she knew it was time to move on.

Why did she always fall for these losers? Did she think she could change them, turn them into cultured, rounded human beings? Her irrational tendency to date camouflage-clad action men had led to numerous disagreements with her parents. 'You're an intelligent young woman, for God's sake,' her mum had said; 'can't you at least find someone who looks like they can hold a conversation?'

Despite her parents' barely concealed disapproval, she had continued to bring home a series of tall, muscular types with war fixations, culminating in husband Roger. Her friends and work colleagues had been very supportive during the break-up, repeatedly telling her that she could do better and that Roger wasn't good enough for her anyway.

Her work became her one purpose, her reason to get up in the morning, her true vocation. Petra's gut feeling was to take a chance on Joe's book and she tenaciously persuaded her fellow book worms that they should meet the author. Although they felt that her previously impeccable judgement had been impaired by recent events, they were prepared to humour her and entertain this man whose literary credentials they seriously doubted.

With wardrobe doors wide open, Joe surveyed his meagre sartorial choices. How to make an impression? What to wear for such a (possibly) momentous meeting? Should he dress, as if for an interview, in suit and tie and his best uncomfortable shoes; or more casually in open-neck polo and jeans?

From their website he had ascertained that Embryo was a trendy, modern publisher, but he didn't want to make a fool of himself by trying to appear younger than his years. Compromising, he chose a plain blue shirt and grey linen jacket and trousers, smart but underwhelming, the ordinary bloke look that he felt reflected the book.

The last time he'd made this train journey it was for an all-expenses-paid work junket to recognise his length of servitude, celebrating with people of equal or higher longevity, none of whom he knew.

'Twenty-five years?' Neville from Birmingham had quipped over the hors d'oeuvres. 'You don't get that for murder.'

This time the trip to London was for himself, the greatest achievement of his life if he could pull this off and get his book on the shelves. As he watched the fields and trees flash by, turning as the locomotive progressed into indistinguishable terraced home after terraced home, he reflected upon the positive part this train had played in his life. He'd met Louise here, the match that lit the flames of his emotional resurrection; Emma and Jamie wouldn't exist if he hadn't caught this train all those years ago. Now it was hopefully taking him to his salvation, to the return of his self-respect, to the publishers who actually wanted to meet the author of 'That Bloody Book'. He would be devastated if he screwed this up.

'Good afternoon, I'm Joe Stamford, I have an appointment with Petra Hunter,' he announced to the young receptionist, who looked at him as if he were in the wrong place.

'I'll take you through, sir. Would you like tea or coffee?'

'Coffee please, black, no sugar,' he replied, feeling as if he needed something stronger.

A little short of six feet tall, slim, auburn haired and not unattractive, Petra looked a little older than he expected, but he still felt ancient as he entered the fashionable office.

'Welcome to Embryo. This is Josh Baxter,' she smiled, introducing him to her youthful business partner. 'Make yourself comfortable.'

I'm old enough to be his dad, thought Joe as he shook Josh's hand

and sank down apprehensively into a plush black leather chair that contrasted sharply with the pristine white walls. His eyes were drawn to the only colour in the room, a single yellow orchid that stared back at him from its ebony vase on the glass table around which the three of them sat. Joe soon realised that each time he shifted nervously a loud farting sound would emanate from his chair. I didn't get where I am today by letting rip in important meetings, he thought, as he opted for the nonchalant, motionless, relaxed look.

'Apologies for the flatulent furniture,' said Petra, 'it's because it's brand new. They tell us that it will stop doing that once it's worn in.'

'So you like my modest attempt at literacy,' he stammered, trying to appear cool and failing miserably.

'Petra likes it. I'm yet to be convinced,' said Josh, looking Joe in the eye. 'Tell me, why should we publish it? What makes it different from all the others?'

'It's from the heart,' replied Joe, that interview anxiousness returning. 'What can I say, it's my masterpiece. I've spent a lot of time and effort on this, though I'm probably too close to judge it. You guys are the experts. You tell *me* if it's any good.'

'My main concern is that there appears to be an element of autobiography,' said Petra. 'Can you assure us that all the characters are fictional and there are no nasty libel cases waiting to bite us on the arse.'

He'd considered the spectre of libel action and thought he had all the angles covered.

'Some of the situations are real, albeit somewhat enhanced, but most are figments of my warped imagination,' he replied. 'The bods who populate the tale are fictitious, though. They're based upon my observations of the human condition, so there may be someone who thinks they recognise themselves; but no character is exclusively representative of one individual. Can't you put something in there about resemblances to persons living or dead being coincidental?'

It seemed like minutes had passed in thought before Josh looked from Petra to Joe and conceded, 'OK, Petra has persuaded me.

We're willing to print a few thousand initially and test the water in strategic bookshops, place a few adverts and produce some flyers. Can you get your local paper to run a piece?'

'Pretty sure I can,' said Joe, trying to supress his excitement. It wasn't quite the Booker Prize contender reaction that he'd hoped for, but he was more than happy that they thought it worthy of a punt.

'Are you available for promotional duties and interviews if we can get them?' asked Petra.

'Do you mean TV?' replied Joe.

'Think we should maybe try local radio stations to start with,' said Josh, his expression questioning Joe's photogenic qualities and implying that he wouldn't allow him anywhere near a TV camera. 'Bookshop appearances, maybe Sunday supplements if it takes off and we go national.'

'I have an idea for the cover,' said Joe, pushing his luck.

'We commission graphic designers for the artwork, but we can put you in touch with them. This is your baby and you should be as hands-on as possible,' encouraged Petra, 'but the risk is ours and we have final say on the layout.'

Purchasing a bottle of expensive champagne on the way, he travelled home on a cloud, high above the other commuters.

Inane grin on face, bottle and signed contract in hand, he proudly entered the house.

'I don't believe it!' smiled Louise, as she hugged him. 'Suppose I'd better read it now.'

10. A413 Revisited

Disconcerted at being recognised, Joe felt uncomfortably self-conscious as people nudged each other, pointing as he sauntered through the market square. A private man, how would he cope if he ever encountered real fame?

As suggested by Josh, he'd arranged an interview and photo session with the local paper, and, as a result, 'That Bloody Book' had prime position in the window of Waterstones. A Friday lunchtime signing session scheduled and, unbelievably, he was a minor local celebrity, at least temporarily on a par with the legendary John Otway.

'This must be a dream,' he said to the bookshop manager, as he looked up at the display with his picture and name predominant; 'if it goes no further than this I'll be contented. My work in print for posterity; there must be at least a hundred copies.'

'Pleasure to meet you, Joe. Could you sit over here and we'll manage the queue. Love the book; would you mind signing a copy for my mum?'

'Queue? Do you really think there'll be a queue?' he asked, as he signed his autograph for the first time.

'Hope so. That's what we're here for, to sell books.'

Smiling, signing and shaking hands with the numerous well-wishers, some of whom he knew - was that guy who just congratulated him the very same that used to bully him at school? Old workmates came to join in. 'You jammy sod!' said one. 'Best thing you ever did, getting out.'

A smartly dressed, imposing man said nothing as Joe scrawled his name once again. Joe's eyes were involuntarily drawn to the scar, from mouth to ear on his left cheek. Like all who met him, Joe was curious as to how this stranger had come by such an injury, but he simply smiled and nodded as the man turned away.

And suddenly there she was. Sandy. Right in front of him, that smile, those legs, holding out her copy to be signed. 'Hi, Joe; long time no see. You've come a long way since we last met.'

'Further than you think,' he smiled, regaining his composure. 'How's things?'

'Oh, you know, married, mortgage, two kids,' she sighed.

'Me too; never been happier,' said Joe, as he signed with two kisses. 'Good to see you again. Take care.' And then she was gone.

Feeling only resignation, sadness and regret about the time he'd wasted on futile fantasy and the hurt caused by his subsequent negative emotions, he moved on to the next in line, a large, formidable lady whose demeanour implied frustration at being kept waiting.

Petra attempted once again to convince her still doubtful partner. 'It could be a word-of-mouth one, a slow burner.'

Although encouraging locally, sales at the other chosen shops had been slow. Embryo had tried in vain to secure radio interviews and reviews in the national press and it appeared that the initial impetus would fizzle out.

'Can't you just admit that we made a mistake on this one?' pleaded Josh. 'We're throwing good money after bad; this guy hasn't got what it takes.'

'Give it one more chance,' she said, convinced that her faith was well placed. Undaunted, she sanctioned a second print run, as the first few thousand dawdled, hardly jumping off the shelves.

'I have a proposition for you,' she told Joe over a business lunch;

'we're not going to sell this through the usual publicity channels, so I think you should tour the country. We'll arrange it with the bookshops and send the blurb to the appropriate local papers. You know – Joe Stamford will be at such and such a shop at this time, signing his brilliant debut novel; that kind of thing.'

'Go on tour, like a rock star?' he said, intrigued. 'I like it, but I'll have to swing it with the boss.'

'Er, not exactly like a rock star,' she laughed; 'you'll be staying in cheap B & Bs, looking after yourself. We have to do this on a budget, sell the book from grass roots. I have taken the liberty of organising the first venue.'

'Don't suppose it's going to be LA then,' said Joe. 'Go on, surprise me.'

'The book is being printed next week in Cornwall. I've arranged for you to be there when it comes off the press. A reporter from the *St Ives Times and Echo* will meet you there for an interview; could be a good angle.'

Joe's grandfather had lived in Cornwall, in a small village near Penzance, and he had vague idyllic recollections of staying there as a child. He'd not been back since his grandad died there in the mid-eighties and he cautiously welcomed the idea of a nostalgic trip down memory lane. He briefly considered taking Louise and the kids with him, spending a few days by the seaside, but it was a school day and not viable.

A long, lonely trip, he thought about the odd occasions when he'd stayed overnight for work, alone in soulless, depressing hotels. Was this to be his life, zig-zagging across the country on his own, the CD player in the car his only company?

At least now he got to choose his own sounds. Usually, car journeys were fraught with heated musical disagreements between Joe, Louise and the kids.

'You can always get out and walk if you don't like it,' he'd said unreasonably, as another Tom Waits growl rattled from the speakers.

'What kind of father makes his kids listen to Tom Waits?' Robin had asked. 'It's tantamount to child cruelty, and I'm sure Social Services would be interested.'

He rarely listened to the radio; he couldn't abide the majority of disc jockeys, more concerned with their own vacuous celebrity than with the music they were meant to be playing. In the scheme of things, it wasn't a heinous crime, but few things annoyed him more than DJs talking over the introductions and endings of great songs. How could their inane babble ever be justified over the sublime sax break at the end of Lou Reed's 'Walk On The Wild Side', or their words be more important than the joyful New Orleans band on the fade of Paul Simon's 'Take Me To The Mardi Gras'? Oh for the days of the late great John Peel, sometimes unlistenable, but mostly cutting edge music played in full with love and without embellishment; a little information about the artist and then on to the next song.

Although these weren't exactly the endless ribbons of the expansive Californian highways and his steed was far from a Cadillac, he enjoyed the illusion of freedom that driving inspired. The open road, sunroof open, the music loud, a lone pilgrim on the road to the wild-west country of Cornwall; his adventure had just begun.

11. Lonesome Town

Printing ink, paper and machinery – it was the smell that hit him first as he entered the building, the unique odour that brought it all flooding back. He was that spotty youth again, on his first day at work at the printers and binders. Though, apart from the vast proportions of the place, the noise and the unmistakeable aroma of newly printed books, this factory bore no resemblance to the ancient, long since demolished surroundings of his earliest employment. Modern, bright and airy, this was a state-of-the-art, efficient manufacturing environment.

Following the shift supervisor along bright yellow health and safety conscious paths, conversation curtailed due to the overwhelming cacophony of printing, folding and cutting, Joe and the reporter made their way to the machine where, coincidentally, his work was at the guillotining stage. These days a smooth, clean, uninterrupted process, fully automated, no labour required to stack the pallet, no books crashing to the floor, no banter from the modern-day equivalents of Chris and Michael, all ears rendered redundant by headphones to protect hearing, the human element nullified: a sanitised, robotic version of work.

Ears ringing, they retired to the relative silence of the Queens, the interview informal over one of Joe's favourite, simple, gastronomic pleasures - a ploughman's accompanied by a pint of excellent local ale.

After paying poignant homage at the graveside of the grandfather he had barely known, he headed back alone to his accommodation, the pattern set for his existence for the foreseeable future.

At least Petra had given some thought to the itinerary, minimising travel by applying some logic to the route, the early dates on the 'Joe Stamford UK Tour' taking in various venues along the south coast. The crumbling, fading romance of seaside resorts in the autumn rain added sombrely to his sense of loneliness, the beeping and flashing lights of deserted amusement arcades like a life support machine for the British tourist industry. Taking in the bracing sea air on an early evening walk along the sparsely populated promenade, he passed a tipsy, teetering priest on his way to read the last rites.

Portsmouth, Brighton, Margate, Southend-on-Sea, Ipswich and up to Great Yarmouth, one town blurring into another as he accustomed himself to a new, solitary lifestyle. The customary interview with a bored journalist who asked the same old questions, meeting with a few disinterested browsers in a quaint old bookshop, booking into the Victoria, yet another run-down, sleazy-looking back-street hotel.

Once showered and shaved, he entered the homely hotel bar, resigned to another reclusive evening of boredom. He observed the only other customer, a tall thin man in his early thirties resembling a stick insect, perched precariously upon a bar stool.

'Good evening,' nodded Joe, as he ordered a pint of best, his heart skipping a beat as he noticed 'That Bloody Book' on the bar. The first time he'd seen someone he didn't know reading it, the bookmark protruding at least two thirds through, a genuine punter who'd actually taken the trouble to purchase it.

'Good book?' he enquired, wanting an honest opinion.

'Not bad,' replied the stick insect; 'quite amusing in places and the story keeps you hooked. Not heard of the author before, but my cousin tweeted to recommend it. Looks a bit like you as it happens,' he said, turning to Joe's convict-like picture on the inside cover. He looked at Joe again. 'Hang on, is it you?'

'Guilty as charged,' grinned Joe, as he introduced himself to the man he would come to know as Spike. 'What brings you to these parts?'

'My stag weekend,' replied Spike, hardly believing that he was talking to the author. 'Just waiting for the others to come down. Hey, why don't you join us? We're going on a crawl, maybe a club if we make it that far.'

Joe hesitated; he'd grown unaccustomed to conversation and crowds and was unsure if he was ready for a night on the lash with a bunch of strangers - but then he thought, why not?

'Don't want to impose, but I could do with some company. If your friends don't mind, then yes, thanks, I'd love to tag along. Can I get you a drink?'

'No thanks, I've got one 'ere.'

'That's what Van Gogh said.'

'Hope that's not your best joke,' said Spike, grimacing; 'we'll be expecting better from a famous writer.'

'Hardly famous,' laughed Joe; 'you're the first person who's ever recognised me.'

Pint followed pint, pub followed pub, some buzzing with weekend revellers, some quiet, until Spike, walking like a giraffe on skates, and his boisterous entourage descended. Joe struggled to keep pace with the Olympic standard drinking of these men who were almost twenty years his junior. Even in his younger days he'd seldom indulged to excess and these guys were serious imbibers.

'I must apologise,' Damien, the joker of the pack, had said when Spike announced that Joe would be accompanying them.

'What for?' asked Joe.

'For my behaviour later,' replied Damien, smiling and shaking his hand.

Now there he stood at the bar, ordering his round with his trousers and pants round his ankles, the barmaid bemused and unsighted, unaware of the source of their childish hilarity, until she glanced at the mirror on the wall behind him and asked the landlord to throw them out.

They staggered on to the next dubious establishment, a buzzing, garish-looking club, the bouncer critically inspecting their attire as he reluctantly allowed them access. A deafening, metronomic beat shook the ground, the dazzling orange lights in sync with the drums while the marginally less unsubtle purple followed the bass line. Mirrors covered every wall, depriving the clientele of all sense of direction as they moved manically across the floor. God forbid if there's a fire in here, thought Joe, we'd never find our way out. Making their way to the bar, they passed a dimly-lit booth, where a passionate couple appeared to be in the latter throes of foreplay.

Joe's eyes weren't the only ones on stalks as the lads inspected the seemingly endless parade of beautiful, immodestly clad young ladies out for a night of revelry and pleasure. They'd obviously stumbled upon the place to be.

'It's a good job I'm aesthetically challenged,' said Spike, his mouth agape. 'I could quite easily be led astray in a place like this.'

His attention diverted, Joe was unaware of the shady character wearing a large hat that hid half of his face in shadow, surreptitiously dropping something into his drink.

Joe felt ancient and decrepit, the oldest one there by some distance, totally out of place, like a dirty old man for the involuntary, uncontrollable thoughts that were in his head. Finishing his drink and making his excuses, muttering something about nightclubs not being his thing, he thanked Spike and his friends for a great evening and stood to leave.

To his surprise, Damien and the quiet, reflective Tim decided to head back too.

'You're the life and soul,' Joe said to Damien as they fell along the street, 'thought you'd be at home in a place like that.'

'Not really,' he replied, as if insulted, 'I find those places soulless and depressing, like a cattle market; besides, I've had enough for one night. This is going to be a long weekend, a marathon not a sprint; got to pace myself.'

* * *

Like many of her compatriots, Maureen O'Hanagan had reluctantly left the beauty of County Kerry on the west coast of Ireland when times had got hard. She dutifully followed her handsome, humorous husband Daniel to wherever the work took them. The English building industry was booming and Daniel had toiled all the hours possible to support them and their young daughter Maeve, until a painful fall from some poorly erected scaffolding left his back shattered and bent. He would never work on the building sites again.

With his compensation, savings and further capital from Maureen's nursing shifts, they had scraped together sufficient funds to take out a mortgage on the Victoria Hotel. "A cosy, family-run hotel with bags of potential, two minutes' walk from the seafront", the estate agent blurb had said. Cosy equated to small and bags of potential meant in bad need of renovation, but there was little else within their price range and they proudly moved in.

Full of optimism, Daniel laboured day and night through the pain of his back and put his heart and soul into transforming the Victoria into a habitable, friendly, moderately prosperous inn. They were happy, running their own business, the perfect, sociable hosts to the varied customers who graced their modest establishment.

Gradually, the bottle took hold. He had always been partial to the odd libation for the purposes of sociability, but now the booze was there, every day on tap, and the temptation proved too hard to resist. Their profits dwindling as Daniel addictively drank them away, spirits sinking lower by the year, he became withdrawn and depressed. Fully aware of what his habit was doing to their lives, their dreams, their relationship, their daughter, their business, he packed his bag and left, ashamed.

For a while he was seen living on the streets, huddled in doorways, begging pathetically for change. Then he simply disappeared, just another lonely, broken vagrant lost to the world, and a heartbroken daughter wondering when her dad was coming home.

Maureen presented her bravest face to the world and carried on, not knowing what else to do. The hotel had Daniel's indelible imprint upon it; it was a monument to the man he once was, a living tombstone for the man she had loved.

The market was faltering as the recession hit, but they were just keeping their heads above water. She saw herself running the Victoria for another five years, before selling up and returning to the green fields of her birth.

She hated the stag trade, some of them were little better than animals, but she could ill afford to turn down the revenue they generated. Maeve was always packed away to her Aunt Pauline's when the stag weekend parties hit town. Maureen didn't want her innocence sullied by these uncouth, unbefitting rabble.

This intake seemed a little more civilised than most, however, affording her some respect, a little older, though not grown up. After all, they were men, they would never grow up. Yes, they would return slaughtered, but they didn't look as if they would wreck the place. Not trusting them entirely, though, she expected a late night, opting as usual to stay up until the majority of them were back and in bed. Her only other residents were Jim the retired sailor (the permanent incumbent of room seven), and a sad-looking, travelling author who had booked for one night only.

Unexpectedly, two of them rolled in laughing just after midnight, with the author in tow, looking much happier than when he'd registered earlier.

'Any chance of a nightcap?' asked Damien, utilising his natural charm 'Will you have one yourself?'

Maureen politely refused the drink – she hadn't touched a drop since Daniel left – but she reopened the bar and poured three double brandies – another sale, another step closer to going home. As the lads made themselves at home, they began to sing, their harmonies uncomfortably off key, at first well-known classics with crescendo choruses – 'Starman', 'Hey Jude', 'Are you Lonesome Tonight?', all ending in laughter as the words and tune jumbled unrecognisably.

Then silence descended as Damien began to sing alone. My god this guy was good, singing beautifully, plaintively recalling his Irish roots, as he crooned 'The Leaving of Liverpool', 'The Irish Rover' and, finally reducing Maureen to melancholy tears, a haunting, majestic version of 'Danny Boy'.

Joe awoke in stages, his senses reluctantly regaining consciousness one by one. As his eyelids partially unstuck, he took a few minutes to recognise his surroundings, his head fuzzy, his mouth like the Sahara, his teeth furry. Levering himself slowly out of bed, holding on to anything static, he stumbled into the bathroom and gradually focused on his reflection. Jesus, what was wrong with him? Panicking, he saw his scary, bloodshot face staring back at him, totally covered in red blotches. This looked serious: what exotic disease had he caught, and how would he find a doctor in a strange town on a Saturday morning?

Deciding to wake himself up to accommodate clearer thought, he filled the sink and cupped his hands, vigorously splashing the cold water on his face, the angry blemishes disappearing as he did so.

Returning confused to the bedroom, his bare feet found the culprit with a squelch: a discarded half-eaten kebab with smatterings of chilli sauce on the wrapper, the same bright shade of red as his recent ailment. Observing his grease-covered shoes and trousers, he slowly attempted to piece together the events of the previous night. He remembered leaving the nightclub, the walk back with Damien and Tim, their painful vocal contortions in the bar, Damien's voice of an angel. But, much as he tried, he couldn't recall going out again to purchase the kebab or how and when he'd made his way back.

Dressing with little co-ordination, arm by arm, leg by leg, he cautiously descended the stairs for breakfast, still in a daze. A resounding cheer from the lads as he entered the dining room, he wondered what on earth he could have done to warrant such a reception.

'You're a bit of a dark horse,' said Damien, leering through his hangover; 'she was all over you and she was a stunner. How did you do it?'

Joe didn't have to plead ignorance, he had absolutely no idea what they were talking about, but still they couldn't buy his incredulous look. Refusing to believe his denial, they grilled him relentlessly about his adventure after he had left the bar, apparently on the arm of a beautiful woman.

The events unfolded as Damien recounted the story. After Damien's lone recital, the lady in question had appeared from nowhere at the bar and Joe had not wasted any time, engaging her in conversation as he brought a round. He had bid them a cheery goodnight as a little persuasion lured Joe away from his new friends and out into the unknown. And there the story ended.

Fantastic, he thought. A rare, intriguing liaison with the tenderer gender and he couldn't remember a thing about it. What had he done? What if Louise found out? But how could she? Nobody knew what had happened, not even him.

12. There Ain't Half Been Some Clever Bastards

What the hell was he doing here? What was Petra thinking of, arranging for him to talk, at Cambridge University of all places? How many great authors who actually knew what they were doing had trod these hallways? Stephen Fry, the font of all knowledge, had studied and performed here. Nick Hornby, Tom Sharpe, Peter Ackroyd, to name a few, and now he was expected to stand up in front of the geniuses of the future and expound upon the virtues of his modest, unworthy effort.

'You've got to be joking,' he'd said, when Petra phoned. 'I've never spoken in front of an audience before, let alone at a bloody university, and we're not talking just any university. And when am I supposed to perform this impossible feat?'

'Two days' time. Just think of the kudos this will give your work. It's for part of a series on contemporary literature. Tony Parsons has cancelled at the last minute and they're desperate for a replacement. I've told them you'll be there.'

'No chance,' he retorted; 'I won't do it.'

Knees trembling as he waited in the wings, he peeked round the curtain to see the hall about three-quarters full of confident young men and women, the academic cream of the country's youth. What could these students possibly gain from listening to him speak? He could only think that they were here as an alternative to a particularly boring lecture, a brief respite from the seriousness of whatever high-brow subject they were studying. The austere décor of russet and beige added further to his sense of being out of place and he felt as if he were in the midst of an old sepia photograph.

Trying to summon up some confidence, he thought of the only other time he'd performed in public. In the days when they still thought he had potential, the powers-that-be had enrolled him on to an internal Management Development Programme, intended to indoctrinate prospective bosses in the ethos and ways of the Company. For one of the modules they had employed the services of an out-of-work actor in a misguided attempt to teach them presentation skills. Prior to the course, they had all been instructed to learn a nursery rhyme; not a problem for Joe, as he'd been routinely reading them every other night for the previous few years.

'After lunch you will be performing your nursery rhyme in front of your fellow participants,' the actor had announced in Shakespearian tones. 'This will be done in a way that is unique to you. I'm looking for something different; you will not simply stand up and recite. Apart from that, the format is up to you. You have the morning to consider how you wish to present your rhyme. In the meantime, we will be working on stagecraft.'

Joe had been terrified as he took to the stage and, asking for audience participation in clapping the rhythm, he'd aggressively rapped one of Emma and Jamie's favourites, Winking, Blinking and Nod, prowling the boards, his outer two fingers protruding on the beat. He'd even grabbed his crotch *à la* Michael Jackson as a climax to his act. Although he would certainly have been laughed out of the Bronx, his performance had been the talk of the course, his colleagues genuinely amazed that such an ostensibly quiet, unassuming man could rap. He'd amazed himself too.

Somehow, though, he didn't think the same technique would work with the esteemed students of Cambridge and he stood tongue-tied and shaking before them, sweating profusely. Fumbling for his notes and faltering, he began to speak, the essence of his ramblings being the contrast between his education and theirs and his view that literature should not be the exclusive domain of the educated.

He wanted to read about the experiences of the ordinary man and woman on the street, written by people who'd been there, about real lives, about their loves and losses, their hopes and dreams. He had a punk attitude to literature – everyone has a story to tell; anyone should be allowed to write their times and tell it on the streets.

He told of his inadequate comprehensive education and of his low expectations upon leaving school, of the years wasted gainfully employed in work he despised, of how it had taken the shock of long-term unemployment to enforce him to realise his potential. He told them that they had been blessed with outstanding ability and their opportunities would be manifold. He advised them to follow their hearts, to avoid the treadmill at all costs, to live their lives with passion and pride. Essentially, to do something they believed in and not to be dissuaded along the way. He said that knowledge was useless without wisdom, that knowledge is the fact that a tomato is really a fruit, but that wisdom is the understanding not to put it in a fruit salad.

To his surprise he wasn't heckled and they appeared to be genuinely interested in what he was saying. Inviting questions at the end, he realised from their knowledge of the characters that some of them had actually read and enjoyed 'That Bloody Book'.

With relief, he left the stage to applause, not exactly a standing ovation, but at least respectful and warm.

In the shadows of the back row, a large mysterious man sat observing silently as he considered his next move.

The whole ordeal had lasted a mere thirty minutes, but to Joe it had seemed like hours.

'How was it?' enquired Petra. 'You obviously survived.'

'Absolutely petrifying,' said Joe, 'but it seemed to go down OK; they didn't lynch me anyway.'

'That's good, because you're doing Oxford next week.'

He needed a drink. His first foray into public speaking had been extremely stressful, but in a perverse way he'd enjoyed the experience and was ready for more, almost looking forward to conquering Oxford. For the first time in his life he felt a degree of confidence.

How long would this promotional voyage last? Petra had implied a few months, but he'd already been on the road for six weeks and had barely scratched the surface.

When writing, he'd longed for the solitude he now had in abundance, for peace and tranquillity to aid his thought processes. Now he achingly missed the constant background noise of his children playing, arguing over TV programmes, fighting over trivialities, their random, inventive songs at bath time and blatant delaying tactics at bedtime.

The next leg of his journey would take him close to home and he was eagerly anticipating a joyful reunion with Louise and the kids, a chance to spend a few nights in his own bed. He'd religiously phoned home every evening to catch up on their news and say goodnight, but he'd missed some milestones that could never be recreated. Emma's show with her dance class at the town theatre, Jamie's hat-trick for the school team, Louise's new hairstyle, which she had described in great detail, but which Joe couldn't visualise. Why a new hairstyle? Who was it for? Was there someone else around when he wasn't there? Attempting to jettison these negative thoughts, he approached his driveway with a mixture of trepidation and excitement.

He didn't get far before the front door burst open and Emma and Jamie ran screaming towards him, arms outstretched. God, how he'd missed them. Looking up as he hugged them, he saw Louise, a radiant, smiling picture, framed in the doorway. The new hairstyle suited her, shorter and sexy, like Twiggy in her nineteen sixties heyday.

Children jockeying for position, vying for his undivided

attention, like a pair of affectionate Rottweilers, they had one leg each and wouldn't let go.

'Hey, hey, go steady, there's enough Daddy to go round,' he laughed.

'More than enough, I'd say,' said Louise, as she joined the group hug; 'you've put on weight.'

It was undeniable. He hadn't exactly been following a healthy diet on his travels. At least a couple of pints every night, takeaways of universal varieties, Indian, Chinese, fish and chips, pizza, and he'd taken full advantage of the breakfast element of B & B.

Sinking into the sofa, he retrieved their presents from his bag: a pirate ship for Jamie, a furry rabbit for Emma, a pair of earrings and a bag of washing for Louise.

It felt great to be back and, as they sat round the table for dinner, Joe considered giving up on his apparently useless jaunt around the country. Sales figures had barely changed and, basking in the warmth of his family, he questioned whether it was worth it.

'You've got to carry on, you can't stop now,' said Louise, 'you've put so much into that book. Besides, what other prospects do you have? You've been out of work for over a year now and the head hunters are not exactly battering down the door. We're managing OK; give it another chance.'

It was evident that domestic life had continued quite successfully without him; the kids and Louise seemed contented enough and, once the novelty of his return had worn off, Emma and Jamie were, as usual, more interested in the TV.

Two days later and he was back on the road.

13. I Heard It Through The Grapevine

A cult following, Petra had called it. 'It's taking off; people are talking about it.'

Ironically, it was the medium of Twitter and Facebook that proved to be his saviour, a technological bandwagon that Joe had thus far stubbornly refused to board. Apparently, people were tweeting and chatting (whatever that meant) and 'That Bloody Book' was proving to be an increasingly popular subject-matter.

A dedicated technophobe and proud of it, Joe distrusted the alien concept of social networking (or any other kind of networking for that matter). Truth be told, it scared him. An off-duty police officer had initiated a presentation at Emma's school to forewarn parents of the dangers and effects of cyber bullying and of the predatory perverts that inhabited these sites.

Joe had been bullied at school, when his mouth had often got him into trouble with his bigger, tougher contemporaries, not to mention his PE teacher. In the days before the authorities and society in general were conscious of bullying, it had been considered part of growing and toughening up, a lesson in the art of survival. Things generally culminated in a one-on-one brawl on the school field, hidden by a circle of partisan, cheering onlookers, before a teacher spied the furore, parted the crowd and aggressively dragged the flailing participants apart.

Both boys would be sent to the headmaster, who would sadistically administer the slipper, ensuring the victim had a sore arse to go with his already throbbing head. The black eye would be worn like a trophy for the following weeks, a talking point as it changed colour from purple to red to yellow. 'You should see the other fella,' he would boast.

Graham Savage was the boy everyone feared, ultimately expelled for hitting a teacher in times when such blatant, rebellious acts weren't commonplace. Predictably, Joe's sharp wit had incurred Graham's wrath and the threat that he would see him after school had occupied his mind all afternoon, resulting in him paying even less attention than usual in double geography. Why didn't he think before he spoke?

When the bell rang for the end of day, Joe had hit the ground running and was on the other side of the playground before Graham emerged from the classroom. Joe was fairly quick over short distances but was no marathon runner and his enemy was soon gaining ground.

Turning a corner, he thought quickly and jumped over David Bodsworthy's fence, through his thankfully unlocked side gate, down the garden, with David's mum knocking angrily on the kitchen window. Vaulting the back gate, he escaped with relief across the allotments, trampling veg as he went. He knew he was only delaying the inevitable, however, and that Graham would catch up with him the next day.

He thought of cyber bullying as altogether more sinister, though; and, apart from the lazy, bastardised version of the English language they used to communicate, he abhorred the spiteful, cruel messages sent by vicious kids, designed to terrorise the weak and vulnerable. Perhaps it was unfair of him to blame the medium for the crime, like lampooning the manufacturer of the axe instead of dealing with the murderer.

Begrudgingly, he admitted that this new-fangled method of communication had its uses; he was grateful for any vehicle for his message as it insidiously spread the word like an invisible soothsayer.

* * *

He'd reached the matching grey town and sky of Halifax (via Worcester, Birmingham, Stafford, Chester and Manchester), when the call came.

'Have you seen this morning's papers?' shouted Petra. 'I thought you said all the characters were fictional. I've already had her solicitor on the phone talking about legal action. What the hell were you thinking of?'

'What? Who?' said Joe, caught by surprise. 'I haven't seen any papers yet.'

'Then I suggest you go out and buy them now! The *Sun's* probably the best one, on page five. Call me back as soon as you've had the chance to digest the gravity of the situation.' The phone went dead.

Head in a spin, he rushed to the nearest newsagents. What had happened? Who was it about? He was certain that he'd been careful about disguising any similarities to people he knew. He'd gone over it a hundred times before submitting it for publication.

His stomach churned as he grabbed the *Sun* and turned shakily to page five. There he was, his own face staring back at him like an accusatory mirror, beneath the headline "LEFT WING LAURA'S LONG-LOST LOVER?"

In shock, he read on with horror.

"Speculation continues to mount today as to whether little-known author Joe Stamford (above) was an early love conquest of leftie Labour MP Laura Bisham. There are striking similarities between Mr Stamford's description of an encounter in his debut novel 'That Bloody Book', and an episode in Ms Bisham's recent unauthorised biography.

The incident allegedly took place during a festival at the Greenham Common women's CND peace camp in the early eighties, where it appears that lusty Laura was smoking weed and evidently administering free love.

In both accounts the steamy liaison took place in the certain lady's tent

77

whilst they sheltered from a violent thunderstorm and shared lager and marijuana. Anonymity is also common to both versions, with neither party knowing the other's name, but new evidence has come to light that may link this unlikely couple.

Ms Bisham has never denied the incident and, in a recent interview, even jokingly speculated as to the whereabouts of this unknown Casanova, saying 'It may have happened; after all, we all do stupid things when we're young. Yes, I smoked the odd joint and I may have succumbed to temptation on occasion. I sometimes wonder who he was and what happened to him?'

The Sun *would be happy to arrange a reunion.*

Joe Stamford's whereabouts are currently unknown and Laura Bisham was unavailable for comment at the time of going to press."

Panicking, he picked up the other papers and rifled frantically through the pages as the newsagent looked on disapprovingly. Was this weirdo going to buy a paper or just read them all in the shop? All had covered the story with varying degrees of prominence.

His phone rang again. It was Louise, sounding very worried. 'Joe, why are the press camped outside the house? What have you done?'

'Er, I can explain, dear,' he said, wondering how on earth he could get out of this one. 'There are some stories in the papers about me and Laura Bisham, the Labour MP; something that may have happened thirty years ago, the bit in the book about Greenham Common.'

'You told me you'd made that bit up.'

'Er, I made most of it up; some real bits may have inadvertently slipped through,' he said, squirming. 'Look, just say "no comment" to the press for now. If it gets too bad, take the kids to your Mum and Dad's for a while. I'm so sorry. I've got to phone Petra to sort out this mess. I'll call you back later.'

'Oh, shit!' he said, waiting nervously for Petra's reaction.

'That's an understatement.'

'It could be a coincidence,' he replied, in vain hope.

'I don't think so. You might have got away with it if you hadn't mentioned her UK-shaped birthmark. It isn't common knowledge, but it *is* Commons knowledge. Apparently, it's on her left buttock and she has been known to show it to Tory MPs whenever her patriotism is called into question.'

'Ah,' he said.

'Ah? Is that all you've got to say. I still can't believe it,' she said, sounding slightly nauseous. 'You and Left Wing Laura? I can't imagine anything more implausible.'

'Well, you wanted publicity,' he said, trying to take something positive from the situation. 'Has she got grounds for legal action?'

'I don't know,' she said, sounding seriously pissed off; 'she's claiming defamation of character, but, given that the incident had already been recounted in her biography, you could argue that her character had already been somewhat besmirched. I'm meeting our legal people this afternoon. I suggest you get your arse down here immediately. They'll want to talk to you too.'

14. Back In The Doghouse

The meeting was well under way by the time Joe got there, and he entered the room sheepishly, his head down to dodge the glares of Josh and Petra.

'This is Simon Cavendish, our legal advisor,' said Josh. 'I think you'd better sit down.'

Joe shook his hand, feeling as if he were back at school, standing before the headmaster, accused of some grave misdemeanour for which the punishment would be severe. Joe was disquieted to observe that they'd saved the farting chair for him and that wear and tear hadn't diminished its ability to embarrass.

Simon, a partner in the well-established firm Bardsley and Cavendish, was a tall, imposing, earnest-looking man in his mid-forties. Dressed in black pinstriped suit, with a wide, garish yellow tie, he oozed authority and confidence, and rightly so, for he knew his stuff. He'd dealt with many a libel and slander case in his time and considered it to be his speciality.

'OK, let's cut to the chase,' said Simon. 'I've read the passage that allegedly concerns our complainant and she may have grounds to sue. The first thing I want to establish is whether she is indeed the lady in question, and whether the chain of events in your supposed work of fiction actually occurred.'

'Furthermore,' he continued, 'Josh here has in his possession a document signed by your good self, proclaiming that none of the characters in your book are real people, thereby absolving Embryo Publishing of all responsibility. Let me make it clear that if this goes to court then you, and you alone, will be liable for any recompense awarded to the plaintiff. Now please, tell us your side of the story.'

Joe knew he was in the shit and words like furthermore, thereby absolving, liable, recompense and plaintiff, did little to ease his troubled mind. And this was the easy bit. He still had to face Louise.

'I can't deny that it happened,' confessed Joe, 'but as neither of us knew the other, I thought it safe to recount the story. It was thirty years ago, for God's sake. How was I to know that someone I fumbled clumsily with in a tent would turn out to be famous?'

'And could your fellow fumbler have been Ms Bisham? Do you recognise her now? Are you absolutely sure of the shape and position of the offending birthmark?' asked Simon.

Joe hesitated. It was a long time ago and events were hazy at the time. He couldn't recall what she looked like, the detail of her appearance lost in the mists of time. He'd seen Laura Bisham on TV and wouldn't in a million years have equated this strident, opinionated, quite frankly scary lady with his rose-tinted recollection of what happened on that fateful day.

'I honestly don't know,' he said; 'the birthmark is the only thing I remember for certain.'

'And can you confirm that you've never read and plagiarised Ms Bisham's biography?'

'Certainly not!' said Joe, insulted by the insinuation.

'OK, we can use your denial. Their whole case is based upon the presumption that you have copied the offending passage from her rather seedy biography. It seems that Ms Bisham had confided in a friend with whom she subsequently fell out. Said friend had then delighted in spilling the beans to her indiscreet and uninvited biographer. I must say his account of the, um, affair, is remarkably similar to yours. You, however, have mentioned her intimately positioned birthmark which, ironically, may work in our favour, as said blemish doesn't feature in the work that you are accused of plagiarising.'

'I can assure you that my book is entirely my own work,' said Joe, 'which presumably means that I lost my virginity to Laura Bisham. Not many people can say that.'

'This isn't funny,' said Petra, cringing. (Joe got the impression that she found the very thought rather distasteful.) 'Where do we go from here?'

'It would seem that our miffed MP would rather pursue the line that you have filched this dubious episode, rather than admit that it actually happened. Maybe our Mr Stamford here wouldn't be good for her image,' said Simon, looking down his nose at Joe. 'I'll talk to her people to ascertain whether there is a case to answer and, if so, whether they will settle out of court. In the meantime, I would recommend that you maintain your hitherto natural low profile and try not to say anything to anyone that could further incriminate you.'

It was nearly midnight when Joe got home, thoroughly exhausted from the day's trials, tribulations and travelling. Realising that they wouldn't get anything from Louise, most of the press had given up and left, but a few remained to accost him as he cautiously approached the house.

'Can you give us a statement, Joe?' shouted one reporter, as the camera flashes temporarily blinded him.

'What was she like?' called another. 'I'd imagine she was on top.'

'No comment, no comment,' he said, as he ran to the door and, fumbling with his key, prepared to face the music.

He'd phoned ahead to tell Louise that he was on his way home and her icy tone had forewarned of hell to pay. As he entered, she was sitting at the dining room table surrounded by the day's papers. He could tell she'd been crying and she had a look of exasperated anger.

'Oh, Joe, how could you?' she said, the tears welling up again. 'Is it true?'

'I'm sorry,' he said, pouring himself a glass of wine from the half-empty bottle. 'You shouldn't have to go through this. I won't deny it, but it was thirty years ago, long before we met. We were both getting on a bit when we got together. You have a past as well.'

'Yes, but I haven't written a book about it for the entire world to read,' she said. 'How many others are there to come out of the woodwork? What about the wife in the story? Is she supposed to be me?'

'Of course not, she's totally different; they met on a blind date, they have twins, there's no comparison.'

'He seems to love her a lot,' she sobbed.

'And I love you a lot; much more than a lot, in fact,' he assured her. 'How can you be jealous of a fictional character?'

'But this Laura Bisham; she's not fictional, is she?'

'Unfortunately not,' he said. 'I only wish she were.'

'I don't know if I can trust you any more. What else haven't you told me?'

'There's nothing more, honestly,' he replied, trying to convince himself as well. 'It's all made up or wildly exaggerated. Look, Charles Dickens was familiar with the streets of London, but he didn't pick a pocket or two; and, as far as I know, he wasn't visited by ghosts at Christmas. All made up, figments of his brilliant imagination.'

'You're not seriously comparing this crap to Dickens,' she shouted, throwing 'That Bloody Book' at him. She'd obviously read it again in the light of the day's events.

'Do you really think it's crap?' he said, deeply offended. 'Anyway, this *crap* is starting to sell and may well yet keep us in the luxury to which we've become accustomed.'

'Until you lose it all in court; and apart from that, I'm not sure that I want to be kept in luxury on the proceeds of this.'

'OK, let me know when you've decided,' he sighed, too tired to argue. 'I was hoping I could rely on you for support. God knows, I've got no-one else. I'm going to bed, I'm absolutely knackered.'

'The spare room's ready for you,' she said, turning her back. 'Good night.'

* * *

'Daddy, what's a leftie lover?' asked Emma at breakfast. 'They were singing in the playground yesterday – your daddy's a leftie lover, your daddy's a leftie lover – I don't like it.'

'Don't take any notice, dear; they'll soon get fed up if you ignore them,' said Joe, his heart breaking.

'Daddy, why were those people outside the house yesterday?' asked Jamie. 'They followed us to school and kept asking Mummy questions. Mummy told one of them to fuck off. What does fuck off mean, Daddy?'

'Just ignore them, they're writers for the newspapers, they're not very nice people,' said Joe, peeking through the curtain to see some of them still there, 'and don't repeat that word again. Mummy only said it because she was angry.'

'Aren't you a writer too, Daddy? Are you a nice person?'

'You better ask your mum,' said Joe, his heart sinking as he saw the packed cases in the hall.

'I'm taking the kids to Mum and Dad's for a while,' said Louise, her mind made up; 'they shouldn't have to suffer this.'

'I'll call you every day till you come back,' said Joe, as he hugged Emma and Jamie. Louise turned away.

Tears not far away, he watched helpless as the car disappeared around the corner. Furious with himself, he returned to the house, alone again, naturally.

Climbing back into bed, moribund, he pulled the covers around him and tried to shut out the world.

Late morning and thoroughly depressed, he called Petra for an update.

'This is not going to go away,' she said with some sympathy; 'she wants her pound of flesh. Look, Simon Cavendish is the best in the business; if anyone can sort out this mess, it'll be him.'

'Can you ask him to come and fix my marriage too?' asked Joe.

'Not in his remit, I'm afraid,' she replied, 'that one's down to you.'

15. Don't Talk To Me About Love

Toothpaste tube squeezed in the middle, teaspoons left lying around the kitchen, towels falling from their rails, the death hazard of toys left on the stairs, clothes thrown on the floor instead of in the washing basket, he now ached desperately for all the mundane irritations that used to drive him mad. He'd been alone on the road, but had consoled himself with the knowledge that home life was proceeding unabated, that the purpose of his solitary mission was to enable that life to continue, awaiting his happy return.

This was an altogether different kind of loneliness, the house full of poignant reminders of his previously under-appreciated ideal existence. Photos everywhere, half-read books and magazines, the board games they played during the school holidays, Louise's broken shoe that he hadn't got round to gluing, Emma's one-legged doll that he'd christened Eileen and Jamie's least-loved teddy bears left behind to keep him company. A constant, deafening silence prevailed, an endless emptiness, a void where the unconditional love of his family used to be.

Pouring himself a glass of red to accompany yet another takeaway, he switched on the TV to witness a familiar catastrophe on the other side of the world. There are people worse off than me, he thought, feeling guilt at his self-pity.

* * *

Laura Bisham had been born into a wealthy family and had enjoyed a privileged upbringing in prosperous leafy suburbia. Despite her idyllic childhood, she had delighted in being a rebellious teenager, much of her activity specifically designed to shock and upset her long-suffering parents. She found her bourgeois life boring, longed for adventure and relished conflict.

She'd initially joined CND as a snub to her nuclear physicist father, but in time grew to genuinely believe in their stance and philosophy. When their initial impetus withered, she became a Labour Party activist, her intention to infiltrate the fortress and change things from within.

Surviving smears against her character relating to her supposedly promiscuous behaviour at Greenham Common, the position of Member of Parliament for an underprivileged ward on the outskirts of London was her reward for tenacious lobbying on human rights and campaigning against the draconian stop and search laws employed by the police in the eighties. No-one was more aware than she of the contradiction between her current membership of the establishment and her youthful ideals.

Laura eschewed marriage and relationships, politics and ambition stealing her once natural sense of humour and ability to love. Her public image the antithesis of sex appeal, men had been known to run a mile.

The biography was an embarrassment, threatening to make her a laughing stock, and she had attempted in vain to block its publication. Her intention was to write her own version of events when the time was right, preferably after her retirement, and she'd been angry at being superseded by this tawdry effort. She strongly disagreed with autobiographies written too young, before the subject had lived life to the full, cashing in on transient fame.

The monthly MP surgeries in her constituency were, she felt, the furthest point you could get from changing the world. A necessary but unglamorous part of the role, dealing with the public wasn't one of her strengths. Frowning, she perused the familiar petty complaints on the day's list: Mrs Jones' consistently late bin collections, objections to the erection of a telephone mast, the old chestnut about inconsiderate parents parking on the pavements outside schools, and a Mr Drofmats whinging about the building of a multi-storey car park that threatened to spoil his view.

She knew that these apparent trivialities were important to people, but they weren't the reason she had gone into politics. She afforded each appointment ten minutes of her valuable time and, on each occasion, promised to look into the issue and come back to them.

Only a few more to go, she thought, looking up and taking a sharp breath as Mr Drofmats entered the room. 'What the hell are you doing here and why are you wearing that ridiculous hat?' she shouted. 'Get out now, before I call security.'

The disguise was probably unnecessary. Even after his new-found infamy, his nondescript features had allowed Joe to walk the streets relatively unhindered. Nevertheless, it wouldn't do any harm to change his appearance to negate any unwanted attention.

If you want to get ahead, get a hat, he'd said to himself as he entered the shop containing a veritable cornucopia of titfers. He'd tried on many, before deciding upon a pork pie number, to be worn at a jaunty angle, giving him the appearance of a roadie from the Specials.

'That suits you,' said an attractive lady standing nearby.

'Sold!' he replied; 'how much is it?'

'Oh, I don't work here. I'm just saying that it suits you.'

'Then it's definitely sold,' smiled Joe, making his way to the checkout; 'thank you.'

He barely noticed the large man in the next aisle trying on leather jackets, the scar on his left cheek concealed by a strategically placed cravat.

Now Joe stood nervously before Laura Bisham, wondering whether this was such a good idea after all. 'Please hear me out. Just give me ten minutes,' he pleaded, raising his hands. 'I have a proposition.'

'I hope it's not the same as your last proposition,' she said; 'look at the mess that got us into. Go ahead, you have five minutes.'

'Look, all we're doing is lining the pockets of solicitors,' he said, trying to sound like the voice of reason, 'how about a deal? I'll donate a percentage of the profits from sales to a charity of your choice and you call off the dogs. Given our common ground on many issues, I thought maybe Greenpeace would be appropriate. Apart from the fact that the money would go to a good cause, it would be good publicity for both of us, a win-win situation.'

'Go on,' she said, curious, not dismissing the idea out of hand.

'It would boost your credibility as a radical champion of anti-establishment causes and portray us both as adults, capable of compromise and reason. Why not use this unfortunate situation for the common good?'

Laura begrudgingly considered his words and couldn't argue with the logic behind them.

'What percentage did you have in mind?' she asked.

'Hadn't really given the detail much thought, only the concept; how about three?'

'Make it five and I'll think about it.'

'OK, that sounds reasonable; should we make a joint statement?' he said, surprised. He hadn't expected her to give in so easily, but she looked tired and stressed. Perhaps she, like him, just wanted this whole sleazy episode to go away.

'I'll get my publicity guys to draft one,' she said; 'they'll be in touch.'

'Thanks for being so understanding,' said Joe, as he stood and proffered his hand. 'It's been the business doing pleasure with you.'

Her hand felt cold and clammy, not at all like the warmth of the hazy memory that he'd replayed a thousand times.

'It wasn't such a bad thing that happened was it?' questioned Joe, looking her in the eye.

'Don't push it,' she said, as she showed him the door.

16. Fame

Louise's parents had downsized when she and her sister had left home, no longer requiring the space afforded by their rambling three-bed semi. Their current living arrangement, a two-bed bungalow, was ill-equipped to accommodate five people, much less two young children with all their associated accoutrements.

They had looked forward to their retirement, a peaceful life and the freedom to spend their time as they chose. Much as they loved their eldest daughter and grandchildren, the chaos they brought with them constantly threatened the tranquillity of their humble home and Louise and the kids were in danger of outstaying their welcome.

'You know you are always welcome here,' said her dad, 'but it's not really practical as a long-term arrangement, is it? You should work at your marriage. Couples give up too easily these days. Joe's not such a bad bloke; what is it he's done that's so bad?'

'You've changed your tune; you always said that I could do better, that Joe wasn't good enough for me,' replied Louise.

'Every dad thinks that their princess can do better. At least he doesn't beat you up like that other thug you hooked up with. He's a steady chap; give him another chance.'

'He used to be a steady chap, bloody infuriating at times, but a steady chap nonetheless,' she said. 'He's been different since the book was published; it's like it has a life of its own that's taking our lives down a route neither of us wants to go.'

'So have you split up with Joe or with what the book has done to him?' he said. 'He's the same man. He's just struggling to come to terms with the consequences of a mistake. I know he loves you and the kids and would never do anything to intentionally hurt you.'

'Then why is he appearing on tonight's Jason Reeves show with that bloody woman?' she asked.

'You're kidding!' said her dad in disbelief. 'He wouldn't do that. He hasn't got the guts to go on the telly for a start.'

'Well he is and we'd better get used to it; you've got a famous son-in-law, at least until the divorce comes through.'

'You've done what?' Petra had shouted, 'I thought we'd agreed to leave this to Simon; he's the expert in cases such as this.'

'I'm not questioning his credentials,' replied Joe, 'but I can't see why we should pay for a solicitor when Laura and I can reach an amicable agreement.'

'On first name terms now, are we?' she said. 'Wasn't so long ago you didn't even know her name. Have you got any more surprises for me?'

'She's agreed to drop the legal action and I've agreed a joint statement with her press office,' he stated. 'It should be in tomorrow's papers. Oh, and there is one more thing. They've arranged for us both to appear on this Friday's Jason Reeves show.'

'What!! Are you serious?'

'Indeed I am,' he said. 'You couldn't buy publicity like that; hope you've got enough copies printed … sales will go through the roof.'

Petra had to admit that his reckless action could prove to be beneficial. 'How did you pull that off?' she said, genuinely impressed.

'It wasn't my idea; her people seem to think we can both come out of this OK, not exactly smelling of roses, but at least with some credibility.'

'Do you know what you're letting yourself in for?' warned Petra. 'You could be made to look ridiculous. Laura Bisham is used to the spotlight and dealing with awkward questions.'

'What have I got to lose?' he said. 'Things can't get any worse. Louise says she's not ready to come back. I'm going to deal with this, um, misunderstanding, once and for all on live TV.'

'Your mind is obviously made up and I'm not going to try to dissuade you. All I can say is good luck. I think the expression is "break a leg"..

'Knowing my luck, I probably will, on the way to the studio.'

Joe had never worn make-up before and didn't see why he should start now.

'Is this really necessary?' he protested, as they prepared him for interview. 'You can't polish a turd, you know'.

'Yes but we can reduce the glare from your head,' the make-up lady patiently explained; 'the lights are pretty bright and if we don't do this you'll look like a Belisha beacon'.

Standing stage left, he turned to Laura. 'Are you sure this is a good idea?'

'Don't worry, just be yourself,' she said, 'and remember what we agreed: let me do most of the talking and no gory detail.'

'I don't remember any gory detail,' replied Joe. 'Are you sure you don't want me to tell them how hot you were?'

Laura glared at him. 'Stick to the facts, a youthful indiscretion, it didn't mean anything, sorry you wrote about it, reached an amicable settlement, etc., etc.'

'It meant something to me at the time,' said Joe. 'I was ready to burst until you came along.'

'Too much information,' she said, still glaring. 'I think we're on in a minute. Just follow me.'

For a moment there, Joe could have sworn he saw her blush.

'You've read about it in the papers, the most unlikely couple in the news and they're here to talk about their *in tents* relationship,' Jason Reeves built to a crescendo, 'ladies and gentlemen, please welcome Laura Bisham and Joe Stamford.'

The sound of John and Yoko's 'Give Peace a Chance' echoed

round the studio as Laura, closely followed by Joe, descended the stairs to applause.

'Thanks for coming on, guys,' smiled Jason. 'This is an incredible story and one that's gripped the nation. Laura, when did you first realise that the lady in Joe's book was you?'

'It was brought to my attention by a fellow MP of a conflicting persuasion, who shall remain nameless. For some reason he thought it would be in the public interest to leak the story. He tells me he was tipped off by an anonymous caller.'

'Must have been embarrassing for both of you when it hit the headlines,' continued Jason. 'Joe, do you regret writing it?'

'Not entirely; it is an important part of the story, the rites of passage, as it were, but I wish I'd written it in such a way that Laura wasn't implicated. We've all said things we regret; however, I don't see how I could have foreseen all of this fuss.'

Jason winked at Joe. 'You can tell us. Was she any good?'

'I have fond memories of the day, apart from the bit where I got arrested,' he said hesitantly, glancing at Laura, 'but I was somewhat inebriated, so the detail is lost. For me it was a positive experience and I think I've written it as such.'

'What about you, Laura? Was *he* any good or have you conveniently forgotten the, um, detail too?'

'I must say I had banished the incident to the back of my mind, until I read the papers the other week,' she replied. 'It was a while back; we were both young and impetuous and, I must admit, a little pissed.'

'Not to mention high,' added Jason; 'did you, um, smoke a lot in those days?'

'A little. Let's just say it was part of the prevailing culture in the circles in which I moved at the time,' said Laura. 'I grew up soon after and have not touched it since.'

'You come across as a very serious politician. Do you feel any nostalgia for those days when you were a little more, um, young and fancy free?'

'Of course, we'd all like to be young again with less responsibility,' Laura smiled, 'but it's a serious, big bad world out there. We can't carry on regardless of the consequences of our actions.'

'Joe, you seem to be of a similar political bent to Laura here and I understand you've reached an understanding with regard to your indiscretion. Can you tell us how that came about?'

'I used to be a Labour Party member and we met at a CND camp, so yes, we have some ideals in common,' said Joe. 'Laura had a right to be pissed off with the situation, but I went to see her with the proposition that I pay a percentage of the profits to Greenpeace instead of making our solicitors even richer than they already are. Thankfully, she has been magnanimous and let me off the hook.'

'It's good to see two people sorting out their disagreements by talking to each other. If only politics worked like that,' said Jason; 'and are you both happy with this arrangement?'

'I nearly kicked him out,' said Laura, 'but Greenpeace is close to my heart and he won me over with his argument. The arrangement suits us both and Joe is right, I'm sure there are cases more worthy of the attention of our legal representatives.'

'Joe, all the publicity can't have had a detrimental effect on sales and I understand that it's now among the bestsellers. A good stunt, wasn't it?'

'You can't possibly be suggesting that I planned all this,' replied Joe. 'It was starting to take off before this all came out, but yes, I would have been traipsing round the country for the rest of my life to get this much exposure. It's not had an entirely positive effect on my life, though.'

'Yes, I believe your wife hasn't taken it so well.'

'To say she was a little upset would be an understatement,' said Joe. 'She's currently staying elsewhere, hopefully just until the furore dies down. The kids are being picked on at school, and this whole mess is my fault. Can I say on TV, darling, please come home, I can't live without you. I'm sorry, I love you and I'm missing you and the kids.'

'No more camping trips planned with the lovely Laura then?' laughed Jason. 'I hope you can patch things up with Mrs Stamford; how can she refuse after such a heart-felt plea? Laura, do you think this saga has done you any disservice? Hasn't it added a human element to your public image?'

'I thought I was a fully functioning member of the human race before, but I guess it shows that there was life before politics. What happened happened and we did no-one any harm.'

'And what's next, Joe? This was your first novel; has this experience put you off?'

'No, I still love writing. Maybe a children's book; hopefully that will prove less controversial.'

'I'll look forward to reading it to my kids, as long as Laura's not in it. Don't want them having nightmares,' concluded Jason. 'Thanks very much and I wish you both all the best in your future ventures. Laura and Joe, ladies and gentlemen. Now my next guest is well known for a decadent lifestyle ...'

In a dingy bedsit in Islington, a man leant forward in his armchair as the interview reached its conclusion. This was getting out of hand; it was time to act.

17. And The Healing Has Begun

Joe entered the damp, musty old church with trepidation, not knowing if he would be welcomed. A few people nodded their acknowledgements as he took his place in a rear pew, trying to remain inconspicuous. To him this was alien territory, to be treated warily, his attendance record poor: christenings, weddings or funerals only.

He was uncomfortable with organised religion, finding the inherent rituals and pomp both ludicrous and dangerous. He believed there was once a man called Jesus, a good, kind man with a message of love and tolerance, but distrusted the bible and the men and women who preached its subjective message. He often used the analogy of Chinese whispers to explain his scepticism, believing that if a message is given to one person and they are asked to pass it on, then by the time that message has travelled through half a dozen people it is corrupted, its original words and intent changed beyond recognition. His view was that the bible had not only been handed down through innumerable generations, it had also been translated into many languages and abused ruthlessly by men of power, each with their own spin and agenda. He couldn't see how the original teachings of Jesus (who would no doubt be dismissed as a crank, or at best a communist, if he lived today) could have survived such a journey intact.

Although he had to concede that the modern world would benefit from somebody turning over the tables of the money lenders, or feeding the five thousand, Joe was unconvinced that these parables actually happened. Hence, he felt hypocritical upon passing through the portal of any religious establishment.

Joe's suit looked like it belonged to someone else, as if he'd stolen it. Ill-fitting and lacking style, trousers too long for his stumpy legs, he shuffled uneasily in his seat until the service began.

'We are gathered here today to celebrate the life of Raymond Arthur Willis,' announced the Reverend Jones, 'a modest life in many respects, but one that touched the hearts of all who knew him. Of humble origins, Ray began life as a farm hand's son, one of five children, only three of whom survived the poverty of their circumstances.

'Ray was a fighter from an early age, beating TB and Smallpox in childhood without the aid of the inoculations we all now take for granted. He never spoke of his Distinguished Conduct Medal received during World War Two, modestly considering it merely to be recognition of adherence to his duty. After the war and with a young family, Ray and Elizabeth moved to town, where he gained the factory employment in which he would remain for most of his working life.

'Ray leaves a caring family, his wife Elizabeth, daughters Mary and Anne, son George, his brother Fred and sister Agnes, not to mention his numerous grandchildren, all of whom made him a very proud man. Please stand for Ray's favourite hymn, "Jerusalem", number 319 in your hymn books.'

How can anyone sum up a life in so few words, thought Joe, as he sang 'Jerusalem' off key and too loud: it was one of his favourite hymns too.

Joe took a deep breath as Louise walked towards him at the end of the service. He knew that carnal thoughts were inappropriate in church, but she'd always looked incredible in black.

'Thanks for coming,' she smiled. 'I know that Dad will appreciate it.'

'Don't mention it,' replied Joe, looking into those eyes he'd missed so much. 'I always liked and respected your Uncle Ray. He was good to everyone, never a bad word to say. How are the kids?'

'They're fine, both at school, bit young for all of this. Are you coming back for the wake?'

'I don't want to impose,' said Joe, hoping she would insist. He would use any excuse to be near Louise again, even if it were just for a few hours.

'Don't be daft, you're part of the family,' she said; 'besides, for some reason Uncle Ray liked you too; he'd have wanted you to be there. You can come with me to collect Emma and Jamie from school later. It'll be a nice surprise for them.'

'Great,' smiled Joe, briefly elated. 'I'd love to, thanks.'

Conversation with Louise had never been a chore, but as they drove to school it felt awkward, stilted, as if things had changed, which of course they had.

'So, what's it like being famous then?' asked Louise, blurting out the first words that came into her head.

'Oh, you know, yesterday's news is tomorrow's fish and chip paper,' he replied. 'The press have moved on to their next victims, so thankfully I can go about my business without being hassled too much. Sales are good though and I must be doing something right, got a crap review in the *Mail on Sunday*.'

Emma and Jamie were overcome with excitement when they spotted Joe, Jamie tripping in his haste to reach him and cutting open his knee.

'Hey, come on, tiger, be brave,' said Joe, as he lifted him on to his shoulders, 'there's a plaster in the car. We'll soon fix this up.'

Louise felt a pang of tenderness as she walked alongside them. Joe wasn't a bad dad and his love for his children was never in doubt.

'Mummy, are we going back to live with Daddy?' pleaded Emma.

'Maybe, if that's what Daddy wants,' she said, glancing at Joe.

'Are you kidding, there's nothing in this world I want more,' he replied.

'Yippee!' screamed Emma and began skipping down the street, Louise bursting into laughter as Joe skipped alongside her with Jamie still on his shoulders, his bad knee forgotten.

'Will you stop grinning, this is supposed to be a wake,' slurred Louise's dad, his arm round Joe's shoulder. The death of his big brother had hit him hard, but the healing qualities of his best brandy and the proximity of his family had at least temporarily eased the pain. 'You two were made for each other, you know. Not only am I delighted for you, but I'm even more delighted to have my house back. Are you taking them home tonight?'

'Just try and stop me,' said Joe, raising his glass; 'to Uncle Ray.'

House once again a home as the children ran around laughing and singing, checking that everything was still the same. Aside from a few extra layers of dust, all seemed to be in order. Zola the goldfish head-butted the side of the tank as if he too felt the excitement. Joe thought about the morning the previous year when they had descended for breakfast as usual, until the routine was punctured by Jamie's anguished cries. 'Zola's gone, Zola's gone.'

Joe had peered into the tank and had to agree that it was indeed fishless. Frantically searching, a glint of gold was soon located behind the cabinet, which Joe struggled in vain to move in order to reach the by now surely deceased fish.

'He must have jumped out,' concluded Joe. 'Don't get upset, but he's probably dead.'

Removing the hundred or so rarely played vinyl LPs, the cabinet was finally light enough to shift sufficiently to accommodate an outstretched arm. To Joe's amazement, Zola wriggled, escaped and dropped back into the corner, his second attempt at this unorthodox method of fishing successful as he dropped the dusty, drowsy, but incredibly still living fish back into the tank.

Now Joe too was grateful to be saved from a slow, dark demise. He was dazed and shell shocked, but still very much alive. With his family back intact, he once again felt able to swim, whichever way the tide would flow.

18. The Poacher

Joe considered happiness to be but a brief transient moment where one's orbit coincides with one's dreams. If lucky, then sufficient orbits are completed in a lifetime for this happy collision to occasionally reoccur. The best that can be hoped for during the remainder of an existence is a drifting contentment achieved through compromise.

He realised that this was his second chance and that if he screwed up again he may not get another. Never feeling that he had earned the right to true happiness, he was forever looking over his shoulder awaiting the sting in the tail. He'd been on this Earth long enough to know that it couldn't last. Enjoy it while it's there, thought Joe; someone will be along shortly to crap in your swimming pool, add grit to your Vaseline, or to rain on your parade.

Had life really been less complicated in his parents' day, or was it a facade? Relationships, at least on the surface, appeared to remain on an even keel, through thick and thin. They had withstood far choppier waters than he and remained stoic throughout, together without question, never considering an alternative.

Joe envied their generation. They didn't have the choices brought by modern vacuous freedom, but nevertheless always seemed content with their share of the cake. Uncomplaining – health, a roof over their heads and food on the table were all they asked.

Unnoticed, he watched his wife and wondered once again at how he'd been so lucky to meet her, at the gifts she had given, their wonderful children. It was almost surreal, as if this idyllic life wasn't his, events happening while he spectated from the periphery.

Engrossed in the contents of a pile of battered notebooks, Louise said without looking up, 'You should read these.'

'What are they?' enquired Joe, switching off the TV. In the absence of anything else on, he was half-watching a repeat of *QI*, one of his favourite programmes, rerun yet again. Louise was bewildered by how many times he could watch this stuff without getting bored with it.

'Uncle Ray's diaries,' she said. 'Dad dropped them round earlier; he said Uncle Ray wanted me to have them, they're fascinating. I had no idea he'd had such a colourful life.'

Joe's interest aroused, he joined Louise at the dining room table and began flicking through the yellowed pages, hooked on the detail, a microcosm of a bygone era.

'Wow, these are good,' he said. 'Let's get them in the right order and start from the beginning.'

It was one o'clock in the morning before Joe yawned, 'We'd better hit the sack and resume reading tomorrow. I'd lost track of time.'

'You could use his story for a book, you know,' said Louise, tapping one of the covers; 'there's history, heartbreak, adventure, everything in here.'

'I was thinking the very same thing,' replied Joe. 'Don't you think the family would mind, though? It's pretty racy in places.'

'Possibly, but that must be why he left them to me, so that his tale wasn't lost. He must have wanted you to adapt them.'

So much for Joe's assumptions about the calm waters of the previous generation; in his lifetime Uncle Ray had been a poacher, a gypsy, a philanderer, a war hero, a strike breaker, a shop steward, a family man and many more things besides.

'Are you sure? I promised Emma and Jamie I'd finish my children's book,' said Joe, stroking his chin in thought; 'it's half-done and I want to complete it before they outgrow it, but "Uncle Ray's Diaries" could be the follow-up; it's one hell of a story. He's had more women than James Bond. I've often wondered, did Roger Moore roger more as James Bond or The Saint? Somebody should do an analysis, but I reckon your Uncle Ray could beat them both. What about your Auntie Liz and cousins, though? They can't know about these diaries.'

'No, Uncle Ray entrusted them to Dad; he was the only one that knew they existed. Can't you change the names like you did with 'That Bloody Book'?'

'I could, but look at the mess that got me into,' he said. 'I shouldn't have to point out to you the dangers of writing about actual events and passing them off as fiction. I can just imagine one of Uncle Ray's octogenarian ex-conquests reading about a brief dalliance that happened sixty years ago and taking umbrage, not to mention what your Auntie Liz would do to me. Hell hath no fury, as the saying goes. Let's sleep on it and talk about it tomorrow.'

Joe slowly poured himself a bottle of John Hampden Ale, sat back in his favourite armchair, closed his eyes and listened intently as Louise read aloud, a synopsis forming in his mind as her silky tones recounted a fascinating lifetime.

Ray Willis came screaming into a poor, ragged existence on October twenty-fifth, nineteen nineteen, his impoverished parents' first born. He saw little of his father, who worked for a pittance as a farm hand for a rich landowner.

Despite their poverty, Ray had a relatively carefree childhood, a daily adventure as he and his ragamuffin companions joyfully ran among the fields and woods. As he grew, he learnt to avoid his father, whose character had been irrevocably tarnished by the slaughter he'd seen on the battlefields of the First World War, by the indignity of kowtowing to the squire and by the lack of hope for a more prosperous future. Once a doting husband and loving father, he'd grown mean and violent, raging against the world, his nearest and dearest caught in the crossfire.

Ray's resilient mother took most of the flak and the blows,

protecting her children whenever possible from their father's brutality. The tragic demise of two of Ray's siblings, a sister at age two from smallpox and a brother age six months from cot death, made his dad angrier, his mum sadder and Ray older than his years. Two further children survived, Louise's father Fred and her Auntie Agnes.

Unlike many poorer boys of the era, Ray could read and write well, taught by the local vicar, who had started a boys' club in order to rein in the criminal tendencies of the youthful dispossessed. Ray had begun his diaries at the age of fourteen, shortly before the enforced end of his inadequate schooling, when he was kicked out, unprepared, into an uncaring world. He'd had little choice but to work on the farm with his dad, who took for granted that his oldest son would follow in his footsteps.

At this point Ray would see first-hand one of the causes of his father's anger at the world and vowed to fight against the injustice of their circumstances in any way he could. It had been easy to steal one of the gamekeeper's rifles and ammunition from the unlocked shed and he found a deserted barn in which to hone his shooting skills, utilising every spare hour of daylight.

Known among his peers as the Poacher, his parents turned a blind eye as rabbit and pheasant appeared in the larder. Ray became adept at hoodwinking the gamekeeper and squire, seeing his ill-gotten gains as just reward for their poorly-paid labours on the farm.

Ever more emboldened by his success, he became more reckless with each poaching escapade, the sport of fooling his adversaries as fulfilling as the spoils of his trespass. Until one evening when, as the light faded to dusk and the gamekeeper lay in wait, he was painfully shot in the arse as he made his escape.

Arrested, after the doctor's betrayal followed the removal of the bullet, he was sentenced to two months' hard labour. Denounced by his father, who feared he would lose his only source of income by association, Ray vowed to make his own way in the world once freed, returning rarely and secretly to visit his mother, brother and sister.

Upon his release, the day after his fifteenth birthday, he set out on the road as autumn turned to winter, accepting intermittent shelter and employment as and when offered. Taken in and deflowered by Rose, a gypsy matriarch widow who became both his clandestine lover and surrogate mother, he spent the following year with the travellers, moving from one town to another, forever unwelcome. Begrudgingly accepted into the fold at Rose's insistence and due to his useful poaching skills, Ray was briefly contented with this nomadic existence.

It was at the village Christmas dance, gate-crashed with three other lads from the gypsy camp, that he met Elizabeth. Love at first sight! They danced all night and kissed, without thinking where their sensuous frivolity would lead.

Beaten to within an inch of his life and left by the roadside by a raging, jealous Rose's two teenage sons, he sought solace with Elizabeth, who secretly hid him in an abandoned shed, fed him and nursed him back to health.

The inevitability of Elizabeth's pregnancy and their subsequent shotgun wedding saw Ray temporarily tamed as her father took him in and gave him work as a labourer, not as an act of charity but to ensure that he toe the line and have the means to support his daughter and her impending child.

Ray, however, had grown accustomed to life on the road and couldn't settle. Despite his love for Elizabeth, he longed for adventure and freedom and, promising to return one day, left to eradicate the wanderlust from his system. Work, food, lodging and seduction would intermittently come his way as he travelled the country for the next four years, his winning smile and gift of the gab his ticket to an occasionally enviable lifestyle.

For a while he dreamed of America, the endless possibilities of freedom in the land of opportunity, but there was never enough money for the fare and he would spend the rest of his life wondering what could have been.

Nagging pangs of lust and love for Elizabeth, though, followed him to wherever he laid his hat, along with a curious longing to see his child. Unborn before he left, he didn't even know if it was a boy or a girl. Begging her father not to kill him, Elizabeth cautiously welcomed him back, their beautiful daughter Mary ensuring he would never voluntarily wander again.

Stopping just long enough to impregnate his wife once more, he was invited to join the Army for the Second World War. Somehow he knew that refusing the invitation would cause offence, so he reluctantly reported for duty on his allotted day.

His inherent distrust and dislike of authority ensured his early military experiences were filled with futile conflict; not with the enemy, but with his superiors. Learning quickly to keep his head down to avoid the petty punishments given for disobeying orders, he soon accumulated methods of ducking and diving to make his servitude as comfortable as possible.

With much of the war spent trying to get one over on the hated Sergeant Collins, Ray would ironically receive his Distinguished Conduct Medal for saving his life, carrying his wounded sergeant for two miles across the trenches whilst avoiding enemy fire.

After joining his colleagues in taking full advantage of the gratitude of numerous mademoiselles at the jubilant culmination of hostilities, he returned home a hero.

A country fit for heroes, however, would be some years away and Ray and his young family were economically obliged to move to town, where the previously itinerant traveller was trapped into factory employment. Like a caged animal, he resented the loss of his freedom and rebelled, both against the big stick of the bosses and the camaraderie of the unions. Never afraid of hard work, he performed his job well, but wouldn't take instruction. He'd had enough of orders during the war. When the strikes came, he refused to take part, seeing the union as yet another body telling him what to do.

Labelled a scab by his workmates, he was initially exiled when they returned to work, having gained many of the concessions for which they had fought. The experience, though, was to change him from loner to comrade as he saw what solidarity could achieve and, by the time of the next strike, he had risen to the rank of shop steward.

The penchant for filching the gentry's grouse and pheasant, though, never left him, and the local butcher would often heed the knock on the back door and provide Ray with his beer money.

Now a family man with a sense of purpose, transformed from lone maverick to man of the people, he became a well-respected figure in the community and a thorn in the side of the factory owners; a stalwart leader, trusted and revered by his peers, with a joke or a tale forever on his lips.

'Phew, these stories have to be told,' said Joe, after they'd consumed the entire contents of the diaries. 'The question is, how can I keep it anonymous? Would Uncle Ray have *wanted* it to be anonymous, or would he have wished for posthumous fame?'

'I shouldn't think he'd care now; he won't be around to take the flak,' said Louise; 'it'll be us that will get it in the neck if it upsets anyone. I'll talk to Dad and see what he thinks; we have to be careful. This could blow the family apart.'

Impending events, however, would dictate that 'Uncle Ray's Diaries' would have to remain on the back burner for some time.

19. Trapped

'Are we doing anything on Friday?' Joe asked Louise, as they washed up, revelling in mundane domesticity. 'With everything that's been going on, I've not seen Robin and the lads for a while.'

In his uncharacteristic single-minded ambition, he knew that he'd woefully neglected one of his life's most important components: friendship.

'Don't know if I should let you out of my sight,' she replied, only half joking. 'Where are you going and what will you be getting up to?'

'A couple of beers and a curry in town, that's all; there's no-one better than Robin to bring me back down to earth.'

'OK, but don't talk to any strangers,' she said, as if to a child, conceding that a dose of normality couldn't do any harm.

To his relief, they were all pleased to see him, slapping him on the back, arms round his shoulders as he caught up on their news. Frank had lost his job and was considering starting his own catering business; John had become a dad for the third time; and Simon was still dragging his guitar round the pub circuit and had a big gig next week.

Incessant questions ensued about who he'd met on the Jason Reeves show, and there was the inevitable piss taking about his infamous conquest; but it felt great to be on safe, everyday territory, among people he knew and trusted.

As the evening came to an end too soon, Joe reflected upon what was important in life.

'I've missed you guys, you know,' he slurred; 'what would I do without my mates? We should do this more often.'

'*We* haven't been anywhere,' said Robin. 'You know where we are when you want to talk to us plebs again.'

Alcohol-fuelled nostalgia and affection for his home town filled his eyes, as he surveyed the familiar surroundings of the market square whilst queuing for a taxi. Since his beating many years ago, he'd been reluctant to walk home alone and, though he knew he needed the exercise, he considered his safety and good looks more important.

'Southside Close, please,' he directed the taxi driver and sat back, warm in the glow of a pleasant evening spent among friends.

Shocked suddenly from his contentment by a huge man opening the opposite door and sitting next to him, he said, 'Sorry, mate, this taxi's taken.'

'It is now,' said the man in an accent that Joe couldn't place. In terror, he felt something solid hidden beneath a newspaper sticking in his side. The man turned to the taxi driver. 'Now, it's time to earn that money. Take us to the Freshwater Industrial Estate.'

'What's this all about?' asked Joe, a cold sweat breaking out. 'Look, pal, I don't want any trouble. I just want to go home.'

'Just drive and don't ask any questions,' the man instructed the driver. Looking nervously in his mirror at his terrified passenger, the driver pulled hesitantly out of the rank.

Despite Joe's desperate pleas, the stranger remained silent throughout the short trip to the darkness on the edge of town, where the once-thriving industrial quarter now resembled a ghost town. As they stopped outside a decaying, deserted warehouse, the man handed the driver a generous fifty pounds and growled, 'Keep the change. Remember that as soon as you agreed to this little trip you became an accessory and don't forget that I know your cab number. If you tell anyone about this, I'll come looking for you.'

Pushing Joe roughly out of the car and transferring the

something solid painfully to his back, he said, 'Now walk, dog breath, in there.'

Taking in his surroundings in the moonlight, the crumbling façade of the building, weeds growing through cracked concrete, the broken security cameras, Joe stumbled ahead with a painful reminder in his back each time he faltered from the designated path.

Louise looked at the clock once again, wondering why she was waiting up, as if for a delinquent teenage son to return, the curfew long since broken. One thirty in the morning; why was Joe so late, where could he have got to? Thinking that they'd probably ended up in some dodgy club, she reassured herself that he was a grown man (if such a beast existed) and retired to bed, tossing and turning, waking every half an hour.

At three o'clock she tried his phone. 'Hello, this is Joe Stamford. I can't be bothered to talk to you at the moment. Leave a message if you want and I'll get back to you when I feel like it.'

Worried sick, she phoned a drowsy Robin. 'We left him at the taxi rank at about 11.30,' he said. 'He was a bit pissed, but I assumed he was on his way home. Let me know if he doesn't turn up.'

Should she call the police? Friday night and they would have their hands full. Would they take seriously the disappearance of a man who hadn't come home after a night out? 'Are you sure he hasn't ended up at a party or a club, or gone off with another woman?' they would ask.

Feeling powerless, she decided to leave it until the morning before raising the alarm.

Arms and legs tied tightly, clueless as to the motive of his adversary, Joe had been left alone for some time before his captor returned to torment him. Hank Schneider wondered how he'd sunk so low, terrorising this two-bit author whose work would surely have been forgotten by now, were it not for recent publicity.

One of the youngest recipients of the Vietnam Gallantry Cross, his was a career set fair when he'd joined the Central Intelligence Agency at the culmination of a discredited war, although the bravery that led to his medal had sullied his *film noir* looks. The distinctive scar, received when rescuing a stricken colleague from the imminent knife of the enemy, had diminished his reputation as a master of disguises and had proved to be a serious hindrance to his aspiration to be an undercover agent.

Despite this disadvantage, he had still been delegated the odd assignment, including a posting to England to infiltrate the Greenham Common peace camp in the early eighties. He'd protested that a female agent would be better suited to the task in hand, but his misogynistic boss had insisted that he was the very man for the job. 'Just don't wear socks with your sandals,' he'd advised; 'not only would it blow your cover, but it's a crime against fashion.'

Whilst there, he'd maybe taken his duties a little too far when instigating a brief fling with one of the protesters, initially as a ruse to find out more about their plans, but ultimately because he liked her. He fell for her kindness, her sense of principle which, although polar opposite to his own, was obviously genuine. When expressing self-consciousness about his facial disfigurement, she simply replied, 'Don't worry about it, there's not many of us has a perfect body', and proceeded to show him the UK-shaped birthmark on her bum.

She dumped him two weeks later when he started getting too serious and thereafter he couldn't bear being at the peace camp, morosely continuing with his assignment and gathering intelligence as ordered. It was the second time he'd been discarded, cast aside by a fickle female who'd gained his trust and affection. He would never again trust a woman, particularly one with left wing tendencies.

Hank had been raised hard on redneck rhetoric in a small town in the state of Mississippi and had a nose for anything that smelt even slightly of liberalism or communism. He was convinced that there would never be a left wing revolution in England, its inhabitants far too conservative to tolerate the inconvenience; but nevertheless he'd made it his life's mission to supress any potential uprising. As his career faded, he'd been dumped there, on the wrong side of the Atlantic, his talents forgotten by his superiors, a chip on his shoulder at being overlooked for promotion.

When his behaviour became ever more erratic, he was reluctantly put out to grass by his superiors. Banished to this sleeping island outpost and left to his own devices, he was a maverick loose cannon, unwilling to move with the times, seeing red in every shadow. A rogue ex-agent obsessively adhering to his obsolete original brief – to supress or discredit any left wing organisation or individual considered a possible threat to the *status quo*, however minor.

In his opinion, they didn't come much more minor than Joe Stamford who, after his brief exploits at Greenham, had dropped off the radar, seemingly for good. Until, that is, Hank illicitly intercepted the e-mailed critique of 'That Bloody Book' from Alistair Ball, a man he'd been monitoring due to his subversive writing. Both Joe and Alistair would have been at once scared, proud and amused, had they known that they were under the scrutiny of a CIA agent, albeit a retired one.

As Hank had read the passage about the supposed hero's sexual adventure at Greenham, it became personal as well as political. In an error of judgement, he hadn't for a moment taken Joe's work seriously and had castigated himself for allowing it to reach publication, not to mention best seller status and media exposure.

He was seriously pissed off with a world that had undervalued his contribution to the cause and a world that allowed such blatant left wing propaganda air time and publicity. In his professionally prepared place of interrogation, he set about putting this irritating little shit in his place.

'Good venue, and no offence, but this is the worst rave I've ever been to,' said Joe, resorting to wit as he often did when scared; 'when are the rest of the partygoers turning up?' A hard slap round the face confirmed what he already suspected, that this guy had no sense of humour.

'H-Haven't we met before?' stammered Joe, trying to recall where he'd seen that scar. Light shining in his eyes, ropes digging into his wrists and ankles, disorientated by the lack of a focal point in the cavernous warehouse. 'I-Is that a real gun?'

'I'll ask the questions,' snarled Hank. 'Now, tell me about your book. I want to know who else conspired in your sordid little communist manuscript. You can't have written it without input from greater minds than yours.'

'I'm flattered that you think it worthy of kidnap,' replied Joe, wondering where the interrogation was going next, 'but it's only a harmless little story; the politics are almost incidental.'

'You commies make me sick. You think you can write anything you want without consequence. Well, I'm here to tell you that we won't tolerate your scheme to topple this government with your conspiracy of words.'

'What? This is absurd,' said Joe in disbelief. 'Do you seriously think that my book is part of a plot to displace the government?'

'Are you denying that *That Bloody Book* is one of a trilogy with *Right Rascals* and *Food for Thought*? All three pertain to everyday life with humour, but all have an underlying subversive message that can't be coincidence.'

Joe was familiar with *Food for Thought* by Cindy Stanton and had enjoyed cooking some of its excellent vegetarian recipes. He had yet to read *Right Rascals*, Alistair Ball's latest rant against all things Tory, but it was on his shopping list.

'Isn't *Food for Thought* a cookery book?' If this guy didn't have a gun and a manic look in his eyes, Joe would have been in hysterics. 'Can't see the connection; what have they all got in common?'

Grabbing him by the throat, Hank growled, 'Not just any cookery book. I don't believe for a minute that you're not part of this conspiracy. Well, I have news for you. Regrettably, Ms Stanton was involved in a car crash this morning whilst under the influence of drugs and Mr Ball jumped in front of a train this afternoon, after a short dalliance with depression. Unfortunately, neither survived. I should have arranged that little accident for you months ago.

Nobody would have missed you then, but it's unfortunate that you have attained a modicum of infamy and that questions would be asked if you disappeared.'

'Sorry to be such an inconvenience,' choked Joe. If he hadn't been taking this nutter seriously before, he was now. 'Let's get this straight. You've killed two innocent authors because you thought they were conspiring with me in inciting the overthrow of the government? Firstly, you're deranged, and secondly, whatever happened to freedom of speech? If you're not going to kill me too, what do you want from me?'

Hank emptied the contents of a brown envelope on to the table in front of him. 'You can start by making a contribution to my campaign fund. I wonder what your wife would make of these.'

At first the pictures just appeared to portray a tangle of limbs and Joe turned his head this way and that, attempting to determine the top from the bottom. Then with alarm he recognised his own face peeking out from beneath a buttock and the more he gained perspective, the more depraved the images became.

'Where in hell did you get these?' said Joe in disbelief. 'They're not real; you've just superimposed my face onto something from a porn site.'

'Oh, I can assure you they are very real,' said Hank, leering in Joe's face. 'You should be more careful who you talk to on stag weekends. And that reminds me, you still owe me for your evening's entertainment and a kebab. Not only am I out of pocket, *vis-à-vis* two hookers, but I had to buy you a kebab to keep you quiet on the way back. You should thank me for getting you safely back to your hotel in one piece; there are some dodgy characters around, you know.'

Bob Marley and the Wailers' 'Stir it Up' emanated from Joe's pocket. He'd always loved its simple but sublime intro and had searched high and wide to obtain it for a ringtone. He was fleetingly reassured by its laid back familiarity, until brought back down to earth by the realisation that Louise must be beside herself with worry. He'd promised he wouldn't be late home. What ungodly hour was this? He'd lost all sense of time during this terrifying, preposterous ordeal.

He thought about the lost hours, permanently erased from his memory, on Spike's stag weekend, as he nauseously studied the flagrant festival of flesh before him. 'How can I have done *that* without remembering a thing about it?' asked Joe. 'I didn't even know I knew that position.'

'You were somewhat beyond full consciousness,' replied Hank with an evil grin; 'the human body is surprisingly pliant when in such a condition.'

'Look, you're crazy, tell me how much you want and let me get home to my wife,' he pleaded, sickened by what he'd seen. 'You won't need to show her these photos, I'm already in the shit. How am I supposed to explain being out all night?'

'That's your problem. We'll start with ten thousand pounds,' he said, handing Joe a piece of paper with five account numbers; 'two thousand transferred into each account on Monday. If it's not there, then you know the consequences.'

'How am I supposed to transfer that kind of money without it being missed,' Joe enquired, 'we have a joint account.'

'Once again, that's your problem. It would be a shame if these works of art fell into the wrong hands.'

'And once you have the money, is that the end of it?' Joe asked. 'You'll hand over those disgusting pictures?'

'Oh, you're welcome to these,' replied Hank, 'but I'll have the originals, saved as an insurance policy in case my commie-catching fund needs topping up, or if your next book proves to be not to my liking.'

'It's going to be a children's book, for God's sake; but I guess if you can perceive revolution in a cookery book, then we're all under suspicion.'

'I hate children,' Hank sneered; 'besides, *Animal Farm* masqueraded as a children's book and Orwell was as radical as they come. You're a lucky man, because I'm going to let you go now; but don't forget our little deal. We wouldn't want the lovely Louise to be made aware of your disgusting behaviour, would we? It would be so tragic, since you've only just reconciled your differences.'

'What do you mean, you fell down a hole?' shouted an exasperated Louise, tempering her relief at seeing him safely home with her anger at being put through hell. 'Go on, tell me, how and where exactly did you fall down a hole?'

During his three-mile walk home, he'd had ample time to reflect upon the night's events and to perfect his story and limp, as well as to smear his clothes and face with mud to aid authenticity.

'That bit where they're digging up the pavement outside the school,' he replied, rubbing his supposedly injured thigh; 'some idiots have removed the safety barriers. It was dark and I couldn't see where I was going. My leg's killing me, but I don't think it's broken.'

'And why didn't you phone me or answer my call?' she asked, ignoring his supposed pain and looking him in the eye in an attempt to ascertain the truth.

'I tried, but there was no signal down there,' he lied. He hated this deceit, but could see little alternative. 'Think I fell asleep for a while; then these lads came by on their way home from a party and pulled me out. I must have been down there for hours.'

'Robin said they'd left you waiting for a taxi.'

He'd anticipated that she would phone Robin and had the answer to this one ready. 'There was a massive queue. I got fed up with waiting and decided to walk.'

Joe raised his eyes slightly to see whether she was swallowing his implausible tale. He'd wondered if she would sleep through the whole thing and be none the wiser, but her three o'clock call had put paid to that vain hope. Louise could normally sleep for England and it would take world war three to wake her; in contrast to Joe, who had always slept lightly, his over-active mind flitting from one scenario to another until the burgeoning daylight would creep through the curtains. When the children were babies it had usually been he who

114

tended to their nocturnal cries. This time, however, when he needed her to sleep, she'd been very much awake.

She looked him up and down. 'Not even you could make up a story like that,' she sighed at last.

I'm an author, he thought to himself, that's what I do, make up stories. Had he got away with it? It would be some testament to his new-found powers as a storyteller if he had. He told himself that falling down a hole was actually more plausible than the truth.

She shook her head, not entirely convinced, but surely even a mind as fertile as Joe's couldn't have concocted something so unlikely and, if anyone could fall down a hole, it was Joe. 'Don't think you're spending the day in bed; you've got the kids today. I've got to go in to work.'

'I thought it was your day off,' said Joe, yawning.

'Nicola's off sick again. I'm short staffed. I haven't slept either, you know.'

'Yes, I know,' he conceded. 'I'm sorry. I shouldn't be allowed out on my own.'

Jamie entered the room, wearily wiping the sleep from his eyes. 'Daddy, why have you got mud all over your clothes? Can we go to the park today?'

Joe picked him up and squeezed him tightly. 'Of course we can, son,' he said through his exhaustion, feeling very lucky to be alive.

20. All Shook Up

Staring at the screen, a cold shiver descended his spine as the news was confirmed regarding the sad deaths of his fellow authors. The article stated that the incidents were unrelated and that the police weren't looking for anyone else in relation to these tragic events. So last night wasn't a bad dream and the mystery maniac had literally got away with murder.

What could he do? He couldn't tell anyone what he knew for fear of the exposure of his own unwitting indiscretions. Anyway, what evidence did he have? He could imagine the police reaction. 'Got a good one here, guv. This fella's just come in, says he was kidnapped by a mysterious scar-faced American, taken to a deserted warehouse, tortured and blackmailed. Says this guy killed those two authors. Shall I book him for wasting police time and kick him out?'

Besides, as far as Louise was concerned, he'd spent the night in a hole in the ground (kinda big and kinda round). Despairing, he reluctantly resigned himself to the fact that he'd have to live with the fear, the knowledge that this psychopath could turn up at any time to demand more money or to irretrievably ruin his life.

'Could you let me have an advance on future sales?' he asked Petra in desperation. He'd begrudgingly decided to arrange the transfers into the psycho's accounts and knew that he would have to replace the ten thousand before Louise missed it. Joe knew that the book was still among the best sellers, but he was useless with money and didn't have a clue as to how much it was making.

'You can't have spent the last royalty cheque already,' said Petra.

'No, just a bit of a cash-flow problem,' he replied.

'I'll have to swing it with Josh, but possibly. How much do you need?'

'How about ten thousand?' he asked hopefully.

'That's some cash-flow problem. We might be able to manage five. Are you in any trouble?'

'Nothing I can't handle,' he lied. He was way out of his depth and he knew it.

'I was going to call you later anyway,' she said. 'We've had interest from an American publisher; they have a ghost writer who wants to adapt 'That Bloody Book' for the US market; if it comes off, then ten thousand would be chicken-feed.'

'You're joking,' said Joe. Judging by the reaction of the one American he knew had read it he was unconvinced as to its crossover potential. 'It's a very English story. Much of it pertains to our green and pleasant land; can't see our distant cousins taking to it, myself.'

'They did it with Nick Hornby's *High Fidelity*,' said Petra.

Immediately picturing himself in a Hollywood studio, overseeing the adaptation with some big-shot director, he said, 'Robert De Niro would be perfect for the older incarnation of the hero. What do you think to Johnny Depp for the younger man?'

'Whoa, calm down, you're getting a bit carried away,' she laughed. 'How are you fixed for next Wednesday? They want us to fly out to New York to meet them. Three or four days should be long enough.'

'I'll have to consult my social diary, but it's likely I will be available.' How could he refuse an offer like that? He imagined that things would be a little frosty at home for a while after his involuntary late night, and a brief sojourn to foreign climes sounded an attractive proposition in the circumstances.

Louise was philosophical. Did it make any difference whether he were on the other side of the world or in his home town? He could probably get into trouble just putting the bins out.

'Please be careful,' she pleaded. 'They have holes in the ground in the USA too, you know. You're not going anywhere near the Grand Canyon, are you?'

'Petra's sensible,' reassured Joe. 'I'll be safe with her.'

Petra and Joe waited patiently for take-off as the pilot announced, 'Apologies for the delay, ladies and gentlemen, but the Air Jamaica plane in front of us has broken down and we're waiting for it to be towed from the runway.'

Joe imagined two laid back, dreadlocked pilots in a ganja-filled cockpit. 'Wh'appen, Rasta?'

'T'ings ire bredren, jus' chill.'

Eventually, their flight lumbered laboriously into the air. Joe had always been amazed at the apparent flouting of the laws of physics that enabled jumbo jets to fly. He was reminded of once being chased around the football pitch by an irate goalkeeper after he'd expressed surprise at his agility in relation to his bulk. 'It's like those jumbo jets,' he'd said, 'you always wonder how the fuck they get off the ground.'

He'd visited the States before, with Louise to Cape Cod and, before they'd met, with friends to LA and San Francisco, but this was his first trip to New York. Like a child embarking on his summer holiday, the excitement was palpable.

'Have we got any sweets, Mum, my ears are popping,' he said to Petra, as the plane rose above the clouds.

'You men are all the same,' she said, as she handed him a packet of Starburst; 'big kids the lot of you.'

'I'm sure these were bigger when they were Opal Fruits,' observed Joe, as he popped a purple one into his mouth. 'Who are we meeting when we get there?'

'A guy called Glen Fiddich; he works for a reasonably well-known publisher based in West Village; they seem to think there may be a market for your work if we can Americanise the characters and change the location to Detroit.'

Glen Fiddich? Is he mature, single and Scottish?'

Petra winced; she was used to his awful puns, but this was one of the worst. 'I wouldn't use that joke when we meet him; apart from the possibility of your work being known internationally, there could be a lucrative contract in this.'

Joe sat back and tried to relax with his iPod on shuffle. He'd never had a problem with flying, as long as he didn't think too deeply about the fact that they were suspended thirty-five thousand feet in the air. To him, the safety instruction ritual before take-off was a waste of time, knowing that there would be little chance of survival if the plane went down. 'In the event of an emergency landing, put you head between your legs and kiss your ass goodbye.'

He was just drifting off to sleep, aptly to the beautiful sound of Van Morrison's 'I'm Tired, Joey Boy', when the turbulence hit, mild at first, but worsening gradually as they flew into thicker cloud. The hurricane season in the Gulf of Mexico had been particularly violent of late and they were flying precariously along the edge of the remnants of one.

The pilot asked the cabin staff to take their seats and informed the concerned passengers in his best reassuring voice that there was nothing to worry about, but that the turbulence could last for the next half an hour. Everyone gripped their arm rests as the elephantine flying machine was thrown around the sky like a piece of paper, Petra's hand on top of Joe's as they contemplated their fate, fearing the worst.

'Ouch,' shouted Joe, as she dug her sharp nails deep into his thigh after an exceptionally turbulent buffeting invoked screams of terror from the passengers.

At the point of contact, hand upon leg, the large bearded man across the aisle remotely operated the camera hidden in the air vent above their seats. Calm and impervious to the tempestuous tantrum of the skies, he'd been in far worse situations and didn't scare easily.

Airborne rattling crate, rivets loosened, fearful first-time flyers, screaming seasoned travellers, all were relieved as the airport emerged from beneath the clouds. Amid laughter and tears, the pilot safely landed the bucking beast on terra firma as appreciative applause echoed round the cabin.

'Welcome to New York, ladies and gentlemen. Apologies for the unpleasant turbulence during the latter stages of the flight. Please inform a stewardess if any part of the plane has fallen off and take care when opening the overhead lockers, some luggage may have become dislodged and unstable. We look forward to welcoming you when you fly with us again.'

'No chance,' said Joe, still shaking; 'you won't get me on one of these again. I'm going back by boat. Are you OK?'

Petra looked pale and shocked. 'I think so. Sorry about grabbing you like that; hope it didn't hurt too much.'

'I'll survive. You can have your nails back when I've had them surgically removed. I need a drink. How far is the hotel?'

As they left the airport, the passenger in the taxi behind uttered those immortal words, 'Follow that cab.'

21. Promised Land

Joe had been reading up on their destination, fascinated by its history. He read that the only reason that Greenwich Village had not been swallowed by skyscrapers is that the ground beneath it is too soft to build upon. Thus, thankfully, this place that was once an actual village had maintained some of its characteristic charm in the midst of New York's hustle and bustle.

As he walked contentedly among its cosmopolitan inhabitants, through its narrow, tree-lined unorthodox streets, in and out of compulsive record and bookshops, inhaling the myriad aromas of the café culture, he imagined the beat poets that had stepped here in days gone by: Kerouac, Ginsberg, Burroughs, along with the many great songwriters who'd spread the Greenwich beat around the world. He'd always loved discovering and strolling around new places and had decided to venture out and soak up the Bohemian atmosphere before dinner.

'Are you sure you don't need a chaperone?' Petra had asked. 'Louise called before we left, you know, asked me to keep an eye on you; she told me all about you falling down that hole. I feel kind of responsible for you.'

'Don't worry, Mum, I'll be back in time for dinner,' he smiled. 'I'm a big boy now. I can even tie my own shoelaces.'

'Go on then, but take care and don't do anything stupid, and if you call me Mum one more time you'll get a slap.'

Joe sipped his coffee, deep in contemplation, as he watched the world go by from a street-corner café; although his visit was just a few hours old, he'd immediately felt at home and had fallen in love with New York. Ironically, Bob Dylan's 'Subterranean Homesick Blues' was playing, one of the catalysts for the disapproval of some of his contemporaries on the Greenwich folk scene who'd objected to his new electric musical direction back in '65.

Joe could barely believe the life-altering events of the last twelve months (was that all it was?). This time last year he'd been on the scrapheap, unemployed and unemployable, signing on and dragging his sorry arse around disinterested employment agencies, suffering the daily indignity of rejection.

Now here he was, beyond his wildest dreams, a semi-famous author in New York, standing at the gateway to international acclaim. He'd put to the back of his mind the small matter of blackmail and the possible leaking of those photos that threatened to seriously derail his train. Life was good and he wasn't about to let some deluded fascist spoil it. Anyway, he wouldn't follow him here, would he? Joe looked all around him with a touch of paranoia and, although surrounded by people of all persuasions, saw no-one suspicious. Realising that he would be forever looking over his shoulder, he made his way back to the hotel to join Petra for dinner.

'I could feed the whole family with this,' said Joe, poking at the huge T-Bone steak nestling among a big pile of fries on the enormous plate in front of him, a mushroom and tomato paying incidental lip service to nutrition. 'How long are we here for? I'll have to buy new clothes to accommodate the inevitable results of these portions.'

'Only three days,' replied Petra. 'Won't be much time for sightseeing, I'm afraid. We meet Mr Fiddich in the morning. Then, if we can agree a deal, you spend the next few days with their ghost writer to discuss how it can be adapted. Any further collaboration can be done via e-mail once you get home.'

'Oh, I was hoping we'd need a few more trips to make it work;

e-mail is so impersonal. If I've got to work with this guy, I'd rather do it face to face.'

'You're welcome to come here as often as you wish,' said Petra, 'if you can afford the fare. Thought you had a, what was it, a cash-flow problem.'

He didn't need reminding and he'd thought about coming clean and telling Louise the truth on his return. He'd have to face the consequences and couldn't bear the thought of being separated, or worse, from his wife and kids again; but at least if she knew, then the nutter would have nothing to blackmail him with.

'OK, e-mail it is then for now,' conceded Joe, 'but when Scorsese or Coppola come a knocking, I want to be there in person.'

Joe nervously followed Petra into the plush, effortlessly trendy offices of Graydon Publishing. Huge cacti sat spikily on every available surface, the azure walls tastefully adorned with geometric modern art. Why did he still feel apprehensive about these situations, as if his work was being assessed all over again? Surely by now he should be confident and assured, successful on his own terms and unconcerned with how he appeared to others. But no, he still sought approval for his scribbling, still on trial, still unsure of the true merit of 'That Bloody Book'.

He sipped on his sparkling mineral water as the conversation went on around him, Petra and Glen doing most of the talking about the nuts and bolts of the deal. Before he knew it, an official-looking contract had appeared on the table before him and he happily signed on the dotted line at his American publishers, he had to say it twice, his American publishers! At one point he thought he may have scuppered the deal, when Glen had introduced him to his ghost writer.

'But, but you're a woman,' blurted Joe.

'Your problem being what, exactly?' replied Deanna, looking both offended and confrontational.

'Sorry, no offence intended, but the book is written from a male perspective,' said Joe, trying to dig himself out, but getting in deeper.

'I'm sure I can get my head round the complexities of the male psyche,' said Deanna; 'this *is* my job and I have successfully worked with men before, you know.'

'Yes, sorry, you're quite right,' said Joe, feeling foolish; 'just took me by surprise, that's all. I'm sure it will be a pleasure working with you.'

'That's settled then,' interjected Petra, before they could change their minds. 'I think we're all agreed on the terms and conditions; it just remains for us to sign up and start work.'

Despite his somewhat embarrassing *faux pas*, Deanna and Joe immediately hit it off once they commenced writing together, she giggling hysterically at his clumsy attempts to explain the Anglicised elements of the book, and he laughing uncontrollably at the misunderstandings that emanated from two different versions of the same language. Although the book contained neither bum nor fag, there was plenty more scope for humorous misapprehension.

He would have liked to have seen more of New York during his short stay, but nonetheless Joe was relishing the experience of collaboration and working with an empathic spirit. Deanna's bubbly personality was infectious and Joe warmed to her sense of fun and seemingly permanent smile.

On their last day, Deanna insisted that they finish early and she took Petra and he to visit Ellis Island and the Statue of Liberty, from where they viewed the famous Manhattan skyline standing proudly against a clear blue sky, its twin giants forever absent.

Joe wondered how Uncle Ray would have fared had he made the journey; he would have loved it here, the endless possibilities, the new frontiers, his wanderlust sated. Over twelve million immigrants were processed between 1892 and 1954 at the immigration station on Ellis Island, the first stop on an amazing adventure, the melting pot for the world's biggest multi-cultural society.

'Thanks for everything, Deanna,' said Joe, as they hugged goodbye' 'I'll look forward to reading your Americanisation of the next chapter. And remember, that's tomato not tom*a*to.'

'You seem to be getting along nicely,' said Petra, grinning' 'I know we're a long way from home, but don't forget you're a married man.'

'Don't be daft. Deanna wouldn't be interested in me,' replied Joe, blushing. 'Besides, I love Louise. I don't want anyone else.'

Joe looked at his watch as he half-heartedly consumed his pancakes with fruit and maple syrup. Following the anxiety of the outward-bound journey, he wasn't looking forward to boarding the flight home. Where was Petra? She said she'd see him at breakfast. He tried phoning her once more, but still no answer. Maybe she's overslept, he thought. I'll knock on her door when I go back up.

He rapped hard, but no response. Worried, he returned to his room to call reception and check if they knew anything. Surprised to see the door open and the maid already cleaning the room, he entered and said, 'Don't mind me, love, carry on as if I'm not here.'

Joe did a double take; he'd been known to indulge in fantasies involving maids in uniform, but this lady definitely wasn't going to feature in one.

Without warning, as he bent to pick up the phone, a muscular hairy arm, bulging biceps beneath lacy sleeves, embraced him and pinned his arms to his side, the free hand expertly covering his mouth and nose with the chloroform. Immediately recognising the dulcet tones of his captor, 'Go to sleep now, there's a good boy', Joe drifted slowly from consciousness, his pitiful struggles in vain.

Hefting limp body over shoulder, the unlikely maid deposited Joe on top of Petra in the laundry, threw in some soiled sheets, checked the coast was clear and pushed the trolley nonchalantly towards the lift.

The dingy street at the back of the hotel was deserted, apart from Ravelo, a Puerto Rican porter on a cigarette break, who observed with interest as the unusually heavy laundry was dumped unceremoniously into the back of a white van, landing with a dull thud. Ravelo cowered back in the shadows, watching in disbelief as the maid slammed the van doors. He was working here illegally; who was he to ask questions or cause a fuss?

Hank surveyed the area to ensure he was not being watched and reluctantly removed his favourite disguise: the shoes that painfully pinched his size twelve feet, the frilly blouse, the tight skirt and the finishing touches, the attention to detail that ensured he got into character, stockings, suspenders and silk underwear. Quickly he changed into a more befitting dark blue boiler suit, jumped into the van and joined the anonymous big city morning traffic.

Ravelo extinguished the remnants of his cigarette beneath twisting shoe and, head down, returned to his duties.

22. Drive South

Petra awoke first, head muzzy and disorientated, in total darkness but obviously in transit, involuntarily bouncing from one side to the other. All she could remember was being woken by the ugliest woman she'd ever seen, her scream for help stifled by a chemical-impregnated cloth covering her nose and mouth, the hideous grin as she wriggled in panic. Was she being murdered? Why...?

She felt around her for clues as to her whereabouts, gasping in terror as her blind fumbling located first an ear, then a nose and a mouth. She jumped and shrieked as the body next to her groaned. 'Who are you, where am I?'

Joe groaned again, his head throbbing as he slowly regained consciousness, Petra's voice finally getting through.

'It's me,' he said, 'and I haven't got a fucking clue where we are. What happened?'

'I don't know, but I think we've been abducted. Why couldn't they have just robbed us and left us in the hotel?'

The dreadful truth was gradually dawning and Joe realised that he owed her an explanation. Petra listened in dismay as he brought her up to date with recent events.

'So you didn't fall down a hole.'

'No.'

'And you didn't think to tell me before we embarked upon this trip that you were being pursued by a homicidal maniac?'

'How was I to know he'd follow me here?' said Joe. 'I've paid him the money. I thought he might leave me alone for a while.'

Their heads banged painfully together as the van swerved erratically along the freeway, Petra thumping him hard as he shouted 'shit'.

'For God's sake, keep your voice down,' she said through gritted teeth. 'It might be better if he thinks we're still asleep. I can't believe you, you're a walking disaster area.'

'I can't argue with that,' conceded Joe. 'I'm so sorry for dragging you into this mess. I wonder where he's taking us. How far do you think we've travelled?'

'There's no telling how long we were out for. We must have left the city. I can't hear much traffic and we're moving fairly fast.'

Remembering that he had a light on his watch, Joe checked the time. 'Ten thirty-five. Think we may be a little late for our flight. I guess all we can do is sit back and wait.'

'Isn't there any way we can raise the alarm?' she said.

'No way that I can think of,' said Joe. 'He's obviously taken my phone; don't suppose you've got yours on you.'

'I don't tend to keep it in my pyjamas,' she replied. 'I left in a bit of a hurry; didn't have time to dress.'

'There's no need for that tone. I'm a victim in this too, you know.'

'Oh, please forgive me if I'm a little crabby this morning,' said Petra. 'I'm never at my best when I miss breakfast.'

Joe considered their options and decided they didn't have any. 'Best make ourselves comfortable and prepare for a long journey then,' he said philosophically. 'How shall we amuse ourselves? I spy with my little eye.'

'Very funny. How can you joke at a time like this? I've got a better idea. Do you know any good stories?'

Two hours later and Hank was getting peckish; he'd missed breakfast too and required topping up, as did the van. Pulling into the services, he found a quiet part of the car park and slowly opened the back doors, the bright sunlight temporarily blinding his prisoners until they became re-accustomed to daylight, the imposing figure of Hank silhouetted against the sky.

'Don't even think about trying to escape or attracting the attention of passers-by,' he growled. 'This is an explosive device that I'm placing on the door. If it is opened without me disabling it I won't be responsible for the consequences. Now I have to fill up with gas and if you're good I'll get you some food.'

'Where are you taking us?' asked Joe.

'That's for me to know and you to find out. Suffice it to say we will be on the road for two or three days,' replied Hank. 'I hadn't planned on this little trip, but I have some urgent family business to attend to and have no alternative but to bring you along.'

Yesterday's call from his aunt had been a major inconvenience and had led to a hasty reappraisal of his plans. 'You better come on home, boy, your Mama's ill; doctor says two weeks max. She's asking to see you before she goes and someone's gonna have to pay for the funeral.'

'Please let Petra go and just take me,' pleaded Joe; 'this is nothing to do with her.'

'She published the book, didn't she? She's as culpable as you are. You had been warned about the consequences of continuing to peddle your propaganda and now you have the audacity to spread your poison on my home soil. Did you think I wouldn't notice? Now please sit back like good passengers and the stewardess will be round shortly with dinner.'

'You're not going to dress up again, are you?' said Joe, cringing at the thought.

'In your dreams. Now, that's enough small talk; the better behaved you are, the longer you stay alive,' said Hank, as he carefully shut out their light once more.

'He's bluffing,' said Petra, as they listened to Hank's footsteps disappearing into the distance. 'If we start banging on the side of the van someone will hear us.'

'Look, I've had the pleasure of meeting this guy before, remember. I'm convinced that he's more than capable of carrying out his threats. We need to bide our time and wait for an opportunity to escape. Anyway, I'm hungry and he said he was bringing food.'

Although quick, the service and ambience left a lot to be desired as, ten minutes later, Hank threw in two Big Mac meals with the instruction 'enjoy', and immediately plunged them back into darkness.

They could hear people talking outside as Hank filled up with diesel and wondered whether to take a chance and draw attention to their plight.

'No, let's sit tight for now,' concluded Joe, 'it's too risky. He'll probably blow up the whole petrol station. I hate McDonalds. This is an insult to my cultured palate, but at least we can't see the anaemic excuse for meat and we can pretend that the salad is real. How are you supposed to remove the gherkin, though, when you can't even see it?'

'Great, I'm sharing a table with a bloody restaurant critic,' said Petra. 'Just eat it and stop complaining; we've more important things to worry about than the quality of the food.'

Hours passed as their mobile prison rattled along, eating up mile after tedious mile of freeway. They made themselves as comfortable as possible, utilising the thoughtfully left contents of the laundry to pad the area beneath them. Conversation was stilted, Petra not having yet forgiven Joe for his part in the nightmare in which she found herself.

'Not wishing to appear indelicate,' she said, wriggling uncomfortably, 'but I'm bursting for a pee.'

'Me too,' replied Joe; 'do you think if we asked nicely he'd stop somewhere?'

Hank was getting increasingly annoyed as the incessant knocking behind his head grew louder and more insistent, but he'd guessed what they wanted; he too was becoming slave to the call of nature. Eventually finding somewhere remote to pull in, he wrenched open the doors and shouted, 'What?'

'Please, sir, can we use the bathroom?' asked Joe, raising his hand.

Hank surveyed the area and, apart from a field full of cows watching them curiously, the coast appeared to be clear.

'That bush over there,' he pointed, 'one at a time, ladies first.'

'I'm not going behind a bush,' said Petra indignantly.

'Fine by me if you think you can last till midnight. We have a lot of mileage to cover; maybe I'll find a motel later if it's safe, but in the meantime I suggest you empty your bladders, or whatever you need to empty, now.'

Robin waited patiently for the last of the passengers to come through Customs. Joe had recently collected him from the airport after his holiday in Tenerife and he was returning the favour. He was sure he hadn't missed them. He checked the flight number once more. Yes, this was the correct flight. Knowing Joe, he'd probably been stopped in Customs. He smiled to himself as he imagined the Customs officer pulling on the plastic glove. After waiting for a further twenty minutes, he went to check at the airline desk.

'I'm sorry, sir, but they never boarded the plane,' said the lovely Lucy; 'maybe they missed the flight and will be on a later one.'

Surely Joe would have phoned to let him know. He tried calling him, but the familiar answer kicked in, 'Hello, this is Joe Stamford. I can't be bothered to talk to you at the moment …' It was about time he changed his voicemail; it was mildly amusing the first time you heard it, but now it was just plain irritating.

'Oh god, what's happened now,' sighed Louise, with phone in one hand and pan of baked beans in the other. 'Jamie, stop hitting your sister. Sorry, I haven't heard from him all day, but I just put that down to the time difference. You'd better come on home. It's not fair on you to wait around at the airport. He'll have to make his own way back.'

Hank had stayed in enough sleazy motels in his time, but he couldn't recall one as run down as this. Discretion was imperative, however, and it was off the beaten track and sparsely inhabited. The unshaven, inebriated blob at the desk had barely acknowledged them as Hank paid in advance and snatched the key to a dank, musty double room on the second floor. He picked at the peeling yellow wallpaper and searched for cockroaches. He found none, but he was sure he would be cohabiting with all kinds of vermin, and not only communists.

'What kind of godforsaken hell hole is this?' asked Joe in horror, as he took in the less than salubrious surroundings. 'You sure know how to treat guests to your country.'

'You can always spend the night in the van if you'd prefer,' replied Hank. He'd been driving all day and was not in the mood for Joe's facetious comments. 'Now, let's sort out the sleeping arrangements. You two in that one by the window and me in this one by the door. We have another long day tomorrow, so we best prepare for bed and get an early start.' He produced two sets of handcuffs. 'And in case you're thinking of doing anything stupid while I'm asleep, you can wear these.'

Petra burst into tears, the trauma of the day finally catching up with her; still in her creased flannelette pyjamas, worn for comfort rather than style, since she generally slept alone these days.

'I'm already prepared for bed,' she sobbed. 'I've been wearing these damn pyjamas since yesterday; my hair needs washing and now you expect me to sleep handcuffed in the same bed as him … no offence, Joe.'

'None taken,' he said, feeling guilty and sympathetic as he looked at Petra, an invariably elegant lady whom he'd never before seen looking anything less than immaculate, now reduced to this dishevelled indignity.

Opening his suitcase, Hank removed a bundle of women's clothing from his varied disguises. 'Here, you can take your pick from these; they may be a little big for you, but there's plenty to choose from. You're welcome to use the shower first tonight, but don't use all the hot water, that's if there is any.'

Petra picked at the clothes before her in disbelief. As well as the maid's uniform, there was a policewoman's, a nurse's and what looked like an exotic dancer's.

'Are you serious?' she said, mouth agape. 'I can't wear these.'

'I apologise if they're not to Madame's taste, but that's all there is for now; take it or leave it.'

Now this was a photo opportunity not to be missed, thought Hank with an evil grin. They'd all taken their turn in the poor excuse for a shower, a lukewarm trickle of murky water that barely wet their heads, Joe thankful for once that he had no hair to wash. Now Joe and Petra tried in vain to attain a modicum of comfort without their positions appearing too compromised, a difficult proposition with Joe handcuffed both to the rickety bed and to a decidedly unhappy Petra in an ill-fitting nurse's uniform.

'Haven't you got enough bloody pictures to blackmail me with already?' asked Joe. 'I don't have a good name to lose, but there's no need to besmirch Petra's reputation too.'

'You can never have too many like this,' laughed Hank, as he admired his handiwork. 'Priceless! The tabloids will be very interested in these as a sequel to your sordid escapade with Left Wing Laura. I couldn't believe my luck when my research uncovered that little affair. From there it was easy to leak the tale to that Tory MP and inevitable that he would deem it to be in the public interest to tell the papers. Unfortunately, I hadn't anticipated that your resulting notoriety would actually sell more copies of the book.'

'So you were responsible for that too; what have you got against me?' pleaded Joe. 'Why are you so determined to ruin me? Am I really worth this much effort?'

'Oh, I'm just a little bored since my enforced retirement,' replied Hank, 'and I've decided to make you my little project to keep me amused.'

'Oh, I give up!' sighed Joe in exasperation. 'You're obviously beyond reason.'

Sleep was predictably fitful as they tossed, turned and pulled each other's arms this way and that, eventually deciding on the spoons position. 'OK, but no funny business,' said Petra.

The crack of dawn arrived too soon as they were roughly shaken from their slumbers by an impatient Hank. 'Time to go, children; vacation time.'

23. Bad Moon Rising

'Mummy, when's Daddy coming home?' asked Emma. 'Will he bring us a present?'

'I don't know, dear,' said Louise, attempting to mask her anxiety. 'Soon, I hope. Daddy's working in America.'

'Is he at Disneyworld? Why couldn't he take us?'

'No, he's not at Disneyworld. Maybe we can go there one day.'

Louise was at her wit's end. Another day had passed without word from her errant husband and she'd spent most of it in tears, imagining all kinds of scenarios. As well as constantly trying his number, she'd been on the phone to the airline and to Joe's publishers; neither had heard from them.

She jumped as the doorbell rang. Who could it be? Not Joe, he would use his key; oh no, not the police with bad news.

'Go and play with Jamie while Mummy answers the door,' she instructed Emma, and, taking a deep breath, she walked slowly down the hall.

Relieved to see Robin, she asked him in. 'No news, I suppose?' he said.

'Nothing, zilch. Oh, Robin, what's happened to him, where could he be? Do you think he's run off with that Petra?'

'I very much doubt it,' reassured Robin. 'Look, Joe can be a bit of a prat, but I know he loves you and the kids; he's told me enough times how lucky he is. Besides, he told me before they left that she's about six inches taller than him and that he doesn't fancy her.'

'Oh, that's OK then,' she replied. 'It's a good job he didn't go with someone he does fancy then.'

'I've always envied you two, you know. You have a great relationship; I can see you both sitting round the fire with your grandchildren when you're old fogeys. How much do you love him?'

'I thought I'd never want anyone else, but now I'm not so sure. How can I trust him after all that's happened?'

Robin looked her in the eye. 'Look, Joe's my best mate and I'd trust him with my life; not with my girlfriend, but certainly with my life. No, sorry, that's in bad taste. Something's not right here. I think he's in trouble. I'm due some holiday and I've never been to the USA. If we've not heard from him by Wednesday, I'm going to find him.'

'OK, but I'm coming with you,' said Louise. 'if he is having an affair, I want to hear it from his own lips before I kill him.'

'What about Emma and Jamie?' asked Robin.

'They can stay with my mum and dad for a while. They're always saying they don't see enough of them.'

'OK, that's settled then. I'll make enquiries about flights. You're sure about this?'

'Positive,' said Louise.

Their second day on the road was much the same as the first, apart from a violent swerve that threw them painfully against the side of the van when Hank successfully avoided a skunk that had wandered into the road. Uncomfortable, junk food, back of nowhere stops, culminating in another dodgy motel, albeit not quite as bad as the previous night.

Joe had always dreamed of travelling the back roads of America, maybe following the trail of Jack Kerouac's *On the Road* or searching for the crossroads where Robert Johnson sold his soul to the devil; but this was far from his fantasy trip, the wind in what was left of his hair on a Harley, or the epitome of cool in a Cadillac convertible.

They'd decided to attempt to engage their abductor in conversation at every opportunity, to try to find a human being behind the macho, cross-dressing, confused persona that he projected.

'We have to find his weaknesses,' reasoned Joe, 'his Achilles heel.'

Still Hank remained guarded, an impenetrable enigma, steadfastly uncommunicative. They slept fitfully once again, handcuffed and helpless in threadbare sheets, Petra angrier with each waking hour.

On the third day, they reached their destination: a rambling, deserted, derelict plantation house, a ghost of its former evil glory.

'Welcome to the State of Mississippi,' said Hank, surveying the vista; 'my neighbourhood.'

'And why have you brought us here exactly?' enquired Petra, as she took in the faded grandeur of their surroundings.

Hank looked around nostalgically. 'I used to play here when I was a kid; it was empty then too. Used to be one of the biggest cotton-picking places in Mississippi, until the slaves murdered the owners and escaped. They were all rounded up in the end and lynched, of course. All happened long before I was born, but the house was never occupied again.'

'So why are we in Mississippi?' asked Joe. 'You said you had some family business to deal with.'

The familiarity of the surroundings loosened his tongue as Hank looked into the distance and replied, 'It's Mama. She's dying; not long to go.'

'I'm sorry,' said Petra; 'must be a difficult time for you.'

Hank stared at her; her sympathy appeared to be genuine and the shoots of an idea pierced his thoughts. His forehead wrinkled as he considered the possibility. No, it couldn't work, could it? But why not, and it would make Mama's passing more bearable.

He looked Petra in the eye. 'You know, Mama's one wish was for me to settle down and raise a family. It's been a big disappointment to her that I never married. You can come with me tomorrow, be my

English fiancée; she'll go to her grave happy if she knows I've finally found someone.'

She returned his gaze in disbelieving unease, the thought of this strange proposition filling her with dread.

'You must be joking! Do you really think you can fool her into thinking we're an item,' she said. 'We're a pretty unlikely couple.'

'What's so unlikely?' he replied. 'I'm an eligible bachelor and you're an attractive woman in the right light.'

'Charmed, I'm sure. And do I have any choice?'

'None whatsoever; you do as I say and your friend here stays alive.'

'And what am I supposed to do while you two are playing happy families?' asked Joe.

'You stay here like a good boy and *she* stays alive,' replied Hank. 'it's a perfectly simple equation.'

'And if we're to go through with this ridiculous charade, do I get to know your name?' asked Petra.

He hesitated, thinking hard. If this was going to work, she'd have to know something about him. 'Hank Schneider Junior at your service, ma'am,' he said, kissing her hand, which she withdrew quickly.

'And what about Hank Schneider Senior? Will I have the pleasure of meeting him too?'

His mood darkened. 'No, the only thing that worthless bum gave me was his name. He left when I was a baby and thank the Lord I never knew him. I was raised proper by Mama and we had nothing but the shack we lived in and the clothes on our backs. Goddam it, there were blacks on the other side of the tracks had it better 'n we did. It was the army that saved me from going off the rails; guess the army was my Papa.'

Joe listened intently as Hank opened up, looking for a chink in his armour, for a hint of vulnerability.

'And what am I supposed to wear to this momentous meeting?' asked Petra. 'Am I to be a nurse, a maid or a policewoman? I don't think you'd want to introduce me to your mother in that other outfit.'

In his haste he hadn't considered the detail, the plan still formulating in his warped mind. 'I'll go to town first thing, bring you back something pretty.'

'Surely you don't want to be seen buying women's clothing in your home town?' she said. 'Could be embarrassing for you. Better if I come along and choose something suitable myself; that way we can be sure it fits and I'll look presentable for your mother. I'll need shoes and a bag to go with it, of course.'

The full moon rose slowly over the plantation. A moon that had seen so much turmoil and heartbreak in this place now witnessed three disparate souls on the porch, brought together in the most bizarre circumstances imaginable. Before Hank went into the house to prepare their living quarters, he handcuffed Joe and Petra to the railings.

'Is this really necessary?' pleaded Joe. 'How far do you think we'd get? Presumably you have our money, passports and phones and we have no idea where we are.'

'Belt and braces, that's all,' said Hank, as he disappeared inside; 'experience has taught me not to take anything for granted.'

'What in the name of God do you think you're doing, going along with his crazy masquerade?' Joe asked Petra when he was out of earshot, 'you're taking one hell of a risk and we should stick together.'

'Look, if I can get into town I can find out where in hell we are and try to get a message home,' reasoned Petra. 'Mississippi's a big place for anyone to look for us. If I can narrow it down to a town, we may stand a chance. Anyway, he's hardly likely to harm me in front of his beloved mama, is he?'

'OK, you're making perfect sense as usual, but please be careful. If he catches you out we're both in the shit. You couldn't get me a change of clothes while you're out shopping, could you? I think these could stand up on their own.'

'I'll try, but might be pushing our luck a bit,' she said. 'Look, we'll find a way out of this and when we do you'll have plenty of material for another book, except no-one would believe it.'

As Hank showed them to their room, he removed an old key from a chain around his neck.

'You have a key to that door?' asked Joe.

'Something special happened here a long time ago,' replied Hank with a wistful look, 'something beautiful. Kept this key 'cause I knew I'd come back some day; but it's not the same, can't turn back the clock. Everything was ruined back then and it can't ever be fixed.'

24. I Found That Girl

As the plane taxied to the runway, Robin sat back and pondered the puzzle of Joe's disappearance. Louise was understandably quiet, looking out of the window at nothing in particular.

What did they have to go on? They knew the names of the hotel where they had last been seen and of the publishers who were working on the adaptation of the book. They had no further clues or ideas as to where they could be and the needle in the haystack seemed way beyond their grasp.

Absentmindedly, he flicked through the pages of his newspaper, the now-familiar tales of worldwide debt dominating the headlines. He wondered what a trillion dollars looked like. Recoiling in horror at the aberration on the next page, he closed the paper quickly before Louise saw it. He glanced left to see her still deep in thought, staring sadly through the window and into the distance.

Curiously opening the pages slightly once more, there was the awful verification of what he thought he'd seen: an outrageous picture that couldn't lie, beneath the headline "LOVE RAT JOE AT IT AGAIN". There was no denying it was him, handcuffed to a bed with a good-looking young lady dressed as a nurse. A smaller, less controversial, but somehow more damning picture depicted them on a plane, Petra's hand undeniably resting on Joe's thigh.

Robin read on in disbelief as the story told of their trip to the USA and of their tawdry affair, the photo allegedly taken in a sleazy swinger's club in New York. The tabloid, that had recently had to apologise and pay compensation for phone hacking and hounding an innocent victim of assault to suicide, went on to take the moral high ground by pointing out Joe's marital status and parenthood.

What was he to do? He couldn't let Louise see this, it would destroy her. He still couldn't reconcile the disturbing images he'd just seen with the friend he thought he knew. Joe wouldn't do that to Louise, would he? Robin had always prided himself on being a good judge of character. He couldn't be that far wide of the mark in his assessment of Joe, could he?

He turned to the sports pages in an attempt to clear his head and to get that picture out of his mind, all to no avail, and he closed his eyes in thought. It was too late to turn back now as the plane gained height and they were irretrievably on their way to the Big Apple. Robin vowed to find out the truth, however unpalatable it may be.

'What's wrong? You look like you've seen a ghost,' said Louise, as she looked at him with concern.

'Oh, it's nothing,' he replied, 'I'm just a little nervous about flying, that's all.'

Petra felt bad about leaving Joe behind, Hank making him less than comfortable in the makeshift cell in the old slave quarters, but she was doing this for them both. Besides, Joe was the one responsible for this mess.

She had been promoted to the passenger seat in the van and sat with trepidation as Hank remained silent throughout the short country lane journey to town. Try as she might, she could see no opportunity to slip the leash and tell of her plight. Hank watched her like a hawk, ensuring that she communicate with no-one, as she chose a smart but unassuming outfit from the town's only clothes shop. It appeared that this was a backwater that didn't even warrant an anonymous out-of-town shopping precinct. The assistant appraised them with curiosity but, apart from a 'can I help you' and a 'have a good day', said nothing. Petra looked for a clue as to their location and found it on the sign above the bank. Where else could it be but Bushville?

Approaching Hank's mother's home, a modest bungalow in an anonymous back street, she glanced at him and noticed for the first time a nervous apprehension as he hesitated before entering. She stood anxiously beside Hank at his mother's bedside, the frail, weather-beaten old lady with piercing blue eyes looking her up and down. A photo of a young Hank filled a beaten frame, looking surprisingly handsome in his army uniform, smiling proudly as he held up his medal, the newly-formed scar adding to a rugged hero look that contrasted profoundly with the desperate older man by her side.

Hank had visibly changed upon entering the room, this huge man almost cowering in deference to the tiny woman who, despite appearances, had once ruled over him with a rod of iron.

'So, you're the fiancée who came out of nowhere?' she rasped. 'And why hasn't Hank told me about you before?'

'Pleased to meet you, Mrs Schneider,' said Petra, trying to sound convincing. 'It's been something of a whirlwind romance; we've not been together long.'

'And can I trust you to look after him?' she asked, with a hint of the menace of her son in her voice. ''Bout time young Hank settled down; he's a good boy really, had a hard start in life, but he's made his mama proud; never been the same since Vietnam, though.'

'I'll do my best, Ma'am,' said Petra.

'He had a girl once, you know,' she continued. 'He was smitten by Mary Morrison before he went away to fight for his country; then he came home to find she'd married that no good Vince Stone, son of a businessman. She only married him for his money, of course. Hank never got over the broken heart she give him; that's why he left to work for the government. There was no future for him here after that.'

'Mama, Petra doesn't need to know all this ancient history,' said Hank, embarrassed.

'Don't know if I'll make it to the wedding,' she coughed; 'doctor says I could die at any time.'

For a moment Petra felt sympathy for this fragile old lady, gasping for her final breaths, until she went on vociferously, 'I'd have liked to see my only child wed; but apart from that, I'm ready to go, been too long in this world. Never thought I'd live in a country with a nigger for president. When I was younger the Klan ruled round these parts; now we have to cohabit with the blacks, use the same shops, buses, libraries.'

Petra said nothing. Ordinarily, she would have argued vehemently against such sentiments, but this old hag was too long in the tooth to change now; let her answer in hell for her bigotry, if such a place existed.

The effort of spewing forth her hatred and reactionary views further exhausted Mrs Schneider and she closed her eyes, her breathing deep and rattling. Hank held her hand, holding back the tears, then turned and left the room, not knowing whether he'd ever see her again. Petra followed, silently seething.

'Thank you,' said Hank simply, as they drove back to the plantation.

'What for?' asked Petra. 'I didn't really do anything voluntarily; you forced me into this, remember?'

'Yes, but Mama liked you. I could tell.'

Petra didn't know how to take what was meant as a compliment; she couldn't think of anyone she'd less like to be liked by.

'Don't mention it,' she said. 'So what happens now?'

'This is a small town; news of my return and my new companion will be all around the neighbourhood by now. There's a barn dance in town on Saturday and I'll be expected by my aunts, uncles and cousins to attend; we're going along … give me a chance to show you off.'

'What? You're expecting to fool the whole town into thinking we're together! How long are you planning on keeping this up?'

'You saw Mama, she ain't got long,' he said with a quiver in his voice; 'we stick around till after the funeral, then we're outta here.'

'And then where to?' asked Petra. 'You can't keep us prisoners forever and people at home will be missing us by now.'

'Haven't thought of our next destination yet; been a little preoccupied with getting here in time. As far as your friends and family at home are concerned, you and that piece of scum have run off together. That's how the papers are telling it, anyway.'

'Oh no,' she groaned, 'you've sent them those photos, haven't you?'

''fraid so; killed two birds with one stone. Firstly, it should stop anyone coming looking for you if they think you've run away to have an affair; and secondly, it will permanently blacken the name of Joe Stamford. It's one thing humping a Labour MP thirty years ago, but it's another thing leaving your wife and kids and eloping with a younger woman. I can't see the great British public being too forgiving of behaviour like that.'

'And what about my good name?' she asked. 'What have I ever done to you?'

'It's unfortunate that you are guilty by association with that lowlife, but all's fair in love and war and the war against communism never ends.'

'Look, we're not your enemies and we're certainly not communists,' Petra tried to reason with him. 'I'm a partner in a successful business in London; I have little choice but to play by the rules of capitalism, and Joe is a minor author with left wing leanings, but he's hardly influential, is he? Wouldn't a politician be more deserving of your attention?'

'Maybe, but I wouldn't have got this far. MI5 and the press would have been on my back if I'd kidnapped that two-timing bitch Laura Bisham, for instance. This way I can make my statement to the world when I'm ready and on my terms.'

A light switched on in Petra's mind. 'Two-timing bitch? You mean you were once associated with the lovely Laura too? She sure knows how to pick her men. This is all starting to make perfect sense now.'

'She has nothing to do with this,' said Hank, realising that he may have given too much away.

'Obviously not, and what do you mean "your statement to the world"?'

'Let's just say that I'll get my fifteen minutes of fame,' he replied, staring straight ahead.

On her return, she found Joe looking laid back on a threadbare sofa. In her absence he'd been amusing himself by formulating the next chapter of his children's book, although, without pad or pc on which to scribe his latest masterpiece, it would remain in his head for now. Startled from his thoughts as the door opened, he looked up as Petra was pushed inside to join him. 'Welcome home. Nice outfit; didn't manage to get me anything, I suppose?'

'Sorry,' she replied, 'Hank said the household budget wouldn't run to stroking your vanity.'

'Hank now, is it? And how did the future Mrs Schneider get on with her prospective mother-in-law?' he asked.

'That's not funny,' said Petra, with hands on hips. 'She's an evil old bag and I can see how her crazy son has turned out like he has. I almost feel sorry for him. He's been dealt a bad hand.'

'How can you feel sorry for him after what he's done to us?' said Joe. 'I don't care how he came to be what he is, he's still a bastard, full stop.'

'I know we're all responsible for our own actions,' she argued, 'but our upbringing and things that happen to and around us shape who we are. His father left when he was a baby, he was raised by that horrible woman in an environment where racists and reactionaries thrived and, on top of that, he fought in Vietnam and his girlfriend dumped him while he was there. Not exactly the recipe for a well-balanced member of society, is it? What chance did he have? It also appears that, prior to your dalliance with Laura, he had feelings for her too.'

'So this whole ludicrous escapade is down to my unwittingly

stepping on his toes all those years ago,' said Joe. 'Unbelievable.'

'It seems so. Laura Bisham's got a lot to answer for.'

Joe shook his head in exasperation. He wasn't a vindictive person, but he'd had more than enough of Hank and his games. 'I can't disagree that he's had some bad breaks in life. From what you say, the man's a walking country and western song. There's not a dead dog in the story too, is there? Look, I'm sure a psychiatrist's report would absolve him of all culpability, but he's probably wrecked my marriage, my reputation such as it was, and my life in general, not to mention what he's done to you. He's blackmailed me, killed two people that we know of and threatened on numerous occasions to kill us too. You'll forgive me if I have little sympathy. Anyway, what else did you find out on your mission to town?'

'Not much, I'm afraid,' said Petra, 'only that we're in a place called Bushville, would you believe. Oh, and that there's a barn dance on Saturday night to which I've been less than cordially invited.'

'What? And how are your line dancing steps?' he asked in disbelief. 'Can't see you fitting in at a hoe-down somehow, but I'm sure you'll have a good time.'

'Do you think I'm enjoying this?' she said. 'Look, the only way we're going to get out of here is if we can communicate with the outside world and get help.'

'Yes, I know, I'm sorry. I've hardly seen daylight for the last five days, been cooped up in that van, motel rooms and now this shit hole. Guess I'm going stir crazy.'

'And how have you been passing the time while I've been out at work?' she asked, looking around for any sign of activity. 'I can see you haven't done the cleaning.'

'I'm trying not to make myself too much at home in case I get attached to the place,' he replied. 'Been doing a bit of thinking about my odyssey to childhood. The next chapter is finished, it's all up here,' he continued, tapping his head. 'I miss the kids so much. It's the only thing that's keeping me sane, knowing that they're still out there waiting for me to return. Got the title too, it's called

The Lellow Hittamapotamus. It's about the loss of innocence when these twins start school and the teacher tries to tell them that it should be a yellow hippopotamus. The children insist that the lellow hittamapotamus is real and go out searching for it to prove the teacher wrong. They look in all kinds of unlikely places and find all manner of previously undiscovered things. It's full of words that are mispronounced, charming, funny words that should exist and be in the dictionary and maybe they will one day, like jabberwocky. Lewis Carroll invented words, why shouldn't I?'

Petra looked at him with pity. 'It must be heart breaking being apart from them and not being able to even call.' She paused, not knowing how to break it to him. 'I may as well tell you that the papers back home are reporting our affair, along with pictorial evidence.'

'Oh God no; that's it then,' said Joe, head in hands, 'we're both ruined. If we ever get back, Louise will never speak to me again, let alone allow me access to the kids.'

'We can only hope that someone will see the story for the fictitious nonsense that it is,' said Petra, 'and that we have friends who believe better of us.'

25. Have A Little Faith

Louise and Robin were losing patience with the hotel manager, but what further information could he give them? 'Look, they're not the first guests to disappear without checking out, happens all the time; all we can do is report it to the police and let them deal with it. I suppose they were a bit unusual in that they left their luggage behind; the police took it away as evidence, good job too, as we needed the room for the next occupants.'

'And did the police investigate, look at their rooms for anything suspicious or interview anyone?' asked Louise.

'I guess so, but we heard nothing more from them, so as far as we're concerned the matter's closed. The bill was paid by some publishers in West Village. They made the booking, so were liable for the costs.'

Ravelo the porter lifted a heavy case on to his trolley as he listened discreetly to their conversation. He hesitated as they walked away and then followed them outside.

Robin put a comforting arm round Louise's shoulder. 'Next stop the police station then; we're getting nowhere here.'

'Sir, Ma'am,' whispered Ravelo from behind them, looking around to ensure no-one was watching. 'I see something; fifty dollars I tell, but no-one must know it me who tell.'

Robin removed the money from his wallet and counted out fifty dollars, holding it tightly to ensure they got the information first. 'OK, what did you see exactly and why didn't you talk to the police?'

'Police send me home, ask too many questions about where I from.'

Louise wept as he went on to inform them in broken English of what he thought were two bodies being taken away in a white van by a maid who changed into a laundry man. 'Were they … dead?' she sobbed.

'I don't know. I just tell what I see,' answered Ravelo nervously, as he snatched his fifty dollars, turned and faded into the anonymous blend of characters loitering in the lobby.

Two drunken prostitutes were centre stage at the police station, shouting and screaming at each other, grabbing handfuls of hair whenever they managed to escape the grasp of their captors. The argument appeared to concern a client who had been about to enter into a transaction with one of the ladies when he saw the other one and expressed a preference for her instead.

Louise and Robin sidled carefully around the altercation and approached the desk, the experienced Sergeant Mahon's attention drawn slowly from the melee to them. 'Good day, Sir, Madam,' he nodded. 'Please ignore our little floor show; just a day in the life of our humble precinct. And how can I assist you?'

After Robin's explanation, the sergeant looked at Louise with sympathy. 'Sorry to appear insensitive, Ma'am, but are you sure they haven't simply run off together, regrettably not uncommon in this day and age. We carried out a thorough investigation and found no sign of foul play; we spoke to the receptionist, the maid, the waitress, nothing. There was no evidence of anything amiss in their rooms and all that we could ascertain is that your husband ate breakfast alone and thereafter disappeared off the face of the earth along with Ms Hunter. The case has been handed over to Immigration as, if they are still in the US, they will be treated as illegal immigrants.'

'And did you not think it strange that they left without taking their things?' asked Louise.

'A little, yes, but maybe a new life, new clothes,' he replied. 'I'm sorry, Ma'am, but we have wives reporting their husbands missing every day. Ninety-nine per cent of the time there's a logical explanation, usually not the one she wants to hear, but an explanation nonetheless.'

Robin went on to tell of the unlikely new evidence they'd uncovered.

'And you can't give me the name of the witness to these events, or a registration plate for the van, or a more detailed description of our mystery transvestite perpetrator?' said the sceptical sergeant. 'Not much to go on, is it? Look, I'll see if there's any CCTV at the back of the hotel and, if so, if there's any footage for the morning in question.'

Retrieving Joe and Petra's luggage from lost property, two small cases for a supposedly short trip, the sergeant said, 'You can take these with you. We'd only give them to the homeless if they're not claimed. Let me have your contact details and I'll be in touch.'

Back at the hotel Louise slowly opened Joe's case and picked through his typically crumpled clothes: he never did believe in ironing. Holding his 'Born to be a Blockhead' t-shirt to her face, the smell of his body spray filled her nostrils and she burst into uncontrollable tears … she'd always hated that shirt. Joe had invariably worn it to Emma and Jamie's parents' evenings, deliberately to wind her up.

'I hope they aspire to greater things than that; it's not exactly a good example, is it?' she'd argued.

'Nothing wrong with aspiring to be a Blockhead,' he'd replied. 'Ian Dury was a fine songwriter and poet, and the Blockheads are great musicians, best live band I ever had the pleasure of bopping to.'

Despite all he'd put her through, she wished he was here beside her, to know he was safe, alive. Yes, she'd berate and badger him, and threaten dismemberment and divorce, but she needed to hold him again, if only by the neck.

She lay on the bed and watched a tiny spider climb its silken, barely visible thread to the ceiling, then fall and start again. She felt alone and weak, powerless and helpless. How could they hope to find him in this enormous country? He could be anywhere.

Joe tried in vain to supress a snigger as Petra appeared in the doorway, a vision in the checked shirt, jeans and cowboy boots that Hank had thoughtfully obtained for her. 'Don't say a word,' she said, 'I'm not in the mood for your sarcastic comments.'

'Far be it for me to comment on your fashion sense,' said Joe, 'just sorry I'm not coming with you, I could do with a night out.'

Since Petra's introduction to Hank's mother two days previous, both she and Joe had been confined to barracks, prisoners in the crumbling, haunted slave quarters. These rooms had hardly been luxurious in their prime; now they were simply derelict, cold and damp. Bored beyond boredom, all their risky escape plans exhausted, their diet consisted of nothing but takeaway junk food.

'For God's sake, let me cook something decent,' Joe had pleaded, after consuming yet another tasteless burger and fries. 'I'll let you have a shopping list and if we can gather some wood I'm sure I can get that old stove working in the kitchen, unless you're intent on inflicting a slow death upon us all by filling us with this poison.'

Hank considered this proposition and had to admit he'd been letting himself go during their little adventure. Despite living alone, he'd always prided himself on keeping in good shape, a belief that a healthy diet and plenty of exercise promotes a sharp mind and fit body. After a week of physical inactivity and eating crap, he could feel his muscular frame subsiding and his usually razor-sharp mind becoming fuzzy and indecisive.

'OK, you can make Sunday dinner,' conceded Hank, handing him a pen and pad. 'Write down what you need on here and we'll pick it up in town today. Now, are you ready?' he said, turning to

Petra. 'I must say, you look the part; ever done any country dancing before?'

'A little, at school under duress; it wasn't considered cool where I come from and we all hated it.'

'Well, all you need to do is follow me and at least try to look as if you're having a good time. And no funny business; remember that if either of you are thinking of communicating your predicament to anyone, or of attempting to escape, then the other will suffer the consequences.'

After the grocery shopping and another visit to the ailing Mrs Schneider (who was deteriorating rapidly and barely recognised them), they approached the venue for their evening's entertainment, Hank visibly upset by his mother's worsening condition.

'Are you sure you're up to this?' enquired Petra, hoping he'd change his mind and not put her through this ridiculous ordeal. 'We can turn around and go back, you know. If you would rather be with your mother, nobody would blame you for not wanting to dance, given the circumstances.'

'No, we're expected. I'll be fine once we get inside. Everyone knows everyone else's business round here and I'd rather avoid the inevitable questions that would be asked if we didn't turn up.'

Although billed as a barn dance, Petra wasn't expecting it to be in an actual barn, a cavernous, draughty structure, laid out with trestle tables and benches, a makeshift stage at one end, bales of hay scattered, like buffalo gals, around the outside.

Heads turned as they entered. The whole town had heard about the return of the war hero and Vietnam had been largely supported in these parts at the time. Although America as a whole had since conveniently forgotten many of its participants, consigned them to the scrapheap, Bushville appreciated those of its own who had fought for their country and held them in high esteem.

Petra considered her options: was there anyone here she could run to and raise the alarm? She observed as everyone they encountered smiled and nodded at Hank; this was his territory, who would

153

believe the word of some crazy English woman against that of their decorated soldier?

Hank's Aunt Maud and Uncle Jim were the first to greet them and Petra could immediately see the family resemblance in his mother's younger sister, those same piercing blue eyes that she automatically associated with the bigotry and hatred she'd recently been forced to listen to. Normally a confident social animal, Petra had never felt so out of place, so far away from home, so ill at ease in the company of people.

As she was introduced to cousins, second cousins, old friends, even his old schoolteacher, she couldn't deny that these strangers were going out of their way to make her welcome. Of course, she had to think on her feet when answering their incessant questions and invent the detail, make it up as she went along with glances at Hank for reassurance. He'd taken the precaution of briefing her on where and when they had met (at a party at the American Embassy in London, no less), but did they live together, had he met her family, where and when were they to be married, did she know Prince William?

It was with some relief that she heard the band strike up 'Stand By Your Man', of all songs, and Hank guided her firmly to the dance floor. 'Well done, you've got them eating out of your hand,' he said, 'though of course they've only got to hear an English accent and they're getting out the best china.'

'I'm going to become an actress when this is all over,' she said. 'If I can convince people that I'm your fiancée, then I can fool anyone.'

Surprisingly agile for his size, Hank instinctively recalled the steps that had been drilled into him as a child and was soon taking charge, turning Petra this way and that as the band got into their stride. As they danced, he scanned the hall for familiar faces and saw many, all much older than when he was last here, but unmistakably the faces that made this his home.

Then he saw him, Vince Stone, as smug as ever in a pale blue suit ill designed for dancing. Projecting all the aura of the richest man in town, with his not inconsiderable backside firmly in the seat of local politics, he stared back at Hank from among an entourage of eager hangers on. Vince nudged the man to his left and they both laughed uproariously.

Hank's gaze was drawn with interest to the grossly obese woman by his side, hair dyed a bright yellow shade of blonde, and he realised with dismay that it was Mary Morrison, his childhood sweetheart, ballooned and bulbous, almost beyond recognition from the sweet girl he once knew, a spoilt by-product of the gluttony of her husband.

Nodding his acknowledgment and falsely smiling, Hank turned his attention back to his dance partner. There was no denying that she looked good in tight jeans and a cowboy shirt and for a moment he thought he sensed a little flirting in her demeanour. Petra winced and drew a sharp breath as he held her tightly by the waist and swung her round joyously. For the first time since his cruelly stolen youth, Hank was feeling good, enjoying the moment and the close proximity of a beautiful woman. He was actually having fun and he wanted Mary and Vince to know it.

Petra had seen it while his attention had been elsewhere, the unattended mobile phone on the corner of a table at the back of the hall. Dare she risk it? It went against all her instincts and upbringing to steal and these people had shown her nothing but welcome and hospitality, but she must do something to get them out of this mess. Joe was helpless, even more so than usual, so it was down to her to take advantage of this opportunity. Subtly, she steered them in the direction of the table, careful to give Hank the impression that he was still leading; and, making sure no-one was watching as they rotated past, she grabbed the phone and slid it into her back pocket.

Joe lay back once more on the now familiar old sofa and studied the cracks in the ceiling, attempting to find shapes and patterns in the random road map of decay. He'd rather be in jail, he thought; at least then there would be some social interaction. A distant noise brought him back to earth. At first he thought he was hearing things, until the singing grew gradually louder and the song became recognisable.

Well, I'm goin' away to leave,
Won't be back no more
Goin' back down south, child
Don't you want to go?
Woman, I'm troubled, I be all worried in mind
Well, baby, I just can't be satisfied
And I just can't keep from cryin'.

He knew the song well – Muddy Waters' 'I Can't Be Satisfied' – but who was singing it so beautifully, so heartfelt, so gutturally, whilst clumsily banging around in the room outside his door?

Joe listened intently for any clues as to the nature and identity of the uninvited guest, but could hear only stumbling and intermittent singing. Eventually, he saw the door handle move as the mystery maestro attempted to enter the locked room.

'Help,' he called, 'I'm a prisoner here. Can you get me out?'

A hesitant pause, then the handle moved again.

'Please, can you help me?' he repeated.

'Who is it? Who's there?' replied a gravelly, lived-in voice, in panic and fear.

'My name is Joe and I'm being kept prisoner. Can you break down this door?'

Joe heard more stumbling, mumbling and grumbling and then footsteps disappearing quickly into the distance.

'Help, don't go,' he shouted in desperation, 'please, get me out of here.'

Then silence once more. He sat back on the sofa and rocked back and forth with his head in his hands. Was he going mad, had he imagined it, or had there briefly been someone there, a fleeting hope of escape?

Leroy James staggered outside into the cool night air, brown paper bag containing a bottle of cheap red wine in hand, a blanket tied in a bundle over his back. He'd been riding freight trains and living on the road for as long as he could remember. First the job had gone because of unjust accusations of stealing from his boss and then, when the money ran out, his woman ran out too. May as well hit the road and find his fortune elsewhere. Town followed town, city followed city, in some places kindness and charity, in others hatred and intolerance. He'd slept in barns, in subways, in shop doorways, on hay, on discarded mattresses, on freight trains, under freight trains, under bridges and under the stars. Drink had followed drink, wine, beer, cider, meths; he could no longer taste the difference.

It had been three days and nights since he'd had a roof to protect him from the elements and he thought he'd finally found temporary shelter, somewhere to lay his weary soul until some heartless policeman would move him on again. How was he to know that the derelict plantation house would be haunted, just like all the other places he stayed? In panic, he retraced his steps, through the back door and across the field, as fast as his erratic movement would allow, and wondered what he had to do to stop those voices in his head.

26. Pass It On

It was Sergeant Mahon on the phone confirming that yes, there were CCTV cameras at the back of the hotel, but the one trained on the spot where the alleged incident took place had been deliberately covered, indicating that criminal activity was potentially involved. They were reopening the investigation but, as there was no further information than when they'd last spoken, there was little the police could do at this stage.

'So you're prepared for the shit that will hit the fan when the British Consulate learns that two of its citizens have been at best kidnapped, or at worst murdered on your turf,' said Robin.

'That's purely speculation, sir, based on the evidence of an anonymous, hardly reliable witness whose testimony was purchased for fifty dollars.'

'Maybe so,' answered Robin, 'but I intend to raise the profile of this case. I'll go to the press if necessary. Something stinks here. I know Joe Stamford and I know he wouldn't just run off with another woman.'

'We're already re-interviewing the hotel staff, sir,' said Sergeant Mahon, 'and I'll be in touch if we uncover any new evidence; but it's a fact that most men keep their brains in their dicks and the lure of the flesh can induce uncharacteristic behaviour in the best of us.'

Robin considered Joe's past record with the fairer sex, his infatuation with Sandy, the car crash that was his relationship with

Rebecca, the press revelations about Laura and, now, those pictures in the paper with Petra. Could this amateur psychologist of a sergeant be right? Were they wasting their time in following them here? Was it simply an affair, an inability to resist temptation?

But everyone knew that Louise was the best thing to happen to Joe; they were made for each other, the perfect family. Even if he could sink so low as to betray Louise, he wouldn't desert his kids, would he? No, Robin was convinced that his instincts were right, that Joe was in trouble and, if he had no-one else in his corner, then it was his duty as a mate to stand up for him and fight his cause.

Louise answered the door with a face like thunder. Robin hesitated before imparting the sergeant's lack of news.

'And am I supposed to care?' she screamed. 'I've just spoken to Mum; she's told me to come straight home, told me that the tabloids are reporting their sordid affair; they've even got pictures.'

'Oh,' said Robin, looking sheepish.

Louise stared at him in disbelief. 'You knew about this, didn't you? How could you bring me all the way here when you knew what he'd done?'

'Now, hang on,' he replied, 'I knew nothing until I read the paper on the plane. We were just taking off. I could hardly go to the pilot and say sorry, we've changed our minds, can we get off, please.'

'And why didn't you tell me?'

'Because I knew it would destroy you,' replied Robin, 'and because I believe in Joe. I think it's a set-up. Someone's out to get him. I don't know who and I don't know why, but I intend to find out. You go home if you want, but I'm staying until I've solved this, once and for all.'

Louise shook her head in confusion. 'You may be right,' she sighed. 'I thought I knew him too. I would never in a million years have believed him capable of what he's done to us, but I'm tired, Robin, I can't cope with this any more. My responsibility lies at home with Emma and Jamie; the bullying has started again since the new publicity and they need me there. I wish you luck on your quest and I hope you find them, but you're going to have to do it on your own.'

Exhausted and limbs aching, it had been a long time since Petra had danced all night, the stress of learning the steps on the hoof adding to her fatigue. She flopped down on the sofa next to Joe and took a deep breath as Hank turned the key in the lock: incarcerated again.

'There was someone here,' said Joe. 'I called for help, but he ran away. Must have been a tramp and I probably scared him shitless. For a moment I thought he was our saviour, a blues-singing angel sent from above. But who would answer an atheist's prayer?'

Petra looked at him with concern and wondered if the stress of their ordeal had finally pushed him over the edge. Was he experiencing aural hallucinations, imagining angels of mercy?

'And how was the dance?' he asked.

'Hard work, but not as bad as I expected. The band were OK as it happens, and the natives were friendly.'

'Friendly enough to help us?' asked Joe. 'Did you get a message to anyone?'

'No, too risky,' she answered; 'he didn't let me out of his sight and everyone knew him; he's quite a celebrity round here.'

'So we're no further forward,' said a frustrated Joe. 'I thought the idea of you going along with his deception was to make contact with the outside world and get us out of here; but so long as you've had a good time.'

'That's not fair,' replied Petra. 'If I'm caught trying to trick him, then you're dead and I dread to think what he'd do to me. Thought this may come in handy, though,' she continued, extracting the phone from inside her pants.

'Wow, well done. I'm sorry, I underestimated you. How did you manage to get that?'

'Very carefully and nervously,' she said. 'What's the first thing you do when you lose your phone?'

'Call the number, so that you can hear where it is?'

'Exactly, I had to make my excuses and retire to the bathroom to put it on silent and then hide it so that it wouldn't show. These jeans are pretty tight, you know. Bloody thing was vibrating all the way back. Under different circumstances I may have quite enjoyed the sensation, but I had to keep talking so he wouldn't hear it, had to tell him that my irregular breathing was down to too much dancing.'

'So who do we call?' asked Joe. 'We don't know anyone's number in the States and all our allies, if we have any left, are three and a half thousand miles away.'

'We don't call anyone, we text,' said a practical Petra; 'we can't risk him hearing us.'

'OK, but the same applies: who do we text?'

'Well, presumably you'll want to let your wife know that you're still alive,' she said, 'though if she reads the papers she'll probably wish you weren't. There's not much battery left, maybe enough for one message each, so make it count.'

'I want to contact Robin,' said Joe; 'he's always been there for me in the past. He'll help us.'

'Robin it is then. I just hope he brings Batman with him. Here,' she said, throwing him the still-warm phone, 'and don't forget to tell him where we are. Let me know when you've finished and I'll text home too.'

Earnestly, Joe typed his message to Robin, asking him to tell Louise that he was still alive, that he loved her and would explain everything as soon as he could and to not believe what she read. He went on to inform him that they had been kidnapped and were in a derelict plantation house in Bushville, Mississippi, but they didn't have the zip code.

'For God's sake, how long are you going to take?' enquired Petra. 'What are you doing, writing your next book?'

'Are there two p's in Mississippi?' asked Joe. 'Here, finished. What do you think?'

Petra read his missive, shaking her head. 'You don't have to punctuate and spell everything so meticulously,' she said, 'it's a text, not a bloody English exam. I guess all the information we have is there, but whether we'll still be here by the time anyone gets to us is another matter.'

She hit the send button and began her own communication, telling her mother not to worry and that she loved her.

'OK, done,' she said. 'Now all we can do is wait and hope.'

27. Town Without Pity

Robin had been awoken by his phone in the middle of the night twice during his brief stay in the States, first by Fat Frank from back home forgetting the time difference and enquiring if he had any news about Joe, and secondly by his boss wanting to know if he could come back early due to high workloads. Not at his best when his sleep was interrupted, he'd told them both where to go, albeit a little more diplomatically with his boss, and thereafter switched off his phone before retiring.

His plan that Sunday morning was to accompany Louise to the airport, followed by a day of sightseeing, before making an appointment with the British Consulate the next day in an attempt to enlist their assistance.

Two new messages greeted him as he held his phone in one hand and brushed his teeth with the other, the limit of his multi-tasking abilities. The first from his boss implied that his career prospects would be somewhat impaired if he refused to help out the company in this difficult time, and the second, from an unknown number, was unmistakably Joe: nobody else wrote texts like that.

So he was right all along: Joe was in trouble. Dressing quickly, odd socks, t-shirt back to front, he rushed to Louise's room to share the good and bad news. Good in that he wasn't having an affair, bad in that he was miles away, imprisoned and in danger.

Comforting Louise as she broke down, he didn't know what to say;

163

he couldn't imagine the inner turmoil induced by this momentous message.

'Robin, Joe couldn't wish for a better friend than you,' she said after some thought. 'Whether he deserves such loyalty I'm not sure, but to come all this way to help him shows faith beyond the call of friendship. I'm still going home today because my first priority has to be the kids, but please find him and find out the truth.'

They exchanged a hug and a tearful farewell at the airport. 'Don't worry. I'll get to the bottom of this,' reassured Robin. 'Give my love to Emma and Jamie.'

Vince Stone trained his binoculars on the old plantation house to verify what he thought he'd seen from his back window. He was not mistaken; that was definitely smoke rising from the chimney in the slave quarters. So there were squatters in the neighbourhood. Wouldn't be the first time that someone had thought they could take advantage of shelter in the old place; wouldn't be the first time they were run out of town. Rounding up his posse of vigilantes, they made their way determinedly along the lanes, about a dozen of them in a convoy of trucks, jeeps and cars, armed with rifles and clubs.

Hank saw them coming from a half a mile away, the dust rising from the road in a mobile cloud, getting closer by the second. Joe was indignant about being interrupted in the preparation of his culinary masterpiece, but Hank, for some reason, was insistent that they return to their room with immediate effect.

By the time the gang had arrived, tyres screeching as they came to a halt, Hank was sitting back nonchalantly on the porch with his feet up, the stray cat he had befriended snuggled comfortably on his lap.

'Hi Vince, been a long time,' he said; 'see you're keeping good company as usual.'

Vince held up his hand and his friends stood back. 'What you doing here, Hank? The hotel in town not good enough for you? Your family not want to put you up?'

'For old time's sake,' replied Hank, 'a little nostalgia. Remember when we played here as kids, those innocent days?'

'Yeah, you were always the cowboy and I was the Indian,' replied Vince; 'you were the slave master and I was the slave. Guess we've both moved on since then. Where's that lovely fiancée of yours?'

'Inside sleeping off a headache,' replied Hank; 'all the travelling is catching up with her. And how's Mary?'

'She's mighty fine thanks, though you'll find those headaches get more regular once you're hitched. This is our eldest, James,' he continued, gesturing to the nearest of the thugs behind him. 'James, come and meet Hank, an old school friend and rival for the affections of your mother.'

'Glad to meet you, sir,' said James, looking far from glad.

'See you've found a friend,' said Vince, pointing at the cat purring contentedly on Hank's lap. 'You always did like your critters. Remember that old dog you had, shot by the farmer when he wandered on to the farm and worried his sheep.'

'No critter ever did me any harm,' replied Hank, as he stroked the contented cat under her chin. He hadn't thought about his old dog Bobby for some time and was surprised that the loss still hurt after all those years.

'Planning on staying long?' asked Vince. 'We're knocking this old place down soon, you know; some developers want the land for a shopping mall to go with the new houses that are going on yonder fields. I'd hate for you to still be here when they start.'

'Not long. Mama's on the way out; only a few days, by the look of her. Once the funeral's done, we'll be gone. This town was never big enough for both of us.'

'True. Swear I saw a hint of jealousy in Mary's eyes when she saw your new lady. I don't want her getting upset now.'

'You've nothing to worry about there,' said Hank; 'all in the past and best kept that way. I wish you both well.'

'Very magnanimous, I'm sure,' said Vince. 'We all made our choices, no regrets.'

'I don't recall having much choice at the time, but no, no regrets,' Hank lied.

'Shame it's just you here,' said Vince, 'me and the boys were looking forward to busting some heads; not much sport round here these days.'

'Sorry to disappoint you,' said Hank. 'Sure you'll find some other poor vagrants more worthy of your attention.'

'You take care now,' said Vince, as he motioned his hangers-on back to their vehicles, 'and sorry to hear about your mama.'

'Don't think she'll welcome your sympathy; she always blamed you for me leaving town. No hard feelings though,' he lied again.

'No, no hard feelings' said Vince.

As he shook Hank's hand, he wasn't quick enough to avoid the lightning-speed claws of the cat. Hank smiled as Vince walked away, blood dripping from a long scratch on his arm.

'OK, you can come out now,' said Hank, unlocking the door once he'd watched Vince and his cronies disappear into the distance.

'It'll be ruined,' said a distraught Joe; 'our first decent meal for over a week and you've let it overcook; a magnificent joint of beef and it'll be shrivelled up like a burger. May as well stick it in a bun and pour ketchup on it.'

'Oh, stop whining, Gordon Ramsay,' said Hank. 'I removed it from the stove. Lived on my own for a long time, you know. I have been known to prepare the odd meal or two.'

To Joe's relief the meal was salvaged and he had to stop himself salivating as he served the slightly pink roast beef, perfectly cooked potatoes and Yorkshire puddings, accompanied by fresh runner beans and topped with gravy made from the juices of the meat. Hank swapped his plate with Petra's and tucked in appreciatively.

'No offence,' he said, 'just a precaution in case you'd decided to add a little something to mine.'

Petra hesitated and looked at Joe, forkful of food half way to her mouth.

'It's OK,' he said, 'perfectly safe to eat. I'm not in the habit of spiking people's food or drink, unlike some.'

'Hey, this ain't bad,' said Hank, as he shovelled in another mouthful, 'you sure know the way to a man's heart.'

'Well, this is all perfectly civilised,' said Petra, sipping at the red wine that she'd suggested as an accompaniment, 'just like a group of friends sitting round the dinner table chatting. You don't seem like a bad guy, Hank. What's this all about, and when are you going to cut us some slack?'

'Friends,' scoffed Hank, back down to earth after the previous night's masquerade, 'I don't need friends. The only thing that friends do is let you down. You won't get round me with your womanly charms and talk of friendship. Just 'cause you been play acting at being my girl, don't mean you can get too familiar.'

'Then tell us what you want,' pleaded Joe. 'Is it money; are you going to ask for a ransom?'

Hank opened his mouth to answer, but was interrupted by his phone' His expression darkened on hearing Aunt Maud's voice.

'Time to get back in your box,' he said, as the call ended. 'Mama wants to see me one last time. Looks like I'm about to lose the only person I ever trusted.'

Tears had been flowing, Petra could see on his return; the tell-tale redness around the eyes, the occasional sniff, the drained expression. So there was a human being beneath that tough, unflinching exterior. For a fleeting moment she felt herself drawn towards him, wanting to offer comfort in his hour of need, but she stood back and held her irrational feelings in check.

'She's gone to a better place,' Hank sighed. 'Mama went to church all her life, every Sunday without fail; time to cash in on all that loyalty. Seen more than my fair share of death in my time, God damn it I've caused some of it, but this was different. She looked at peace, though, just like she was sleeping, almost child-like.'

'We're truly sorry for your loss,' sympathised Petra. 'When's the funeral?'

'Tuesday morning,' he replied. 'Got most of it organised in anticipation, only the formalities to go. Have to get you something black to wear, of course.'

Petra had been dreading this moment, though she knew it was coming. As his supposed fiancée, she would be expected to attend.

28. Goodbye To Love

The British Consulate had taken some convincing as to the urgency of the situation. 'The earliest appointment we can offer, sir, is Wednesday morning.'

It had taken all of Robin's persuasive powers and threats of press involvement to convince them to see him earlier, eleven thirty that morning with the only person available, a junior member of staff. To his surprise he had little problem finding the building, despite being given the vague direction of 'Third Avenue, between Fifty-First and Fifty-Second Streets'. He'd been told that it was easy to find your way around New York and that the city's grid system had inspired the road layout in Milton Keynes, a place he'd driven around hopelessly lost on numerous occasions. As he approached the glass-fronted midget tower block, he caught his reflection and felt like a tiny microcosm in this buzzing metropolis, Joe and Petra's disappearance probably insignificant in comparison to the Consulate's important business.

'The responsibility for conducting searches for missing persons rests with the local police force, sir,' stated Tony Corsini, as if reading from the rule book. 'I can find you the number of the police station in Bushville, but as your friends have only been errant for a short time the police may not treat it as priority. You may wish to enquire as to whether or not their travel insurance runs to search and rescue costs.'

'But can't you do anything?' pleaded Robin. 'I thought you were here to help British citizens in trouble. Don't know about you, but I would classify kidnap and imprisonment as in trouble, or is it that you don't believe me?'

'If foul play is suspected, sir, then once again the police would be your best avenue. I can give you this leaflet with some useful information and numbers. It will explain the procedures you have to follow and there are contact details for private detective agencies or charitable and voluntary organisations that specialise in tracing missing people.'

Despairingly, Robin perused the leaflet, which went on to explain that the Consulate could not use public funds to finance rescue operations or, chillingly, to pay for the repatriation of bodies should it be necessary. It suggested that, to assist with identification, a personal item belonging to the person being sought should be provided for DNA purposes.

He felt helpless. Navigating bureaucracy was soul destroying enough back home; here it seemed even more frustrating. How could he combat this blanket indifference and find a person or organisation willing to help, to take any kind of responsibility? He'd already returned to the police station to show Sergeant Mahon Joe's text, but he'd simply replied, 'Mississippi's out of our jurisdiction, sir. I suggest you go to the British Consulate or contact the police in Bushville.'

Deep in thought as he called the number, he wondered what to say to get *someone* to take him seriously. He had to admit it was a pretty unlikely story and he could understand the scepticism encountered at every turn.

The patient police officer listened intently to Robin's long and amazing tale. He said nothing until Robin concluded by reading out the content of the text about the plantation house, adding a desperate plea for help.

'There's no-one living there, sir, place is uninhabitable; only people we get there is vagrants. Had one of my officers check it out only yesterday. I can assure you that the place is empty.'

Maurice Schneider considered the new information that Robin had imparted. What was Cousin Hank up to? Vince Stone had informed him of Hank and his English fiancée's unorthodox living arrangements. 'I want him out of there and out of town as soon as the funeral's done,' he'd said. 'If you want to keep your job, then you make sure it happens.'

Maurice had always looked up to Cousin Hank, following in his footsteps by joining the army as an impressionable youth. After his five years' service, he'd chosen a career in the police force and was proud that he now oversaw a relatively law-abiding town, albeit one effectively run by corrupt politicians and businessmen whose only concern was lining their own pockets.

He was all for the easy life afforded by the sleepy town of Bushville, his only gripe being the interference of Vince Stone and his cronies in matters more appropriately dealt with by the law. Things had been quiet for weeks, not even a case of domestic violence to interrupt the station card school, the most serious recent crime a missing phone after the barn dance.

He knew of Hank's undercover work with the CIA, but was unaware of his enforced retirement. He figured that whatever Hank was involved in (probably some top secret operation of national importance) was none of his business, so he'd pleaded ignorance when Robin had called. Should he warn Hank that someone was asking questions? Yes, but best stay away from the house, as he would be keeping his location and guests a secret for a good reason. He'd have a quiet word in his ear after the funeral. After all, this crank was calling from New York. He couldn't do anything from there.

Apprehensively, Petra entered the silent, grey, cold church on Hank's arm, observing many of the faces that she'd seen at the dance, albeit with sadder and more mournful features. She felt Hank trembling by her side and glanced up to see him wipe away a tear, more evidence that this psychopath actually had feelings. Once again an emotional pull took her by surprise; she wanted to support this bereaved man at his most desperate time.

She pulled herself together, told herself what he'd done to them and reminded herself of the inner evil of the man. Could she appeal to his human side when he was at his most vulnerable? Would the death of his beloved mother render him more reasonable, or would it push him over the edge?

Suddenly, the peace was shattered by the passing siren of the town's only fire engine, the Reverend Wilson pausing before beginning the service, waiting for the ominous wailing to disappear into the distance. Maurice nodded his apology and stood to leave to investigate the source of the emergency; he would have to return later to pass on his warning to Hank.

The service was long and dull, the vicar expounding upon the virtues and life and times of May Schneider, telling of her good work in the community, of her dedication to the church and to the Lord, of how a place in heaven would surely be her reward.

Petra glanced to see how Hank was taking this heartfelt eulogy and caught him nervously checking his watch. He'd instructed Joe to be ready to leave as soon as they got back; they would be moving on immediately after the burial. Hank wasn't one for wakes, he'd said, and would prefer to mourn alone, away from here.

Petra felt nothing for the deceased as the casket was lowered into the ground. Good riddance, she thought, hoping that maybe May Schneider's prejudice would be buried with her; but deep down she knew that there would always be another generation of bigots to pick up the evil torch of intolerance and hatred.

Standing head down by the graveside, Hank looked resigned to the inevitability of the end as he threw in a few handfuls of soil, the vicar mournfully uttering 'ashes to ashes, dust to dust', and then it was over. The mumbling congregation walked slowly from the ghostly churchyard and Hank and Petra slipped silently away.

Upon their return, Joe was ready and waiting as instructed,

self-consciously wearing his new clothes, provided by Hank not out of consideration for his comfort, but merely because he'd been starting to pong a bit. Not exactly the designer threads befitting of a contemporary author of his new-found stature, but badly fitting, well-worn jeans and a red plaid shirt with a small Confederate flag on the pocket, purchased from the town's charity shop.

He was actually looking forward to moving on, if only to swap the stifling confines of his makeshift cell for the discomfort and darkness of the van and the feeling of mobility. A change is as good as a rest, he thought. Stepping outside, an uncomfortable feeling of disorientation came over him, the daylight temporarily hurting his unaccustomed eyes.

As the bedraggled Joe was unceremoniously manhandled into the back, Petra was politely invited to take her place alongside Hank in the passenger seat. He didn't want to admit it, but he was growing accustomed to her company.

A strange orange glow filled the sky above the town as Hank negotiated the potholes in the long, tree-lined drive and turned right on to the country lane, heading without deviation towards Interstate 55. A shiver descended Petra's spine as a news flash rudely interrupted the cloying country music on the local radio station, the words jumbling and re-forming in her head, their meaning gradually hitting home.

'This is your favourite country channel KKYJ FM with breaking news. Bushville councillor Vince Stone and his wife Mary have been tragically killed this morning in a fierce fire at their home. In his statement to the press, Officer Maurice Schneider said it was too early to speculate as to the cause and that the Chief Fire Officer would be investigating once the flames were extinguished and the building made safe. Fire crews are on their way from neighbouring towns to help out, but it looks like the inferno will be raging for some time yet. It has been confirmed that both Vince and Mary were in the house and were unable to escape. Their brave son James has been rushed to hospital with severe burns received in a vain attempt to rescue his parents. We'll keep you informed of events as they unfold, but in the meantime our sincere condolences go out to Vince and Mary's family and friends. This is Johnny Cash with "Ring of Fire".'

As the familiar trumpet intro resounded, Petra looked nervously to her left at an inscrutable Hank, his white-knuckled hands gripping the steering wheel as he stared purposefully and cold-bloodedly ahead, a barely noticeable glance in his wing mirror at the flaming sky his only acknowledgement of the chilling news.

29. I'm Gonna Run Away From You

'It's a job, I suppose,' said Paul Hooper, leaning nonchalantly on the bar; 'been at it for the last four years and I've seen more of the USA than most people will in their lifetime. There's places I never knew existed, places I'd have liked to spend more time in and places that quite frankly I never want to see again. Have to go wherever the job takes me.

'Used to be in Security, guarding cash delivery vans in Texas. Got held up nine times; figured I'd used up all my lives, so didn't stick around for the tenth. Worked for a private detective agency for a while, but jobs weren't guaranteed; only called on me when they wanted pictures taken of some poor sucker having an affair so their wives could sue for adultery.

'At least with this job I'm employed regular; there's always some punter thinks they can get away with it, but not any more: this microchip tracker technology can keep tags on them right across the States. So, what brings you to Bushville? One-horse town, a bit off the regular tourist trail and this hotel ain't exactly the Ritz.'

Robin took a swig from his Bud. 'Searching for a friend of mine; he came to your country for three days and never came home. I have reason to believe that he and his companion have been in Bushville recently.'

Paul flicked back the thick black hair from his seen-it-all eyes, felt his stubble and took in their surroundings. 'Shouldn't think he was here on vacation; guess there would be no other reason to visit here unless you was working or looking for someone.'

'It's a long story,' replied Robin. 'So, how does it work? The car hire company calls on you when their vehicle isn't returned and you use their tracking device to hunt down the thief?'

'That's about the size of it. Once the vehicle is a few days overdue, they give me a call. I track it down, report it to the local police and show them the paperwork; they arrest the perpetrator, hand the keys to me and I drive it back; usually pretty straightforward, unless they've dumped it and done a runner. Don't get to spend too much time at home, but the work's OK. I'm my own boss and I was always comfortable in my own company.'

'And the one you're after at the moment,' asked Robin, 'are you close to catching them?'

'No, looks like they moved on a few days ago,' replied Paul. 'I'll be back on the road again tomorrow, heading south. They sent me here because the vehicle had been here for best part of a week. They've sure covered a lot of miles; thing was hired in New York.'

Robin's heart skipped a beat. 'What kind of vehicle is it?'

'Just a bog standard white van, nothing worth stealing, kind of thing people hire when they're moving apartments. If you're going to all the trouble of purloining a wagon, might as well make it worthwhile; a Cadillac or a Buick, maybe.'

Robin couldn't believe his luck. Could this be the very same white van that had been used in the abduction of Joe and Petra? It couldn't be coincidence, could it, hired in New York and ending up in Bushville?

His enquiries at the police station had proved unproductive, the stressed-out officer having no knowledge of any English people in town or of anyone living at the old plantation house. Preoccupied as they were with a recent fire that had taken the life of some local dignitary and his wife, he'd made it perfectly clear that their investigation had higher priority than missing persons.

Robin had paid the house a visit, but there was no sign of life apart from the frightened mouse scurrying beneath his feet, with a stray cat in hot pursuit that had caused him to jump out of his skin. Another dead end, he'd returned to the hotel deflated; he'd have to ask around town tomorrow.

Paul listened intently as Robin told his story, shaking his head in disbelief.

'So you've come all this way to find him; wish I had friends like you, man. And what makes you think he ain't just run off with this, what's her name, Petra?'

'Everyone I've spoken to asks that,' replied Robin. 'It's a cynical world we live in; even his wife's not sure. Came to the conclusion that the only way to track him down is to come looking myself. Listen, I've run out of leads; is it OK if I tag along with you? It's my only chance of finding them.'

'Fine by me,' said Paul, 'be glad of the company. I don't have any wheels, though; restricted to trains, Greyhounds, local buses, taxis or hitch-hiking. Have to keep my expenses to a minimum and be in a position to drive the recovered vehicle back when I find it.'

'No problem,' said Robin, 'I hired a car at Jackson airport; show me your thumb and you can hitch a ride with me. Joe will owe me big time when I do catch up with him: flights, hotels, hire cars, and I'll probably have no job to go back to when I get home. The dozy bastard will be paying me back for years. Where do you think they're heading?'

'Looks like they're on their way to New Orleans. Can't get no further than that without a boat; should be able to corner them there.'

A newspaper rustled on a nearby table, its apparently studious young reader adjusting his glasses: he'd heard enough to confirm his theory.

Fighting back the tears, Louise lifted the last of the cases into the back of her dad's old Vauxhall Astra hatchback, her heart breaking as they drove away, their family home receding behind them. Six o'clock in the morning, an early start to avoid the daily onslaught of the preying press. She sighed. 'Thanks, Dad'.

'What for?' he replied. 'You know your mother and I will always be there for you, whatever you decide to do, wherever you decide to live.'

They'd stayed with Auntie Agnes before, an idyllic week by the seaside, a week of sunshine, ice cream and pebble castles.

'Bexhill-on-Sea: isn't that where you go while you're waiting to die?' Joe had said when Louise had suggested it. 'Best holiday I've ever had,' he'd conceded, when they got home.

Emma rubbed the sleep from her eyes and yawned. 'Are we going away for long, Mummy? Will Daddy come too, like last time? Don't I have to go to school any more?'

'We're going to stay with Auntie Agnes for a while,' Louise explained for the tenth time. 'Daddy won't be coming and I've found you a new school to go to.'

'Are we there yet?' asked Jamie.

Increasingly withdrawn, Emma had taken recent events badly. She knew about the publicity surrounding the man she used to worship: he was her Dad, no-one else's, and she was proud of it. The things they said about him at school, though, had made her very angry and she'd been in lots of trouble for punching Molly Brown and Mummy had to see the headmistress.

Louise had explained everything to the school admissions manager in Bexhill and she'd been very understanding in finding Emma and Jamie a place.

'Can you guarantee anonymity?' asked Louise. 'No-one must know who we are. We will be using my maiden name Willis and we just want to fit in and lead a normal life.'

'I will have to confide in the headmaster, Ms Willis, but there's no reason why anyone else should know the details.'

So that was it then, she thought. It had been a long time since anyone had called her Ms Willis and it felt strange and solitary, the confirmation, as if she needed it, that she was on her own.

Auntie Agnes showed the children to the room that they would share during their stay. Unsure of how long that would be, she'd gone to the trouble of buying new duvet covers for them: princesses for Emma and footballs for Jamie.

'Do I have to share a room with Stinky Pants?' asked Jamie, over a fish and chips lunch. 'We have our own rooms at home.'

'Jamie, it's very kind of Auntie Agnes to put us up,' said Louise. 'Remember, we're guests here; you behave now.'

'I want to go home, I don't like it here,' shouted Jamie, kicking his feet on the table.

'Now listen,' said Louise, 'we'll be staying here for a while until we get things sorted out. We had a good time here on holiday and you'll make friends at your new school. We'll be fine once we get settled in.'

'This is all Daddy's fault,' shouted Jamie with angry tears in his eyes, 'I hate him; why did he have to leave us?'

'It's not Daddy's fault,' replied Emma. 'He'll be back, you'll see, and then we can go home and he'll put everything right. And if you call me Stinky Pants again I'll punch you, just like I did to Molly Brown.'

Auntie Agnes looked from one to the other in dismay, wondering what she'd let herself in for.

'I'm so sorry,' said Louise, 'this has been a big upset for them. I'm sure they'll be fine once we get into a routine.'

'Don't worry,' said Auntie Agnes, 'I understand. After lunch we'll walk down to the seaside and get some ice cream. What do you think, kids?'

'Yippee!' screamed Jamie. 'Can I have choc chip?'

Paul leant forward in the passenger seat to get a better sight of the wing mirror. Yes, it was still there. 'Think someone's on our tail,' he said; 'anyone been following you?'

'Not that I know of,' replied a perplexed Robin, as he spotted a blue Subaru in the rear-view mirror.

'Been with us since we left Bushville,' said Paul. 'All part of the training for the security vans; force of habit, you get to know who's behind you. Never stopped the bastards holding me up, but sometimes it helped to be prepared. Drove into the police precinct once when I knew we were being tailed, suckers followed us and jumped out with sawn-off shotguns; should have seen their faces when they realised where they were.'

'So what do we do?' asked Robin. 'Are you sure he's following us?'

'Pretty sure. There's one way to find out: pull in at the next rest stop and see if he joins us. I'm getting hungry anyways; time for some lunch, I think.'

'But what if he's trouble?' said Robin. 'We don't know why he's after us.'

'He's hardly likely to do anything in a public place, is he?' replied Paul. 'And I'd rather have him where I can see him. Look, I'm just after the van. You're the one who wants the bandits that took it. Is there anything you're not telling me about your friends? Why do you think this guy's likely to be trouble?'

'Don't know, just a feeling,' said Robin. 'All this is way out of my realm of experience: kidnap, subterfuge, ex-private detectives. I used to love the *Rockford Files*, but I'd rather not be involved in a real car chase if it's all the same to you.'

'You've been watching too much TV. Besides, you're driving an economy Chevy and he's in a Subaru, hardly classic *Starsky and Hutch*, is it? Pull in here and let's see if he follows.'

Hitting the kerb as he nervously entered the car park, Robin found a space and asked, 'What now?'

'We wait and let him park. Try to get a good look at him, but be subtle. We don't want him to know we're on to him.'

Sure enough, the Subaru passed them and nestled in the corner of the car park.

'OK, now we know,' said Paul. 'That guy was in the hotel last night, on the table near us, reading his newspaper. Tried to engage him in conversation before you came in, but he didn't want to know. Figured he was just another loner; meet them all the time when you're on the road.'

'I don't like it,' said Robin; 'can't we just drive away?'

'Then he'll be behind us again and we'll be none the wiser. Aren't you even a little curious? Don't you want to know what his angle is?'

'I guess so,' said Robin, 'but first sign of any trouble and I'm out of here.'

The sparsely populated, run down roadside diner was in a state of permanent anticipation, for a lunchtime rush that somehow never materialised. Red and white was the predominant theme of the cracked décor, with faded black and white photos of old movie stars scattered randomly around the walls. The heads of its few customers turned as one as Robin and Paul entered and sat down on uncomfortable metallic chairs at a corner table with a view of the whole dining area. They each picked up a laminated menu, Paul struggling with the adhesive qualities of an old coffee spillage that had stubbornly stuck his to the table.

Robin peeped over the top of his menu and kicked Paul under the table as their mystery pursuer nonchalantly surveyed the premises and took a table on the opposite side of the diner, taking care not to look directly at his quarry.

'OK, here we go,' said Paul, standing and walking purposefully in his direction. Robin followed apprehensively.

'Mind if we join you?' asked Paul, not waiting for an answer and planting himself firmly opposite the tall, bespectacled, smartly dressed young man. He offered his hand. 'Paul Hooper, and this is my travelling companion Robin Barker. Now, let's cut the crap. Why are you following us?'

He doesn't look like trouble, thought Robin, as he sat alongside Paul, can't be much older than twenty-one. Still got the remnants of youthful acne and those Buddy Holly glasses invoke the innocence of a bygone era; he could have stepped out of one of those old pictures on the wall.

'Harry Vance,' he answered, nervously shaking hands with them both. 'Oh dear, is it really that obvious? I'm not very good at this, am I? Let me buy lunch and we can talk while we eat.'

Tony, the diner's browbeaten owner, approached their table, a patch over his left eye the result of an accident with the wrong end of a barbeque fork, his greasy black hair apparently lubricated with bacon fat. He tilted his head to one side to accommodate the use of his one good eye as he took their order.

'OK, so that's two grille sandwiches, one Chicken Rueben – grilled chicken, kraut, Swiss and dressing on rye; one Blackened Tuna – Cajun-style tuna steak with cucumber sauce and sprouts; and one Chicken Caesar Salad with three side orders of fries and coffee for three, refills are free of charge. So where are you guys heading?'

'New Orleans,' answered Paul, trying to give the impression that any elaboration on those two words would not be forthcoming.

'That business or pleasure?' he persevered.

'Mainly business,' said Paul, 'but you can't visit New Orleans without incorporating a little pleasure.'

'And what line of business would that be?' asked Tony, not taking the hint that his questions were unwelcome.

'We're restaurant critics,' replied Paul. 'I trust we'll be able to write good reviews about this place?'

'You sure will, sir, coming right up,' said Tony, as he scurried away to supervise their order personally.

'OK, now we're asking the questions,' said Paul, turning menacingly toward Harry. 'What's the game? Start talking.'

Harry paused, wondering how much to give away. 'I overheard you fellas talking in the hotel last night in Bushville; think we may be trying to track down the same people.'

'And how much did you hear?' asked Robin. 'Who are you looking for?'

'I'm not interested in your friends exactly, except to try to prevent them coming to any harm. No, I'm after the guy who's with them; we've had him under surveillance for a while, but he gave me the slip in New York. As I said, I'm not very good at this.'

'You say *we've* had him under surveillance,' said Robin; 'who's we and who's he?'

'I can't tell you who we are, sir, but has your friend ever mentioned an acquaintance with a guy named Hank Schneider?'

'Never heard of him,' replied Robin. 'If you lost him in New York, how did you trace him to Bushville? Who is he and why have you been watching him?'

'There are some questions I cannot answer,' said Harry, 'but our Mr Schneider has connections to Bushville. I took a long shot that he may have returned there. We have been watching him because his behaviour has become increasingly unpredictable of late. Please be assured that I am on your side and it is in all of our interests to find your friends and their abductor as soon as possible.'

Conversation was interrupted by the arrival of their food, immaculately presented by Tony, who instructed them to 'enjoy and please let me know if you require anything else'.

'Hey, this looks good,' said Paul, his mouth watering, 'have to try that restaurant critic angle again.'

'So what does he want with Joe and Petra?' Robin asked Harry. 'Is he dangerous?'

'We believe his motive may be both personal and political. I understand that your friend has been known to dabble in left wing causes.'

'In his youth, yes,' said Robin, 'but Joe's harmless, for God's sake, nobody ever took his views seriously.'

'Well, it appears that our Mr Schneider has, particularly since your friend decided to resurrect his youthful idealism in print. As to whether or not he's dangerous, we believe that his mind is somewhat disturbed and we're anxious to dissuade him from doing anything rash.'

'Anything rash!' said Robin. 'Bit late to use your powers of persuasion, isn't it? He's already dragged them half way across the States in the back of a crappy van. God knows what state they're in, that's if they're still alive. And what's his personal motive? What could they possibly have done to him to warrant such treatment?'

'We have reason to believe that your friend and he have a past love interest in common and that this conflict of interest may have contributed to his current state of mind.'

'Well, that narrows it down a bit,' said Robin. 'I can count Joe's love interests on the fingers of one hand. Think I'm starting to get the picture. This nutter had the hots for Left Wing Laura, didn't he? My god, this is more serious than I thought. He must be completely unhinged.'

'That's for you to speculate,' said Harry, worried that he'd said too much already. 'Needless to say that we must treat the discovery of their whereabouts with some urgency.'

'Hey, this is getting more intriguing by the minute,' said Paul, as he polished off the last of his sandwich. 'I don't get paid much for retrieving stolen hire vehicles; if we help you find this guy, is there a price on his head?'

'Not as such, but we are anxious to avoid the potential embarrassment of an international incident. You may find that we will be grateful for your assistance.'

'You keep referring to yourself as we,' said Robin. 'Does that mean you're not working alone?'

'I am working alone,' said Harry, 'but I have swift access to back-up should it become necessary.'

'And what do you intend to do when you find this Hank Schneider?' asked Paul. 'He doesn't sound like the kind of guy that would come quietly.'

'I will have to assess the situation at the time,' said Harry seriously. 'Our strategy will depend upon a number of factors, not least the safety of your friends. Now, I suggest that we pool our resources and get back on the road. What do you say?'

30. Papa Was A Rollin' Stone

'Choc chip, please,' said Joe, 'just to remind me of the simpler times, the special times that you have stolen from me.' He thought sadly about Louise, Emma and Jamie, about his friends and his home town, so far away, both physically and emotionally. Would he ever see them again? Could he ever return to his old life?

Petra had somehow used her charms to persuade Hank that they had been good and therefore deserved an ice cream to cool them down following a particularly spicy jambalaya.

'OK,' conceded Hank, 'our journey is nearly at an end, can't see the harm in a little treat, but don't think I'm going soft. If either of you have any thoughts of escaping into the crowds here, then remember that I won't hesitate to put a bullet in your back.'

Chilled by the ice cream and by Hank's threat, they stepped out of the quiet Cajun restaurant into the early evening humidity and walked the sparsely populated streets, too early for the night-time revellers. Beneath elaborate wrought iron balconies, the steamy sound of blues and jazz faded in and out behind elegant colonial facades as they passed. It took them a while to find the address on Hank's scrap of paper, an unostentatious bar called the Blue Moon, which Petra and Joe viewed with trepidation. Joe took in their surroundings: a quiet, run-down back street at the arsehole end of the French Quarter. Among the bins and litter, a mangy cat picked at the bones of a discarded fish, not another soul in sight.

'You surpass yourself once again,' said Joe, with a wave of the hand. 'Are you determined to take us to all the shitholes in the US? I won't be using this tour company again and the travel agent will be hearing from my solicitor upon my return. New Orleans, I've always wanted to come here, the birthplace of so many of the world's most wonderful sounds. The offspring of New Orleans have influenced almost everything I love listening to and you have tainted my visit to this holy shrine of music with your ludicrous vendetta. And why exactly have you brought us to this particular dubious establishment? I would never in a million years have imagined this to be your scene.'

Hank grabbed Joe by the throat and towered above him, angrily looking down upon his bald head from what seemed like a great height.

'Do you think I've enjoyed your snivelling company?' he growled. 'I hadn't intended to drag you halfway across the country. It was all supposed to happen in New York, where my message would have reached a wider audience; but once we'd started along that road south, I couldn't turn back, I had to find my roots and put right some injustices.'

Despite Hank's obvious anger, Joe was well and truly fed up. Jumping on his high horse, a reckless feeling prevailed and, damning the consequences, he continued, 'It's all about you, isn't it? Never a thought for anyone else. You talk about injustice. Do you think you're the only one who has suffered injustice? What makes you so special? Yes, you may have had more than your share of bad luck, but everyone goes through some hard times in their life, whether self-inflicted or otherwise. We've had the misfortune to meet you, for instance. Whoever said that the world was fair? Quite frankly, all this self-pity is becoming a little boring. You are an intelligent man and more than capable of changing your life for the better.'

For a moment Joe thought he'd got through, a flicker of empathy with his argument in Hank's eyes, but hope was short lived as Hank lifted him higher. Joe wriggled in terror, thinking he'd maybe gone too far this time and that these were to be his final minutes. 'Tell Louise I love her,' he choked, fighting for air.

'The song is "Tell Laura I Love Her",' raged Hank, tightening his grip, 'which you well know. When will you learn that winding me up is not good for your health?'

'Hank, put him down now,' shouted Petra, surprised at her own assertiveness.

Eventually, Hank dropped him to the ground like a rag doll and Joe scrabbled around in the gutter, coughing and spluttering. As he staggered to his feet and they approached the premises, a slovenly old man met them in the doorway, wondering what all the fuss was about. 'Hey, what's the commotion?' he asked, studying this unlikely trio with curiosity. 'You're scaring away all my customers. Are you sure you're in the right place? I can direct you to the tourist part of town. I would recommend Preservation Hall on St Peter Street; some great jazz, if you don't suffer from claustrophobia.'

Hank looked him up and down with obvious distaste, as if he were something recently scraped from his shoe and still pungent. The man looked straight back at him. His back was bent with age and his clothes matched the bar's decor, various shades of brown, threadbare and shabby. His grey hair was unkempt, but his eyes were defiant, as if proud of his profession and premises.

'No, this is the place,' replied Hank, gesticulating at the less than salubrious surroundings. 'We want to see the real New Orleans, the seedy, scum-infested underbelly, the place where rats thrive.'

'Hey, I'm looking for someone to handle our publicity,' said the old man; 'don't fancy the job, do you? Who the hell are you, journalists looking for a story? If you've just come here to look down your nose, to sneer at people earning a modest living, then you can hit the road. I don't want any trouble.'

Hank surveyed their surroundings again, a bad-smell expression still on his face. 'You've sure done well for yourself. Tell me, was this place, this lifestyle, this career worth deserting your wife and baby son for?'

The old man stepped back, overcome with panic. 'Who are you, what do you know about my wife and son?'

'Oh, I know more than you think, Dad,' sneered Hank. 'Been asking around back home. Uncle Bobby told me where to find you; he figured you might want to know that Mum had died and that you may want to tell me your side of the events that led to your desertion.' Hank pulled up a chair. 'Go on, I'm all ears; can't wait to hear your pathetic excuses.'

Petra and Joe looked from one to the other, the resemblance obvious now that they thought about it: the same deep brown eyes, the high cheekbones, the flawed, handsome ruggedness, all present and correct, though somewhat withered in the older man. Hank Senior had turned as white as a sheet, the shock hitting home as he sat nervously opposite his long-lost son. Now he could see that it was his boy. He always thought that he'd know him instinctively should they ever meet and was angry with himself for not recognising his own flesh and blood.

'Sure you don't want us to leave?' asked Joe hopefully. 'You've obviously got a lot to talk about.'

'You sit tight,' ordered Hank; 'whatever he's got to say he can say in front of my fiancée and friend.'

Hank Senior shakily regained some of his composure and nodded politely at Petra. 'Pleased to meet you, Ma'am. Forgetting my manners; can I offer you a drink?'

'We'll have three double whiskies on the rocks,' said Hank, before Petra could reply.

Hank Senior motioned to the bartender to oblige and looked Hank in the eye. 'I'm genuinely sorry to hear about your Mama. We did have a bond once, long time ago; a fair bit of water under the bridge since then. Heard a lot about you – your Uncle Bobby kept me up to speed – a war hero who went on to serve his country overseas; not much detail, top secret, he said.'

'Oh, it's a bit late to show an interest in me, isn't it?' said Hank. 'Tell me about you. How does a fine, upstanding citizen such as yourself end up in a place like this?'

The bartender set the drinks down on the table, listening to the conversation with interest.

'Think I'll have one of those for myself, Jed,' said Hank Senior, 'and quit earwigging. Bring my drink and take yourself off; bar's closed tonight until further notice.'

He turned his attention back to Hank. 'So, what did your Uncle Bobby tell you? How much do you know?'

'He told me nothing except a little about this dive you run. All I know is that you ran out on us, left Mama to fend for herself, left us in poverty and left me without a father. What more is there to know?'

'The truth, maybe,' replied Hank Senior. 'You've every right to hate me, but I'm gonna tell you what really happened. Then it'll be up to you to make up your own mind.'

Hank took a slug from his whisky. 'Go on, I'm listening.'

Hank Senior hesitated, then took a deep breath. 'I had no choice but to leave town; they ran me outa my home, Sam Stone and his thugs, your pal Vince's Papa. There was this black boy, 'bout the same age as me, they accused him of attacking a white woman; brutal it was, but I knew he didn't do it, see. He was a good lad. I was with him at the time it was supposed to have happened, helping me chop some wood for the fire he was. I hid him for a few days then helped him to escape; somehow they got to know about it, so they came looking for me. Tantamount to treason in those days, helping a black man on the run. Knew they were in no mood to listen to reason, so I high-tailed it over the back fence; didn't have time to take anything with me, all I had were the clothes I was standing in. They chased me half way across the county with their dogs, but I was always one step ahead of them. Eventually, I swapped clothes with some tramp to throw them off the scent, then hitched a ride under some hay on the back of a farm wagon. I sent a message for your Mama to join me after a few years, once I'd gotten settled here, but she sent a message straight back that she wouldn't have nothing to do with no nigger lover. Her father, your grandfather, was in the

189

Klan, you know. Often wondered if it was her that tipped off Sam Stone, but I'd like to think better of her than that.'

Hank said nothing as his father continued. 'And that's basically the story. If I'd have gone home they'd have lynched me, so I headed south and made New Orleans my home. I came to love it here, to love the people, the cosmopolitan nature of the place; nobody judges no-one, it's live and let live and you can simply go about your business, no-one bothers you. Only regret is that I missed you growing up. Bobby kept me up to date with how you were doing and I was proud of what he told me; seemed you were doing OK without me. Maybe I should've tried to make contact when you were old enough to understand, but Bobby said you were in England on government business and out of touch.'

He nodded toward Petra. 'Some things turn out for the best and you must be happy with such a beautiful girl on your arm. Ain't a day gone by when I haven't thought about you and wondered what might have been, but I had to live my life. You have three half-brothers and a half-sister, you know. Hey, this must be a lot to take in; let me get you guys another drink.'

He gathered their empty glasses and walked unsteadily to the bar to refill them. Again Petra felt an involuntary pang for their kidnapper and noticed the twitch in his right eye, a sign that she'd seen before when he was on edge. It had been insidiously creeping up on her, this uncomfortable and unlikely feeling, and she was disturbed to realise that she genuinely cared and it wasn't just through sympathy.

She wondered how he would react to his father's story. From a tender age he'd been indoctrinated with the belief that his father was the villain of the piece. He'd loved his mother and had accepted everything she ever told him without question, a deep hatred of his father profoundly ingrained in his fragile mind. How would this new information register? It would be like telling a child that Santa Claus isn't real, a previously indisputable truth cruelly denied. Petra had now had the pleasure of meeting both of his parents and, although her impressions had been formed from fleeting encounters, she knew which one she preferred.

Joe's storytelling instincts held him fascinated, waiting with bated breath for the next page to be turned, for the next chapter in the curious saga of the enigma that was Hank Schneider Junior. He knew Hank was armed and was unsure whether this heartfelt tale would push him over the precipice or ease his troubled mind. Joe was ready, if necessary, to grab Petra and dive beneath the table at the first sign of his unpredictable volatility.

Whether it was the second whisky that calmed him or the seeds of doubt planted in his mind, Hank sat impenetrable, an intent expression concealing his thoughts.

'Thank you for your hospitality,' he said eventually, emptying his glass and standing to leave, 'you will be hearing from me again.'

Hank Senior held out his hand and with a forced smile said, 'Don't be a stranger, son. I'd really like to get to know you.'

Hank ignored his outstretched hand and turned purposefully towards the door. Petra and Joe looked at Hank Senior, shrugged and followed.

Extracting conversation from Hank was proving to be even more strained than usual and unlocking his thoughts would require more than a penny. He'd rented an apartment on the edge of the French Quarter, considerably upmarket from their recent accommodation, a little luxury acquired with the remnants of the ten thousand he'd blackmailed from Joe. A high ceiling fan kept the humid air circulating around the lush, antique-adorned living room and they sat silently while Hank mulled over the latest twist in the tale.

After what seemed like hours, Petra broke the silence. 'Are you OK? It must have been quite an emotional moment, meeting your dad for the first time.'

Still Hank said nothing, oblivious to any sounds other than the mixed up ones reverberating around his head.

'You should give him a chance, you know,' Petra persevered; 'meet him half way, make up for lost time.'

Joe gave her a warning shake of the head, as if to say 'don't push it'. He knew all too well the importance of a father's relationship with his son, the gravity of a father's influence, the damage that can be done if that relationship is negative.

'For what it's worth, I can sympathise,' conceded Joe. 'Having spent some time in your company and listened to your life story, I can understand how you've turned into the bitter, twisted individual that you are. But it's not too late, you know; you can turn the corner, get some help.'

Hank looked up wearily. 'Just leave me alone, will you. I need to think.'

'Does that mean we're free to go?' asked Joe.

'No, it does not. It means go to bed and don't disturb me until the morning.'

'Well, goodnight then,' said Joe, retiring to his plush new room which Hank locked behind him: luxurious comfort, but a prison still.

Petra stood also and bade him goodnight, but Hank held up his hand and said quietly, 'Not you. Will you stay and help me? Please.'

31. Stormy Weather

Morning came too soon and a hearty breakfast prepared by Joe was eaten in silence as Hank mulled over his options. Petra and he had spoken long into the night and, despite his suspicion that she was leading him on to make him drop his guard, he felt a bond had formed. But of all the qualities required for friendship, trust wasn't one that Hank had in abundance and bitter experience had taught him not to get carried away with the kind of feelings that were formulating.

Increasingly, throughout their strange journey, Petra had seen glimpses of vulnerability in Hank, a man lost and lonely, lost to the ravages of his past, lost in an outdated ideology.

'Don't prejudge people,' her dad had once told her, well aware of his own shortcomings, 'there's good in everyone.'

'What, even Hitler?' she'd asked.

'I may be getting on a bit, but I didn't know him personally,' he'd replied. 'Who knows what turned him into the monster that he was? But I know one thing: he was once a child and no child is born evil.'

Against all her better judgement, Petra knew she was falling for Hank, that old weakness for men of action waiting to trip her up once again. She glanced sheepishly at Joe. Had he heard them talking? Did he know that she hadn't gone to bed at the same time as him? Hank winked at her, appearing calmer and more at peace. Had she helped him to come to terms with recent events?

Outside, the still air and slate grey skies foretold of imminent rain, a portent of stormy weather. Suddenly, Hank looked up and smiled over a forkful of bacon, a light switched on in his eyes in contrast to the darkness of the day, as if a revelation had entered his mind from nowhere.

'I know now what I have to do,' he said. 'I must start again, a new birth. I will wash away the past, wash away the lies, the disappointments, the betrayal, the fear. I will be rechristened. I will be as a child again.'

Joe stopped mid-chew and stared at him. 'What?'

'We must prepare,' continued Hank, 'for this is the day. At last I feel alive again. The resurrection of Hank Schneider starts here.'

'Bloody hell,' sighed an exasperated Joe, 'a born-again Christian; that's all we need.'

Hank went on undaunted. 'Come on, we have places to go; you will join me at the start of my new life.'

'Is that an invitation or an order?' asked Joe wearily. He wasn't sure whether he preferred the old Hank, menacing and miserable, or this new, exuberant, rejoicing character.

Hank smiled again, an expression that looked unnatural and unsettling upon his furrowed features. He put his arm gently around Joe's shoulder. 'It's an invitation that if not accepted will cause offence, and you wouldn't want to offend old Hank now, would you.'

Petra watched Hank with curiosity, a more amenable side of him revealed, albeit still with an underlying menace; unstable, that was the word. 'So what happens now?' she asked.

'Now that would spoil the surprise, wouldn't it?' replied Hank, still smiling. 'Please go and prepare; we leave in half an hour.'

'Feels like there's a storm coming,' said Joe, looking through the window. 'Shouldn't we wait till it blows over?'

'Hey, a few raindrops never hurt anyone,' said Hank; 'they're just God's tears, Mama used to say.'

As Joe reluctantly followed instructions and returned to his room, Petra hesitated then found herself involuntarily following

Hank toward his. She was aware of what she was doing, but wasn't in control, an almost magnetic pull dictating her movements. Hearing the shuffle of her feet behind him, he turned and said, 'We don't have long; please go and get ready.'

'Hank,' she said, 'please listen. I'll come with you and help you to start again, but on one condition.'

For a moment he stood motionless, mulling over her implied commitment.

'Condition?' he said. 'There always has to be a catch. What condition?'

'You have to let Joe go; he's suffered enough. Let him return to his family. You say you're a new man, resurrected. There must be room in your heart for forgiveness.'

He was unsure how to react; this was unfamiliar territory. His head was spinning, the roller-coaster ride of the last twenty-four hours rendering him dizzy with confusion. Could this be happening to him, a chance of a new beginning? He stared into her eyes. Could he trust her? He'd been lied to before, more than once, but she seemed sincere.

Petra stared back, her gaze unwavering. Yes, she'd dallied with action men before, but compared to Hank they were just playing with the concept. This wasn't War Hammer. Hank was the real thing, been there, done that, got the t-shirt.

'What's to stop him going to the police as soon as he gets around the corner?' he asked.

'Leave that to me. I'll convince him that it wouldn't be in his best interests to squeal.'

'OK, it's a deal,' he said at last. 'He's free to go as soon as I have assurances that he'll keep quiet about our little adventure. Tell him not to forget that I still have the insurance policy of your safety and of those photos.'

Petra shuddered. There she was promising to help and accompany him and still there was the thinly veiled threat that he would harm her should things not go as planned.

195

'I'm not going anywhere without Petra,' said Joe, when the surprise announcement was made that he was free. 'If I go, she goes; if she stays, I stay.'

'Very chivalrous, I'm sure,' Hank sneered; 'never knew you had it in you; but if I say it's time for you to leave, then leave you will.'

'It's OK, Joe, I want to stay,' said Petra, her voice steady. 'I want to stay with Hank.'

Joe looked at her in disbelief, the penny finally dropping. 'What, you and *him*? In the words of John McEnroe, you cannot be serious. What the hell are you thinking of? I can tell you one thing – there will be no future in it, no happy families.'

'I'm well aware of that, but I've made my decision and Hank's keeping his side of the bargain in setting you free.'

'You're crazy, both of you,' said Joe, shaking his head. 'I can't get my head round this. Say hi to Charles Manson for me when you meet him in jail, or were you planning on a Bonnie and Clyde ending?'

'I ain't ever going to jail,' replied Hank; 'they'll have to kill me first. Besides, I'm a master of disguises, remember. They'll never catch us.'

'Hmm, guess you could travel as mother and daughter,' said Joe, grimacing at the thought. 'And how am I supposed to get home? I have no money, no passport.'

Hank handed Joe his passport and wallet. 'Don't forget that I still have those pictures and if I think for a moment that you two are double-crossing me, then Petra here is dead. Now get out of my sight before I change my mind.'

'He means it, Joe,' said Petra. 'Go home and sort things out with Louise; forget about us and tell no-one.'

Joe hesitated and studied her expression, looking for any signs that she was being forced into this unorthodox collusion against her will, but he saw nothing but contentment and a determination to follow her chosen path, however uneven and rocky.

'And you're sure about this?' he asked her in amazement.

'Positive.'

'Then I wish you luck,' said Joe, as he hugged her, 'you're going to need it.'

'Yes, very moving,' said Hank, impatiently opening the front door. 'Now get out. The fact that I'll never see your ugly face again is cheering me up already.'

Turning as he stepped on to the street, Joe saw them framed in the doorway, to the passer-by a picture of domestic bliss. Petra waved weakly as Joe hesitated, shook his head again, then turned the corner and disappeared.

'We don't have to go just yet, do we?' said Petra, as she took Hank by the hand and led him back inside.

32. Walkin' To New Orleans

Joe had felt it as soon as his feet hit the sidewalk, an overpowering heaviness in the air, an ominous stillness, the proverbial calm before the storm. His new-found freedom had a hollow ring as he wandered aimlessly for some time, unsure of his next steps. All of his escape plans had included Petra and he felt alone and scared, looking over his shoulder and into every shadowy alleyway for danger.

Institutionalised from his relatively short time in captivity, he was confused and, with no-one to tell him what to do, he had some decisions to make. This must be what it feels like to be released from prison, he thought: suddenly you're on your own and responsible for your own actions again.

He wasn't entirely convinced by Petra's proclamations and, even if she had really fallen for Hank, he couldn't desert her and leave her to a surely disastrous fate. He knew his first priority should be to contact Louise and get home, but something was stopping him, something was pulling him back. He was hardly an authority on relationships or indeed hero material, but he had to save Petra from herself, from the clutches of this despot. Besides, he was responsible for her being in this situation in the first place. It was up to him to get her out.

Attempting to get inside the warped mind of Hank, he speculated as to what he would do next, where he would go. 'You will be hearing from me again,' Hank had said to his father. It was the only lead he had.

Joe tried to get his bearings, but to him the unfamiliar backstreets of New Orleans were labyrinthine. The buildings had changed from the elegance and romance of the French Quarter to brown-brick three-storey projects, with the occasional boarded-up window. How long had he been walking? He was utterly lost and disorientated. Obviously out of place, he may as well have had "TOURIST" tattooed large upon his forehead, a camera round his neck the only missing accoutrement. He was in a strange city, incidentally the one with the highest homicide rate in the US, and didn't know whether or not this area that he'd wandered into was safe. It would be somewhat ironic if, having escaped from the clutches of Hank, he was to be mugged and left for dead in some back alley.

Although it was heading for mid-morning, the grey skies enclosed the city, creating an aura of dusk and adding ominously to his fear. The impending storm had all but emptied the streets, the few people he passed looking him up and down with curiosity. He searched in vain for something to give him a clue as to where he was, for a sign to point the way. On the other side of the street an old lady pushed a battered shopping trolley, her back bent against the ravages of time. Warily, Joe crossed to ask directions. 'Good morning, Ma'am. Please would you be so kind as to direct me to the Blue Moon bar.'

'Hey, that's some accent you got there, boy,' she replied, raising her head to inspect him, 'where you hailing from?'

'From England, Ma'am. I appear to have lost my bearings.'

'You sure have,' she laughed and wheezed, 'you a long way from home; we don't get many visitors down here. I sugges' you get back to the civilise part of town, boy; shouldn' be walkin' roun' here on your own. Why you lookin' for a bar at this time o' day anyways? You don't look like no alcolic.'

'I have to meet some friends there and we got separated,' replied Joe, bending the truth slightly; 'be grateful if you could point me in the right direction.'

Just then, two large, menacing youths appeared from nowhere

and stood behind her. 'Wha's up, Grandma? This man botherin' you?'

'No problem, boys, he's only asking directions. Either of you know the Blue Moon bar?'

'I know it, but it'll cost you twenty dollars,' said one of them, his tone implying that the fee was non-negotiable.

Resigned to the inevitability of losing the wallet with which he'd only so recently been reunited, Joe carefully reached into his pocket. The old lady interjected angrily. 'You put your money away, boy. We'll be happy to help a stranger in trouble, won't cost you a dime.' She turned on her contrite grandsons. 'What kinda reputation you gonna give us? This gen'leman will go back to Englan' an' tell his countrymen 'bout us an' you asking for money jus' to tell him the way somewheres. Ain't you got no pride?'

Begrudgingly, the boys apologised, in deference to their grandmother, and began imparting a convoluted route, far too long and detailed for Joe's limited memory to retain.

'Whoa, slow down,' said Joe, holding up his hands. 'Look, boys, if you want to earn yourself twenty dollars, do you want to take me there? That's twenty dollars each if you'll act as my bodyguards too. What do you say?'

'Sounds cool,' said the more reasonable looking one, 'ain't got nothin' else to do. What you think, Jayme?'

It was like a knife to the heart and Joe bit his lip. 'Jamie, that's my son's name,' he said. 'God, how I miss him.'

''Then you better get this man to where he need to go, boys,' said Grandma; 'no child should be without their papa.'

'Appreciate your help, Ma'am' said Joe, shaking her hand. 'Come on, guys, let's get started; quicker I can get there and sort out this mess, quicker I can go home to my wife and kids.' He turned back to the old lady. 'Pleasure to meet you, Ma'am, and thank you.'

'Pleasure's mine, sir,' she replied. 'You boys look after this gen'leman, you hear.'

Feeling at once safe and small, Joe sauntered down the street, flanked on either side by the imposing figures of Jayme and his older brother George.

What the hell was he doing, voluntarily returning to the lion's den after being granted his freedom? It wasn't likely that he'd be shown any mercy the second time around. He didn't have a plan, merely a vague intention to return to the Blue Moon to see if they were there and to attempt to get Petra on her own and persuade her to see sense. Now that their relationship had changed from one of captor and prisoner to one of fledgling lovers, there was a chance that Hank would cut her some slack and allow her some freedom of movement. Yes, Joe decided, he would simply hide and await his chance.

As he said his goodbyes and thanked Jayme and George, he handed them an extra ten dollars. 'Buy some flowers for your grandma too boys, and you look after her, she's a good lady.'

A shiver ran down Joe's spine as he realised that Hank could be nearby and he quickly found a secluded nook in the wall, an ideal place from which to view the goings on at the Blue Moon.

'What time is it?' said Hank, as he awoke in panic, sitting up straight and searching for his watch.

'Who cares,' yawned a drowsy, contented Petra, 'just relax. Where's the fire?'

Hank jumped out of bed and dressed quickly, his every movement exhibiting a sense of purpose and determination, a man on a mission, a man with somewhere to go.

'Hank, if this is going to work you'll have to trust me,' said Petra. 'Please tell me where we're going.'

'All will be revealed in good time,' he answered, as he sat on the end of the bed and fastened his boots, 'you have to trust me too.'

'I will, once you've convinced me that you've changed. No more pointless vendettas, no more killing, no more running.'

'And no more conditions and ultimatums,' he said. 'If you want to come along for the ride then fine, but this is me, take it or leave it. Firstly, I have unfinished business to attend to; we're going to see my father.'

Petra sat up and gathered the flimsy sheet around her. 'And will you make peace with him? Seems to me he was the victim; wasn't his fault that he had to leave.'

'He made his choice,' said Hank. 'He chose to help that boy; must have known what the consequences would be if he was found out. He should've had other priorities, Mama and me.'

'Yes, but he was a principled young man; you don't always think about consequences when you're young and idealistic. You can't say that you haven't made mistakes.'

'One or two, yes,' conceded Hank, 'but I wouldn't have deserted my son if I'd been fortunate enough to have one.'

'One or two? That's something of an understatement. I understand that it hurts,' she said, wrapping her arms around his neck, 'but he's an old man now and you should take this second chance before it's too late.'

'Maybe you're right, but we can't stick around here much longer. There's people who'll be looking for me; won't be too long before they pick up the trail again.'

Big, bulbous drops hit the windscreen as they pulled out of the drive, few and far between, but enough to suggest a coming storm of biblical proportions. They sat in silence, the importance of meeting his father again weighing heavily upon Hank's heart. He'd decided that, whatever the outcome, they would be moving on later that day, fugitives on the run from the law and from the past, in search of a new life, somewhere remote and private.

The heavens opened as they pulled up outside the Blue Moon, the rain cascading down the sidewalk and forming a torrent with which the drainage system struggled to cope. A metallic cacophony filled their heads as the rain played a manic, tuneless calypso on the roof of the van and the wipers were impotent as stair rods bounced off the windscreen.

'Doesn't look like this is gonna stop any time soon,' said Hank, peering through the window. 'Are you ready to make a run for it?'

'Ready when you are,' replied Petra, 'just say the word.'

'Go, go, go!' shouted Hank, as if giving orders in battle, and they both jumped from the van and ran laughing to the shelter of the bar entrance.

From his vantage point across the street, Joe watched as they skipped through the puddles like teenagers in love and he realised that Petra was happy. Maybe he should go home; she wouldn't thank him for interfering and she was a grown woman, perfectly capable of making and living by her own decisions and mistakes.

He was in two minds. On the one hand, he wanted justice for the ordeal that Hank had put them through, justice for the people he'd ruthlessly killed; and he wanted to take Petra home with him to the safety of her friends and family. On the other hand, he wanted out of there, with as much distance as possible from that lunatic, back to the arms of Louise and the kids in the unlikely event that they would still welcome him home.

He took a look at himself: ill-fitting secondhand clothes, soaked to the skin, a beard that itched like buggery and a prevalent feeling of desperation. If he hung around here much longer he would surely be picked up for vagrancy. A large drip dropped from the gutter above him, inevitably finding its way down the back of his trousers to the path of least resistance. Ugh, let this all be over, he thought; I'll go home and face Louise, face the media, face the music. He gave little thought about how he would explain the course of events to an incredulous wife and public; he thought only of home and the somehow enhanced attraction of his sedate, unremarkable old life. Determining to cross one bridge at a time, he was about to creep from his cranny and take the first step on his long journey home, when a silver Chevy containing three unidentifiable men came to a cautious halt behind the van.

'This is it,' said Paul, from his hunched position in the back, 'at last!!' He was far from happy with the travelling arrangements, but Harry had subtly pulled rank and commandeered the passenger seat.

'So, what happens now?' asked Robin.

'Looks like they're parked outside that bar, so chances are they're in there,' said Harry.

'Hardly an inviting looking place, is it?' said Paul, straining to get a better view of the decrepit Blue Moon. 'So, what do we do? Can't just saunter in and order three beers like old friends, can we?'

'*We* can't, but you can,' said Harry, instinctively weighing up the options. 'Hank will know me, and Joe will know Robin, but you're anonymous. You could go in and check the lie of the land and report back.'

'What, you want me, a civilian, to go in there, where there is a potentially volatile armed man? Seems to me I'm the only one without a vested interest in how this turns out, but I'm the one who's gotten you here and I'll be the one with my cock on the block.'

'It's only a simple reconnaisance mission and we'll be right outside if you need back up,' encouraged Harry. 'Put my number on your phone and hit the call button if you're in any trouble.'

'Don't you think I'll look a little out of place?' replied Paul, unconvinced. 'Not exactly the sightseeing side of town is it? How do I explain how I come to be frequenting this crumby-looking bar?'

'You'll think of something,' said Harry. 'Tell them you're seeking shelter from the storm.'

'Got an answer for everything, haven't you?' said Paul. 'I don't like it; anything could be happening in there.'

'Look, I'll make a deal with you,' said Harry. 'You assist us and I'll make sure it's worth your while when this is all over.'

Paul considered the implied financial reward and replied at last, 'OK, but as soon as I hit that call button I want you in there with both barrels blazing.'

'Hey, that's my friend in there,' protested Robin, 'and an innocent woman. We don't want this turning into a bloodbath. Just order a beer, try to appear inconspicuous and come back and tell us what's happening.'

'Inconspicuous, that's me,' said Paul, secretly relishing the adventure. 'Don't worry, I'll not do anything to endanger your friends. If I hit the call button once then there's trouble but it's too dangerous for you to come in. If I call twice then I need help and you come straight away, OK? Well, here goes.'

The scene that greeted Paul as he entered the bar, wiping the rain from his eyes, was somewhat bizarre and far from welcoming. A bemused police officer stood in the corner with his hands on his head and his trousers round his ankles. Next to him, looking proud and defiant stood an old man, his arms held out as if pleading for common sense. And centre stage, in full combat gear, stood a huge man that Paul immediately assumed was Hank, with a gun pointing at the head of a tall, attractive lady that had to be Petra. He looked around in an attempt to find someone resembling Joe's description, but could see no-one else.

Taken aback by the drama unfolding before him, he stammered, 'Er, sorry to disturb you', and turned casually back towards the door.

'Not so fast,' said Hank. 'Stand over there with your hands on your head and don't even think about trying to leave.'

Slowly, Paul did as requested and took his place next to the police officer, to whom he nodded and said, 'Hi there. I'll wait till we're formally introduced before I shake hands if you don't mind.'

'Who are you and why are you here?' asked Hank, getting straight to the point.

'The name's Paul and this is a bar. Came in for a beer and to get out of the rain. May have escaped your notice, but it's pretty damp out there. Figured it was either find shelter or start building an ark. Not looking for any trouble and I'll happily find somewhere else to drink if this is a private party.'

'No, you've seen too much,' said Hank, 'you'll have to stay now.'

Hank wasn't a happy man; things weren't going as planned. His mood had changed in a flash, from optimistic contemplation of the future to defensive despair when Petra and he had entered the Blue Moon exuberant and still laughing. There stood Cousin Maurice in full uniform talking to Hank Senior with a serious expression. They both turned at the noise of laughter and stared at Hank with a mixture of trepidation and discernment.

Maurice spoke first, trying to conjure up a mixture of joviality and the necessary authority. 'Good to see you again, Hank. How are you?'

'I'm fine thanks, Mo. And would you be here for business or pleasure?'

'Business, I'm afraid. We're investigating the murder of Vince and Mary Stone and I'm here to ask that you accompany me back to Bushville to answer some questions.'

'Ha,' Hank sneered, 'and you've come alone. Do you really think you can take Hank Schneider by yourself?'

'We simply want to eliminate you from our enquiries, that's all; and I thought that, as we are family, you may want to co-operate.'

'Oh, I'll co-operate,' said Hank. 'I'll make a full confession: I did it, but you ain't taking me back to Bushville.'

'Then we'll have to do this officially,' said Maurice, taking his gun from the holster. 'Hank Schneider, I'm arresting you on suspicion of the murder of Vince and Mary Stone. You have the right to remain silent ...'

He got no further as in one movement Hank grabbed Petra and held his gun to her head, while she gasped in fear and wriggled. 'Hank, no! I thought we were a team; don't do this, please.'

'I'm no use to you dead or in jail,' he whispered desperately in her ear; 'you help me out here and we can get out of this.'

He turned his attention back to Maurice. 'Now, put your gun on that there table, step back into the corner and drop your pants. I find that people ain't so brave when they ain't wearing pants. Dad, you go stand there with Maurice now. Quite a family reunion this is turning out to be; shame Mama and Uncle Bobby couldn't be here. Must have been him that told you where to look for me.'

It was at this point that Paul had gate-crashed the proceedings, his timing immaculate. In his pocket he pressed the call button on his phone once to alert Harry and Robin. He considered his options and, having been briefed about Hank's reputation, decided he didn't have any. There was no alternative but to do as he was told and await help. Surely Harry would be calling for back-up and notifying the police by now.

Hank Senior tried the stern father-to-son approach. 'Hank, you stop this now and that's an order; you can't treat people like this.'

'Ha, and what are you going to do, ground me? If it's all the same to you, I'll pass on the fatherly advice, thanks, even though it is the first I've ever had.'

It was Petra's turn to try and talk some sense into him. 'This has gone too far, Hank, there's no way out. Give yourself up and I'll act as a character witness and tell them about your extenuating circumstances.'

'I told you before, I ain't going to jail.' He took a few moments to think, then concluded, 'We have to get out of here. Cousin Maurice ain't so stupid as to come after me without telling anyone and it's my guess that the place will be crawling with cops before long.'

Outside, Robin and Harry had retreated to the end of the street, from where they could still see the Blue Moon, but at a safe distance. Harry had checked the area and it appeared that the front door was the only exit.

Paul's signal had indicated trouble and soon it was evident when a policeman staggered out in his underpants, immediately followed by a seriously pissed off Paul in a similar state of undress. An old man emerged next, looking fearfully over his shoulder at Hank and his hostage.

Nooks and crannies were what Hank was looking for as his eyes darted up and down the street, potential hiding places for Maurice's accomplices. The shady figure wasn't hard to spot, a shiny head curiously peeping round to get a better view of proceedings. Hank held Petra tight and close, pointed his gun and shouted. 'Hey you, step out slowly with your hands in the air.'

With the word bollocks under his breath, the drowned rat that was Joe emerged from his hide and stood sheepishly before them.

'Joe, you bloody fool,' shouted Petra. 'What the hell are you doing back here?'

'Came to save you, as it happens,' he replied with a weak smile. 'Always was a sucker for a damsel in distress.'

'Oh no,' said Hank in dismay, 'thought we'd got rid of you for good. I guess one extra hostage wouldn't do any harm though; you know where to go, in the back with these gentlemen. Petra, you're driving.'

Feelings of exasperation, pity and respect for Joe were jockeying for position as she took the keys and asked with a sigh of resignation, 'OK, where to?'

'They'll have the airport and roads covered,' said Hank, deep in contemplation; 'they'll have the licence plate of the van; only way out is by boat. To the river please, driver; take a left at the end of the street.'

The rain had eased slightly by the time they'd taken the short journey to the muddy Mississippi, but still it continued in a steady flow to add to Petra's already dampened spirits. At the third attempt, she successfully reversed the van into a reserved parking space and surveyed the quayside through the gloom. Hank seemed to care little when she pointed out that they would get a ticket for parking here.

'And did you have a particular boat in mind?' she asked.

'How about that one over there?' he replied, with a nonchalant wave of the hand.

'You've got to be joking!!'

33. Crying in the Rain

Louise again awoke in some discomfort on the sofa, her neck cricked from lying awkwardly between two cushions. A token glassful remained at the bottom of the bottle of wine that had accompanied their evening meal. In fact, it had been Louise alone that it had been accompanying, as Aunt Agnes was strictly teetotal.

After the ritual battle had finally been won and the children were sound asleep, she'd joined Aunt Agnes in a viewing of a classic from her extensive collection of old movies – *Singing in the Rain* – just the kind of escapism that the doctor had prescribed. She'd stubbornly refused the anti-depressants that he'd offered, his standard prescription for marriage break-ups. 'I'm not going down that route,' she'd said. 'I have no desire to end up like a zombie, brain dead on Prozac. I'll not let this beat me.'

'Then the only thing I can suggest is to keep active, find an interest to take your mind off things.'

Maybe crashing out on the sofa with a bottle of vino wasn't quite what he had in mind, but it worked for her, at least temporarily. They hadn't been living with Aunt Agnes for long, but a daily routine of sorts had already been established – collect the kids from school, an hour of CBBC, help with the homework, evening meal, bedtime stories, followed by a sentimental old film watched in her nightie, at the end of which Aunt Agnes would retire to bed and leave Louise lounging, depressed, in front of the TV. Not much left in the bottle, no point in saving the dregs for tomorrow. May as well finish it off; it helped her to forget.

Rubbing her eyes, she poured the final glass and turned her head slightly to view the clock above the mantelpiece. It was almost midnight as she flicked aimlessly through the channels (over a hundred of them, but still nothing on) and ultimately settled on catching up with the day's news. The weather bulletin ended with a promise of blue skies in Bexhill, then she immediately recognised the iconic Mississippi steamboat that filled the screen as the headlines rolled, the *Natchez* slightly blurred from the effects of fatigue and wine.

The previous year, when he'd still been earning good money, Joe had excitedly brought home a holiday brochure and, with wide eyes, suggested that New Orleans would make a great holiday destination.

'And what are Emma, Jamie and I supposed to do while you're out paying homage to some obscure, half-dead soul singer?' she'd asked. 'I'm sure that the nightlife's brilliant, but it doesn't exactly strike me as being a child-friendly place and I'm not going all that way to spend my holiday babysitting.'

Louise had never shared Joe's passion, his child-like enthusiasm, his unhealthy obsession with music, preferring instead to be lightly entertained by a chronological series of boy bands. In more innocent times, she'd had a thing for Wham and still carried a clandestine torch for George Michael, despite his well-publicised preferences; then, much to Joe's disgust, she'd added Take That and Westlife, among others of the same ilk, to her meagre collection. These days she tended to get her entertainment from the latest TV talent shows, enjoying the competition element and the overwrought emotional reactions of the contestants and judges.

'I'm sorry, I can't stay in the same room as this,' Joe would complain vociferously, as somebody murdered a Bob Dylan song; 'it's appalling. Britain's got the X Factor? I think not. I shall retire to the drawing room and listen to some real music whilst reading the newspaper. I may be some time.'

It would make his day when sometimes Jamie would follow and sit beside him, listening intently and asking questions about the Stones' 'Exile on Main Street' or whatever classic he was listening to at the time, genuinely interested. The frustrated music critic in Joe saw it as an important part of his education, but knew that Emma shared her mother's dubious tastes and couldn't be saved. Periodically, Joe would poke his head round the door and ask, 'Is it safe to return? Oh God, now you're watching I'm An Ex-celebrity Get Me Some Publicity? What time is "Match of the Day" on?'

Louise returned from these memories of relative normality and tried to focus on the TV. The headlines ran repeatedly along the bottom of the screen, some breaking news from New Orleans. "Crazed gunman hijacks Mississippi steamboat", "Five hostages held in river boat drama".

She sat up with curiosity and turned up the volume to get more detail. The newsreader had on her serious face, the one she used when reporting an event of real gravity, a war or a gangland killing or something.

'And in news just coming in, New Orleans is at the centre of a hostage situation today as a heavily armed man has hijacked the *Natchez* steamboat. Police say he is holding five currently unknown people hostage, four men and a woman, and has issued a warning that he intends to kill them one by one unless he is allowed safe, unhindered passage along the river. He also claims to have enough explosives with him to blow up this beautiful boat that is so synonymous with the city of New Orleans. The police are attempting to communicate with the gunman to negotiate a peaceful end to the situation and to identify him and his captives. Now over to our New Orleans correspondent, Bob Fletcher.'

Louise watched with interest as, from beneath an umbrella, Bob Fletcher attempted to capture the mood on the ground.

'And do we have any idea who this man or his hostages are, Bob?' asked the newsreader, as the camera zoomed in to capture the scene in the middle of the muddy Mississippi river. Through the rain, the

211

outline of six figures could be seen on the deck immediately above the steamboat's enormous rotating red paddle, a gun apparently pointed at the head of one of the hostages.

'Not as yet,' replied Bob, 'but the authorities are taking this very seriously and it appears that they are not taking any chances. The man who has made the threats has promised to make contact with the police at four o'clock and the police are appealing for any witnesses who recognise the kidnapper or his victims. Due to the inclement weather, the boat was not intended to sail today, so there are no other passengers on board. We believe, however, that the captain and his mate are driving the boat.'

There followed the usual interviews with so-called experts, whose opinions would be looped endlessly whilst the item remained newsworthy.

Louise strained her eyes to get a closer look and the implausible, daunting possibility occurred to her that Joe could be involved in this. No detail could be determined through the mist and the distance, but one of the hostages looked like a man of about Joe's build. The camera panned to a helicopter hovering precariously above the boat, the wind and rain making life very difficult for the pilot.

Louise looked at the remnants of her glass of wine beside the empty bottle and pinched herself. Was this a bad dream? Had she really drank that much? She went to the kitchen and splashed cold water on her face, then returned slowly to the living room. No, the image was still there, a little clearer now as she spotted the bald head of the man on the wrong end of the gun. Oh my God, it was Joe. What should she do? What the hell had he got himself involved with now? Simultaneous emotions vied for dominance – relief that he was still alive, anger at whatever reckless decisions he'd taken to land himself in this mess, fear of the consequences, and desperation at her inability to do anything about it. She fumbled for her phone and in a blind panic called Robin. Suddenly she felt at once hysterical and sober.

* * *

'New Orleans? Yes, I know,' said Robin. 'No, we've just got here, been a couple of days behind them since Bushville.' He held the phone away from his ear. 'Hey, calm down,' he said; 'please stop shouting and I'll explain what I know. ... 'We, yes I've joined forces with a couple of guys who are looking for them too, but unfortunately one of them is now a hostage too. ... No, there's a police cordon, they won't let us near. ... Because I didn't want to worry you. ... Guns, explosives, yes, we've heard that too. ... Guy called Hank Schneider. ... No, me neither. ... Well, it seems they both shagged Left Wing Laura thirty years ago and he's also taken offence to the political element of Joe's book. ... That bloody book, yes, exactly. ... Hang on, Harry's showed some ID to a police officer and they're letting us through. ... No, I don't know who the hell Harry is or what he does. ... Of course I've asked, but he wouldn't tell me; could be the CIA for all I know. ... No, there's nothing I'm not telling you; you seem to know as much as I do. Look, I'll call you back as soon as I find out more. ... No, I didn't know that it's gone midnight back home. You called me, remember. Got to go, the police want to speak to us. Don't worry, I'll do everything I can to get him out of this. ... Yes, I'll be careful. Now try to get some sleep and I'll call you later. ... Yes, no matter what the time. Bye.'

As the curious crowd looked on, Robin followed Harry through the makeshift cordon to the police crisis co-ordination headquarters – in short, a large trailer van with 'Police' written on the side – where sat Don McPherson, the rotund New Orleans chief of police, projecting an aura of importance. Harry wielded his ID once again and shook his hand. 'Harry Vance, sir. I have intelligence on the suspect. This here's Robin Barker, a friend of one of the male hostages. Can we speak alone?'

'Hey, whatever you've got to say affects Joe,' protested Robin. 'I've a right to know what's going on.'

'I'm sorry,' said Harry, 'but some of the information I have to share is classified. Once we've finished, you'll be interviewed too.'

The chief beckoned to one of his officers. 'Jim, take Mr Barker for a coffee will you and bring him back in fifteen minutes.'

Whilst Robin reluctantly left the trailer, Harry sat down opposite the experienced police chief. He felt like the new kid on the block, a rooky on his first case, out of his depth, his only authority held in the ID card that could open more doors than he'd yet earned the right to enter.

'OK, what's the beef on this clown?' asked a seriously pissed off Chief McPherson. 'I swear that if anything happens to that boat, then someone will face the consequences.'

Harry got the impression that Chief McPherson was more interested in the steamboat than in the safe release of the hostages. He tried to express himself with confidence. After all, he was the one with the facts.

'His name's Hank Schneider and he's an ex-government agent who's gone a little off the rails. I have been detailed to keep him under observation and report back any unusual behaviour.'

Chief McPherson gestured disdainfully through the rain-covered window towards the grey outline of the *Natchez*. 'And would you classify this as unusual behaviour? I assume that you have reported the fact that he's gone "a little off the rails" to your superiors.'

'Yes, sir. I called them as soon as we arrived at the quayside and found out what was going down. Needless to say, they're not too happy.'

'You don't say. And how, if you've been observing this heavily armed maniac, has he managed to kidnap five people and hijack a fucking great boat without you noticing?'

Harry attempted not to cower in front of this authoritative colossus and answered feebly. 'My observation was interrupted when he gave me the slip in New York. I've only just caught up with him again. A senior agent is on his way here and we will place all of our resources at your disposal.'

'A great comfort, I'm sure,' said Chief McPherson. 'And when exactly will he be gracing us with his presence?'

'Within the hour,' replied Harry. 'I've made him aware of the urgency of the situation. What have you done to make contact with Hank, er, Mr Schneider?'

'Nothing as yet. I seem to have mislaid his number. We have a police boat in the vicinity with a megaphone and a trained negotiator. A police marksman is also on board; but, as you can see, the waters are a little choppy and it will be too risky to take a shot while he's near the hostages. We are waiting for your Mr Schneider to contact us. He's told us that he has a laptop with webcam and he's requested a conference at four. Say, do you know this guy personally? Should you speak with him?'

'I have made his acquaintance,' said Harry, 'but it may be best if the initial contact is with you. Find out what his demands are before we determine strategy. He may get a little spooked if he sees me.'

'And the hostages? Who the hell are they?'

'Joe Stamford, a limey author, and Petra Hunter, his publisher; his grudge against the author is both personal and philosophical. I think the publisher was just in the wrong place at the wrong time. Paul Hooper, a guy employed by the hire company to track down the stolen van they've been driving; he helped us to find them with his GPS tracking system. An old fella from a bar back in town called the Blue Moon; haven't a clue where he fits in. And an unknown police officer.'

'There's a police officer on board?'

'Well, either that or he's a member of the Village People on his way home from a party. Oh, and last I saw he wasn't wearing any pants.'

'And what about the guy with you?' continued Chief McPherson, shaking his head. 'I'd rather not have any more civilians mixed up in this.'

'Robin Barker is the best friend of Joe Stamford and may come in useful if it comes to reassuring two of the hostages. Have to be careful how much we tell him or the public in general, though. I don't need to emphasise that it could be somewhat embarrassing internationally if Mr Schneider's former allegiances are made public.'

'Embarrassing for whom exactly?' said Chief McPherson. 'Let's get this straight, my one and only concern is the welfare of the hostages, of the captain and his mate and of the *Natchez*. That boat *is* New Orleans, man. I don't give a damn if the fact that the CIA have fucked up is plastered over every newspaper in the world, so long as I can stop this crazy fool from killing anyone and from blowing up that boat. The press are all over this like a rash and if things come out that embarrass the government, then so be it. The government did nothing for us back in 2005 when Katrina hit town and I will not let considerations of bad publicity jeopardise the success of this operation.'

A knock on the door precluded Harry's reply and the chief ushered the curious Robin back in. Ensuring that Harry knew who was in charge, he approached Robin, put a reassuring hand on each shoulder and sat him down. 'Now, Mr Barker, tell me about your friend and how he came to be in this precarious situation.'

Joe stared back towards the city through the rain, attempting to get his bearings, to pick out any distinguishing features on the landscape. Apart from a queasy rocking with the swell of the tide, the *Natchez* didn't appear to be moving, the captain treading water some way from the shore, as ordered by Hank. The giant paddle was stationary and silent and the five reluctant passengers cold, wet and miserable.

Joe had given up trying to reason with Hank, all pleas for discourse on the subject of their release falling on deaf ears. He'd offered him money – no dice. He'd expressed a willingness to publicly retract some of the more contentious elements of his book – too late. He'd told him that Laura Bisham had meant nothing to him, simply a youthful mistake and a one-off. Somehow this only served to further infuriate Hank and his threat to finish him off there and then and toss him over the side for fish food rendered Joe silent at last.

Petra had said nothing throughout their ordeal, her head down, avoiding eye contact with Joe. Her emotions were all over the place, one minute severely doubting her illogical feelings, the next in awe of Hank's conviction and machismo. She was oblivious to his evil intent, unaware that he had enough explosives to blow them all to kingdom come.

Retreating thankfully to the bar area of the boat, they all sat shivering around Hank while he set up his laptop and webcam. Vainly he combed his sodden hair as he prepared to speak with Chief McPherson, a precursor to his intended demand for later contretemps involving the mayor and maybe, once they knew he was serious, the president. The technology worked first time and the no-nonsense face of Don McPherson filled the screen.

'Good afternoon to you, Mr Schneider,' he said, trying not to appear confrontational. 'Please be assured that we are willing to talk with you to reach mutual agreement on a peaceful resolution to this situation.'

He wanted to tell him that at the first opportunity his marksman would blow his fucking brains out, but he knew that, for the moment at least, Hank held all the cards.

Hank was a little thrown. 'How do you know my name? Who have you been speaking to?'

'We have our sources, Hank. Is it OK if I call you Hank?'

'No it is not,' he said irritably. 'I assume that you must have Harry Vance there with you. Wondered how long it would take him to pick up the trail again. It was far too easy to lose him back in New York, but that's what you get for sending a boy to do a man's job, I guess. Hi there, Harry, a long time no see.'

The chief beckoned Harry to sit beside him. 'Hello Hank, how's it going?'

'I'm good, thanks. And how are you enjoying my old job? I obviously didn't teach you well enough if you've failed on your first simple surveillance mission.'

'Following you is hardly simple, Hank' said Harry, attempting the right mix of familiarity and flattery.

'I guess by now you'll have reinforcements on the way,' said Hank, putting himself in Harry's shoes. 'Well, you can tell them not to try anything clever. Remember that I know all the tricks in the book, wrote some of them myself, in fact. Just one code punched into this little box will detonate an explosion and KABOOM, a watery grave for all of these good people.'

'No-one's doubting you, Hank', said Harry, conscious that a Hank in this mood was more than capable of mass murder.

'I hate to break up this little reunion,' said Chief McPherson, reclaiming centre stage, 'but can you assure me that your hostages are all safe and unharmed?'

'For the time being, yes,' said Hank, as he motioned for them all to get in shot. 'Can't guarantee their safety if you don't do as I ask, though.'

The chief nodded his acknowledgement to the bedraggled and weary, but obviously still living, prisoners. 'Which brings us to your demands, Mr Schneider. What are you hoping to achieve from this situation?'

'Oh, lots of things,' replied Hank: 'an audience for my message, revenge for all the injustices I have suffered, baptism in the waters of the Mississippi and redemption from the sins of the world. We'll start with another chat in one hour and this time I want the mayor present, and then one hour after that I want an audience with the president.'

'You mean you want to speak with the president of the United States?' said Chief McPherson.

'No, I mean the president of the golf club. Of course I mean the president of the United States.'

'I suspect he may be busy, but I'll see what I can do, Mr Schneider. Can you assure us that you won't do anything rash whilst I'm attempting to set up these meetings?'

'You have my word that, providing I'm speaking with the mayor in one hour, everyone's safe for now. Oh, and you can call off that helicopter. The noise is making me irritable and you wouldn't want that now, would you.'

As the screen went blank, they all stared at Hank with mouths agape, the scale of what they were in the midst of becoming evident. Petra spoke first, her voice cracking with emotion. 'Hank, you can't go through with this. Think about these innocent people, your cousin, your father, this man Paul here, what has he ever done to you? Please stop this now, release these people and take me as a bargaining tool so they'll let you go.'

'Do you really think they'll let me go after this?' sneered Hank. 'No, I'm well aware that this is my final act. They'll shoot me dead as soon as they get the chance. The CIA will be here soon and do you know what? I'm glad it's nearly over.'

Cousin Maurice tried a different approach. 'You know, you were always my role model, Hank. You were my hero when I was growing up and all I ever wanted was to be like you. You were a war hero and a government agent, an important man. What the hell's happened to you, Hank? How has it come to this?'

Hank listened to him intently, but the gravity of his argument was somewhat dissipated by his lack of trousers. 'Life happened, Maurice; it's got a way of giving you things and then taking them away, raising your hopes then dashing them to the ground. Guess I just couldn't take any more.'

'Listen, son, we can work it out,' pleaded Hank Senior; 'there has to be a way to end this peacefully. You know, all those years ago when I had to run, I nearly came back for you, figured that they wouldn't shoot at me while I was holding a baby, but I couldn't do it. I left you with your mama 'cause I loved you and I couldn't risk you being hurt, but the emotional hurt you been through is far worse; can't ever recover from that. I guess what I'm trying to say is that I understand and I'm asking for forgiveness.'

'Maybe could have happened,' said Hank, 'given time and a different set of circumstances; but time is something I'm running out of. They ain't gonna cut me any slack for the things I've done and it's too late to turn back; have to see it through now.'

'Then can you at least allow us the dignity of dying with our pants on,' interjected Paul, shattering the dramatic father/son moment.

34. My Way

... Try to get some sleep, Robin had said, but Louise knew that any attempt at slumber would be futile. She made herself a large cafetiere of strong coffee and settled in front of the TV for the night. Interspersed with trivialities about the economy and some celebrity gossip, the main news was from New Orleans and she sobbed into her Wonder Woman mug (a present from Joe in happier times) as the story unfolded. She'd never felt so helpless and alone.

The news appeared to be on a loop with the same headlines and interviews repeated endlessly, reported with some vigour and dramatic effect. Bob Fletcher was an experienced reporter, but he'd not previously had the opportunity to get his teeth into something like this and, although he would never admit it, he was enjoying every second of his moment of fame.

Louise rubbed her eyes and stared at the TV: this couldn't be happening. People like Joe didn't end up in situations like this, did they? A few years ago she would have thought that she'd never met anyone so ordinary and safe; how wrong could she have been? He was a best-selling author and he'd been on the telly, twice if you included what she now saw before her.

Although Joe had often told her that he knew after the first date that she was the one, for her it had taken longer, a slow evolution to a reassuring feeling of comfort in his company. Could you call it love, or was it just the same feeling she had when wearing that favourite old jumper? A cold shiver told her how much she cared and that she desperately wanted to see him safe and unharmed; but could she forgive him for what he'd put them through? Since the publication of the book they'd spent more time apart than together. Despairingly, she turned her attention back to the unbelievable scene before her, trying to tell herself that it couldn't be real.

From his one-syllable answers, it was obvious that Chief McPherson had little time for the press and saw the press conference as a necessary evil, the most efficient means of communicating with the public. He'd made his statement (short and to the point) and was now eager to get back to the task in hand, in no mood to answer vacuous questions.

Undaunted, Bob tried again. 'Does this man really have the means to blow up the *Natchez*? Do you know who he is and why he's doing this?'

'Yes, sir, he does have the means. We know he's had access to weapons and explosives; we've checked it out and I can assure you that the threat is very credible. He is not formerly known to the police and we currently have insufficient information to speculate as to his motive. We will continue dialogue with him until we have a resolution.' Ignoring a barrage of further questions, Chief McPherson left determinedly to a flurry of camera flashes.

Louise curled up into a ball and drifted fitfully off to sleep, hoping that in the morning it would all be gone.

'Nowt,' said the mayor honestly, when asked what influence he had with the president. 'T' gaffer's out of country at t' moment at some summit or sommat; can't do owt about it.'

The mayor of New Orleans was born in Sowerby Bridge, West Yorkshire, England, and emigrated to the US with his family when he was nineteen, gaining citizenship some years later. He entered politics with the Democratic Party and became sufficiently prominent in 2009 to win the nomination for mayor. His most notable achievement to date is to accommodate the improbable

222

phrase 'some summit or sommat' in some dodgy author's increasingly implausible tale.

''appen I'll pass thee over t' someone thee may know,' he continued; ''e can tell thee 'ow things stand.'

'The president doesn't negotiate with terrorists, Hank,' said Mike Farrell conclusively. 'You'll have to talk to me, I'm afraid.'

'But I'm not a terrorist, Mike,' replied Hank. 'I've spent my life serving this country and I demand to be heard.'

'You're sure terrorising those good people you have with you. Maybe you should ask them whether or not you're a terrorist. Look, I've spoken with the president's office and they've assured me that any dialogue is out of the question.'

Mike had not been happy about the interruption of his golf match, but he was the most senior available CIA agent within spitting distance of New Orleans. He'd been decidedly unimpressed by Harry's handling of the Schneider case when briefed. 'And why didn't you report the fact that you'd lost him? Did you think it unimportant?'

'Because I knew I would find him again, sir,' replied Harry. 'And I did.'

'Oh, sure, you found him alright. Not too difficult now he's on every fucking TV screen in the world, is it?'

'And how was I to know he was this crazy?' whined Harry, gesturing towards the river.

'Because you were meant to be watching him; that's what surveillance means.'

Harry cowered and said nothing; maybe he wasn't cut out for this kind of work. Maybe he should seek more sedate employment.

Mike Farrell had been assigned to work briefly with Hank back in '83 on operation RYAN, and had found him quiet, withdrawn and unforthcoming, conversation stilted. He'd put it down to the fact that they were undercover and to the prevalence of moles in that era; trust was in short supply and it wasn't unusual for an agent to keep his own counsel. Unbeknown to him, though, Hank's seething silence was the inevitable result of his two broken hearts, the objects of his desire irrevocably unattainable. All these years later and Hank was still not getting his own way, circumstances dictating that his relationship with Petra would be short-lived.

Like a spoilt child, he made his demands, in the certain knowledge that he could throw the toys out of the pram whenever he desired.

'I'm sure you're doing your best, Mike, but unless I see the president on this screen in one hour's time then it's God save this boat and all who sail in her. Do we understand each other?'

The screen went blank before Mike could answer, end of conversation.

'Hmm, that went well,' said Chief McPherson. 'So, what happens now?'

'Well, I know one thing,' replied Mike, 'he's not gonna be talking to the president and, as he appears to be unprepared to negotiate, we have no alternative but to try to get our people on to that boat and take him by force.'

From his seat in the corner, Robin listened fearfully, potentially witnessing the decision-making process that could end Joe's life. 'And how will you get the hostages out alive?' he asked.

Mike jumped. He hadn't seen the unobtrusive figure of Robin in the shadows. 'Who the hell are you?' he asked.

'This is Mr Robin Barker,' Chief McPherson answered on his behalf; 'he's come from England to find his friend, who is one of the hostages.'

'And why the hell is he in here? This is a sensitive operation. Is there anyone else you've invited to the party, any sisters, uncles, girlfriends?'

'I can vouch for him, sir,' said Harry; 'we've been working together to track Hank and his captives.'

'Oh, that's OK then,' said Mike. 'So this is the civilian that you've managed to keep out of Hank's clutches, is it? I understand that the other guy who's been helping you is now a hostage too. Not a bad day's work, is it?'

He addressed Robin with polite deference. 'Mr Barker, please allow me to apologise for the incompetence of my colleague here; this operation will be undertaken by trained officers under the supervision of Chief McPherson and myself. There are no guarantees, but we will do everything in our power to save those people. You heard what our Mr Schneider said and, unless you have any other suggestions, then I think we have no choice but to storm that boat.'

Robin couldn't disagree with Mike's appraisal of the situation and he nodded his assent, even though he knew it wasn't required. Mike addressed Chief McPherson decisively. 'Now, we have no time to lose. Rain's easing a little, but we still have some cover from the mist. I suggest that we use your guy out there with the megaphone as a diversion while we send another boat around the blind side. What do you think?'

'I have a more subtle idea,' answered Chief McPherson, the cogs of his mind still turning as he thought out loud; 'bit unorthodox, but it could work. We have an Obama lookalike here in the city. He introduced the Jazz and Heritage Festival back in April; went down a storm, he did. Whether he can fool him for long on a webcam I don't know, but he looked pretty convincing up there on that stage. We could give him a script and set him up here with the stars and stripes in the background, maybe make the image a little fuzzy somehow, might buy us a little time and we could get our men on board while he's talking.'

'Aye, I recall t' fella,' said the mayor, 'reight good 'e were.'

'Hmm, Hank likes to think of himself as an expert on disguises,' said Mike; 'this guy would have to be damn good to fool him. Get him over here suited up and we'll audition him for the part. In the meantime, call your team in for briefing. Sooner everyone knows what they have to do, the better. We may have to stall him while we set everything up. Tell him that the president's been delayed getting to a camera, maybe.'

Harry was feeling aggrieved and persecuted. How could he have envisioned what had ensued here? Who could have predicted this?

How could he make amends for his perceived dereliction of duty?

'Sir, I'd like to be part of the team that boards the boat,' he volunteered. 'You'll need CIA presence and I know Hank Schneider. I may be able to reason with him.'

'I doubt that there will be any opportunity for reason,' replied Mike, 'and anyway, what makes you think he'll listen to you?'

'He taught me my job, sir. I've spent a lot of time with him and I think I know a little about what makes him tick.'

'OK, but you don't do anything without agreeing it with me first. This is your second chance and if you fuck up this time I'll ensure you never work for the CIA again. Comprende?'

'Wake up, Mummy. Mummy, wake up.'

Louise stirred slowly, wondering where she was, Jamie shouting insistently. The cold mug of coffee stood on the table before her and she stared sideways through half-closed eyes and throbbing head at the TV screen beyond. Jamie shook her again, then climbed on board for a cuddle. He took in the scene of the empty wine bottle and his crumpled mum and, whippersnapper though he was, knew she'd been there all night.

Gradually, the room filled with the sound of morning as first Aunt Agnes then Emma surfaced, wiping the sleep from their eyes. Louise sat up and tried to clear her head. There was the haunting image of the *Natchez*, drifting calmly in darkness on the screen, night time in New Orleans. Suddenly, the unmistakable sound of gunfire shocked her to the core, her whole being went cold and she gasped in horror.

'Louise, dear, whatever's wrong?' asked Aunt Agnes.

Louise took a deep breath and sat up straight; she must put on a brave front for the children. 'Emma, take Jamie in the kitchen and get his cereal ready, please,' she said, biting her lip.

'Joe's on that boat,' she said when they'd gone, pointing at the TV, 'he's mixed up in this. A siege, they're calling it, they're using words like heavily armed, explosives, hostages. Didn't you hear it, didn't you hear the guns?'

'Are you sure, dear?' said Aunt Agnes, taking a closer look. 'Seems pretty unlikely. I thought you said he'd gone to New York.' She'd been growing increasingly concerned about Louise, what with her drinking and moody silences, and this seemed like further evidence that she was close to the edge.

'I saw him last night,' insisted Louise, 'right there on that steamboat, with a gun pointing at his head.'

'Now don't be ridiculous, pull yourself together, come and have some breakfast, then I'll help you get the children ready for school.'

Louise blotted out Aunt Agnes's scepticism and focused her attention on the news, realising that what she was watching wasn't live. It was a recording of what had happened two hours ago. She saw the words before she heard them. "Two dead in New Orleans riverboat siege" ran the headlines. "Two people killed and one wounded during rescue attempt."

'I'm deadly serious,' she said, 'he was there. I've spoken to Robin too and he confirmed it. Please, go and make sure Emma and Jamie are OK. Keep them away from the TV until I've found out what has happened.'

Aunt Agnes shook her head in dismay and headed for the kitchen, leaving Louise in her strange world.

Bob Fletcher was in his element as he excitedly imparted the news of the night's events, still unfolding as he spoke. 'Two people have been killed tonight in a dramatic conclusion to the New Orleans riverboat siege. One of them is believed to be the gunman, but the identities of the hostages (one dead and one wounded) are as yet unknown. Details are still emerging, but it is believed that a team of police marksmen raided the *Natchez* whilst the gunman was speaking to negotiators via webcam. The surviving hostages are coming ashore as we speak and we hope to be able to broadcast a statement from New Orleans police chief McPherson shortly.'

The camera panned to the chief as he emerged importantly from the trailer. Louise knew it was a dream when she saw him shaking hands with President Obama and then, accompanied by another man, head towards the quay, where a small boat was docking. She knew it wasn't a dream when Emma came in and asked 'Are you alright, Mummy?'

She obviously wasn't alright: eyes red, cheeks streaked with tears, hair a mess, head in hands. 'I'm fine, dear; just had a bad night, that's all. Go and see Auntie Agnes and ask her to help you pack for school. We'll talk later, OK?'

Louise watched numb as, one by one, a bedraggled, wet and shocked group of people disembarked from the boat. The emergency services were there, gently and sympathetically placing blankets round their shoulders and leading them to safety. A shiver ran down her spine as the last of them were led away. Joe wasn't there.

35. The Message

Hank's conversation with the president had been going well. He had to hand it to Mike; he hadn't thought for a moment that his demand would be met and that he would be granted an audience with Barack Obama, but there was no denying he was there, the man himself on the screen before his eyes, a little fuzzy due to a bad signal, but there nonetheless and calling him by his name.

'I'm told you have asked to speak with me, Mr Schneider. And how are you today?'

'I'm good, sir,' Hank stammered nervously. 'Thank you for making the time to listen. I know you're a busy man.'

'No problem. It seems that we have a situation here and I'd like it resolved without anyone getting hurt. What can I do to help?'

Hank took a deep breath. 'I have been a loyal servant to our country, sir, and I'd like to ask one favour in return.'

'Go ahead.'

'You are the most powerful man in the world, sir, and I have a message that I would like you to pass on, a message that is applicable globally for the benefit of the whole of humanity.'

'Sounds intriguing, Hank; what is it that you have to say?'

'Well, it's like this, sir ...'

It was at this point that all hell had broken loose as the door was kicked open and in stormed six armed policemen, closely followed by Harry. Petra screamed and ran towards Hank, all her irrational instincts to protect him, but Joe had read her intentions and in an instant dived on top of her, pushing her to the floor as the first shot rang out. 'Aaaggghhh!!' He'd been hit.

Taking advantage of the distraction, Hank ducked behind a table and returned fire, as bullets ricocheted indiscriminately around the cabin. Petra couldn't move, the motionless, bleeding body of Joe lying heavily on top of her. The still trouserless Paul and Maurice took cover behind the bar as bottles and glasses smashed around them.

It was all over in minutes, although everything appeared to happen in slow motion. Hank Senior ran to be by Hank's side as fast as his ageing body would allow, but a bullet intended for his son cut him cruelly down just as he reached his outstretched hand.

As Hank stood like a colossus with a primal scream of 'DAD, NO ...', he clutched his heart and his face creased in pain. Time stood still as he glared at the apologetic face of his assassin, the still smoking gun in Harry's hand, and defiantly he drew his final breath, his message unheard.

'I suppose I should thank you,' conceded Petra as she sat by Joe's hospital bedside two days later. 'In some people's interpretation of events, you saved my life.'

'Don't mention it,' replied Joe weakly; 'always wanted to be a hero and there was no time to think about what I was doing.'

'Good to see you're on the mend, pal,' Robin grinned, as he tried to make sense of Joe's chart at the end of the bed, 'unless this is upside down, in which case I'll call the priest.'

'So what's the prognosis?' asked Petra. 'How long before you can go home?'

'Lost a lot of blood, doctor says, maybe a couple more days in hospital. You better ask my wife about whether or not I can go home.'

Louise had sounded so far away when he'd called, the distance between them immeasurable, on different continents both physically and emotionally. Because the doctor had assured him that his injuries were no longer life-threatening, they'd agreed that she should stay in England for the sake of Emma and Jamie and that they'd catch up on his return. Secretly, though, Joe was hoping that Louise would jump on the plane anyway to be by his side; after all, that's what he'd have done if, God forbid, the roles had been reversed. It was an indication of the enormity of the bridge that he needed to rebuild.

'Let me talk to her when we get back,' offered Petra. 'I know we've never met, but I can explain how it was, how you weren't to blame for this. Well, not all of it anyway.'

'Thanks, I'd appreciate any help that's going. Think I'm going to need it.'

Joe coughed and wheezed, catching his breath. The pain racked his whole body and he sank back, pale and exhausted. The loss of blood had drained him, but the emotional toll had accumulated too, insidiously depriving him of his pride, his dignity, his humanity. He summoned some strength from somewhere and pulled himself up.

'And what about you?' he asked Petra with concern. 'You've been through the same hell as me, worse in fact, because you've lost someone you cared about. They've taken the bullet out of me, but there's no cure for a broken heart. Hated the bastard myself, but you obviously saw some redeeming features that weren't obvious to the naked eye.'

Petra supressed a tear. 'You can't always choose who you fall for and sometimes it just creeps up on you. Suppose I'll be OK, given time. I've had a few days to consider the irrationality of my feelings. Deep down I always knew what the conclusion would be. There was never going to be a fairy tale ending, was there? But he wasn't a bad man, Joe. He was just a man who did some bad things.'

'Well, I'm not going to argue about the distinction,' rasped Joe, 'but surely it is our actions and the way in which we interact with others that defines us, makes us who we are.'

'You're obviously feeling better,' said Robin; 'same argumentative old git that you've always been.'

'No, there's more to it than that, Joe,' said Petra. 'He was a victim too, you know.'

'Maybe you're right. I guess we're all victims of something or other.'

'And what about this message that he wanted to bequeath to the world?' asked Robin. 'Did he ever tell you what it was?'

'Yes, he did,' said Petra sadly. 'He was convinced that most of the bad things that happen in the world are the result of what parents do or say. Kids are a blank canvas until they are painted by their upbringing. All he wanted was to tell all the parents out there that when they have a child they have a responsibility to teach them good, to lead by example and to show them love. He knew he wasn't the only one affected and that there are too many mums and dads who pass on bad things; that's if they stick around at all. His theory was that the world is in such a mess because of generations of parents abdicating their individual responsibilities.'

'Can't say I disagree with any of those sentiments,' conceded Joe, as he thought guiltily about how far and how long he'd been away from his own kids. 'Must admit that I was expecting something a little more religious or political, something right from centre of the bible belt. Never thought he'd come up with something so, so human.'

'Like I said, he wasn't a bad man.'

'You'd better rest, mate,' instructed Robin; 'you're going to need all your strength to get home. I'll book us a flight for Thursday. In the meantime, I'm going to take Petra for a drink and try to cheer her up; maybe take in some jazz. My new friend Paul is going to join us.'

'You insensitive bastard,' complained Joe; 'you know I've always wanted to come to New Orleans and the only part I'm going to see is the inside of this bloody hospital.'

'You got a trip on the *Natchez*, didn't you? What more do you want? Get some sleep and we'll come and see you tomorrow.'

The fleeting fame that Joe had encountered during the Left Wing Laura affair was nothing compared to the clamour of curiosity that met him as he cautiously left the hospital. It seemed that everyone wanted a piece of him, to hear his and Petra's story and their feelings towards their kidnapper. A police presence at the hospital had temporarily kept the press at bay, but Petra, Robin and Paul had been mercilessly pestered as they'd tried to relax for the few days they had left in New Orleans.

The CIA debriefing had left them in no doubt that any sensitive information they'd gleaned from their ordeal with Hank must be kept confidential, or there would be unspoken consequences.

'Some interesting pictures we found on Hank's laptop,' Mike Farrell had said. 'Wouldn't want those falling into the wrong hands now, would we?'

Oh God, here we go again, thought Joe. He couldn't be bothered to argue; he'd had more than enough of threats and subterfuge and he longed for privacy and the refuge of home. It went against the grain to agree to their version of events, the whitewashing of Hank's past, the airbrushing of his links with the CIA, but for now he would keep quiet and toe the official line. He knew that his life was no longer his own, that his and Petra's adventure would capture the public imagination, that the vultures that were circling around the corpse of his reputation would demand their pound of flesh, but they would have to wait for now – he had more important things to do.

Robin and Joe had come to a mutually beneficial arrangement. Robin needed a job and Joe needed an agent that he could trust to field the incessant questions and requests for interview.

'Please be patient, my client has just had a life-saving operation and he needs time to recuperate. We would appreciate it if you would give him and his companion some space and we will accommodate selective interviews when they are ready and not before. Please leave me your cards and I'll be in touch.' Robin was a natural.

The flight home was spent in quiet reflection, the whole sorry tale replayed endlessly in their minds, as if it had all happened to someone else. There was palpable relief that the nightmare was finally over and that Hank couldn't hurt them anymore, at least no more than he already had.

Petra sobbed with relief as they stepped back onto UK soil, then glared angrily at Joe when his comforting arm on hers was snapped by the first paparazzi photographer they encountered.

'When are you going to learn?' she said, as Robin stood between them and led them through the terminal.

The next day saw a pale and contrite Joe walking on the beach with Louise. Instinctively, he lobbed a pebble as the sun glinted off a camera lens behind a rock. What was he doing? This was one picture he wouldn't mind appearing in the papers. Louise looked tired and stressed and Joe looked weak and defeated, all the fight gone from his body and soul.

'So, do you think you can simply come back and pick up where we left off?' said Louise. 'I'm genuinely glad to see you home and safe, but how dare you put us through that and expect to just waltz back in to our lives.'

'I'm not presuming anything. I just want to explain and then it's up to you. You can ask Petra and Robin what happened if you don't believe me. All I know is that I love you, Emma and Jamie, and you're all that I've thought about throughout this whole nightmare.'

'But we can't live like this, Joe,' she said in frustration, 'with the press watching our every move. We'd found anonymity here, Emma and Jamie were just getting settled again and now you're back with the whole media circus that follows you.'

'But the world's our oyster, Louise. We can go wherever we wish. Petra says that the book's bound to sell in the States with all the publicity and there'll be renewed interest here too; then there'll be the follow-ups, the Lellow Hitamapotamus, Uncle Ray's diaries.'

'The Lellow Hitamapotamus? What the hell's that?'

'It's written for Emma and Jamie; it's going to be huge.'

Louise shook her head. 'It's not what I want, Joe. I want our old life back. We were doing OK, weren't we, before all this? I'm sorry, but I don't want to live our lives in the public eye;. I think we should have a trial separation. You wanted fame and fortune. Well, now you've got it and I hope you'll be very happy together.'

'A trial separation? Isn't that what we've just had? One thing I've learnt from this experience is that the only place I want to be is by your side and I don't care where on this planet that may be. Believe me, if I could wave a magic wand and put things back together, then I would. Listen, all the publicity will die down when the dust settles. The press are very fickle, you know; they'll soon get bored with me, just like you have.'

'Oh, Joe, I'm not bored with you,' sighed Louise; 'you're probably more interesting now than you've ever been. It's not you I don't want, it's all the baggage. How do you think those pictures in the paper made me feel? Even though you say they were a set-up, how do I know there are not more to come?'

Joe flinched; with the CIA holding those stag weekend pictures, he knew he couldn't promise anything.

'Please don't do this, Louise,' he pleaded; 'what about Emma and Jamie? They need their old dad, don't they?'

'I'm not going to stop you seeing them; we'll just have to work out a time and place away from the spotlight.'

'You've obviously given this a lot of thought,' he said. 'Can I see them now? I've missed them so much.'

'Not now, Joe. I need to prepare them first. They don't even know you're back yet; maybe tomorrow.'

'And what about you? If this is a trial separation, is there a maybe tomorrow?'

'I don't know, Joe. Perhaps, given time; but at the moment I can't separate the anger and hurt from my feelings for you.'

'You know I couldn't believe my luck when I met you,' said Joe; 'always knew you were too good for me, of course, but when you agreed to be my wife I was the happiest man in the world. I'll be waiting for you, for as long as it takes, because I know there's no-one else I want.'

A devastated Joe and a philosophical Robin booked into the luxurious five-star seafront hotel, a big step up from the run-down B & Bs of Joe's earlier jaunt, but still just another lonely venue on the Joe Stamford world tour.

'So, is this part of the job description, picking up the pieces after you've screwed up yet another relationship?' asked Robin, as he downed his first pint.

'Seem to recall you used to do that for free,' replied Joe. 'Listen, thanks mate, thanks for believing in me when no-one else did.'

'Hey, that's what friends are for, isn't it?' said Robin, elbow on bar. 'Another beer?'

'Yes, I think so, don't you?'

36. Who's Gonna Shoe Your Pretty Little Feet?

Laura Bisham has resigned her position as Labour MP amid rumours of a second sexual encounter at Greenham Common. She is currently working on her autobiography.

Sandy is still happily married and her two daughters are growing up to look just like her. She occasionally drops into conversation that she once knew Joe Stamford.

Rebecca is also happily married with three children and has chosen to forget that she ever set eyes on that no good son of a bitch.

Harry Vance took the decision to resign from the CIA and is now enjoying working on his father's farm in Iowa.

Maurice Schneider returned to Bushville, where he has taken on the corrupt politicians and insists on administering the law without interference.

Paul Hooper was sacked for spending a few extra days in New Orleans, thereby delaying the return of the van to the hire company. He now works for a top private detective agency in New York, his dream job gained as a result of adding his part in the pursuit of Hank Schneider to his CV.

Joe is currently living in Greenwich Village in an apartment he shares with Robin. The collaboration with Deanna on the US translation of 'That Bloody Book' proved to be a great success, mainly due to Joe's high media profile and the curiosity of the American public.

In between flights back to England to see his children, he spends his time writing and taking in the Village atmosphere.

'The Lellow Hitamapotamus' has been released to widespread critical acclaim and Emma and Jamie are very proud that they've had a book written especially for them. Some reviews have questioned whether there is a political slant, due to the chapter in which the lellow hitamapotamus collaborates with the blue snake to defeat the red mouse.

Louise is planning on taking the children to New York for a holiday and maybe spending some time as a family again. Joe has asked her to help him write 'Uncle Ray's Diaries'.

Joe is also considering an offer to work on a screenplay for a Hollywood movie called 'Hank's Revenge', directed by Martin Scorsese.

Petra is also a regular visitor to Greenwich Village, where she is working on the set-up of a New York branch of Embryo Publishing. She has been seen in restaurants and cafes accompanied by Robin, who has thus far steadfastly refused to wear the camouflage jacket that she brought as a birthday present.

... and the Mayor of New Orleans is not really from West Yorkshire!!

Soundtrack

KC and the Sunshine Band – Get Down Tonight

Mott the Hoople – Hymn For The Dudes

Roxy Music – Virginia Plain

David Bowie - The Prettiest Star

The Who – My Generation

Smokey Robinson and the Miracles – Tears Of A Clown

Sam and Dave – Soul Man

Roy Orbison – Only The Lonely

The Rolling Stones – Get Off Of My Cloud

The Kinks – Waterloo Sunset

Manfred Mann - Do Wah Diddy Diddy

The Who – Won't Get Fooled Again

Pulp – Do You Remember The First Time

The Clash – White Man In Hammersmith Palais

The Buzzcocks – Love You More

Steel Pulse – Handsworth Revolution

Al Stewart – Year Of The Cat

Nick Lowe – What Lack Of Love Has Done

Billy Fury – Halfway To Paradise

Michael Jackson – Rockin' Robin

Tom Waits – Blue Valentines

Bruce Springsteen – 4th Of July Asbury Park (Sandy)

The Smiths – How Soon Is Now?

Tom Petty and the Heartbreakers – Even The Losers

Linda Ronstadt – Hasten Down The Wind

Tom Waits – Tell It To Me

Groove Armada – By The River

The Dixie Cups – Going To The Chapel

The Rascals – A Beautiful Morning

The Animals – We've Gotta Get Out Of This Place

Jungle Book – The Bare Necessities

The Clash – Working For The Clampdown

The Beat – Whine And Grine/Stand Down Margaret

The Clash – London Calling

Elvis Costello – Every Day I Write The Book

The Jam – The Girl On The Phone

Bruce Springsteen – The Ghost Of Tom Joad

The The – This Is The Day

John Otway – A413 Revisited

Lou Reed – Walk On The Wild Side

Paul Simon – Take Me To The Mardi Gras

The Undertones – Teenage Kicks

Ricky Nelson – Lonesome Town

David Bowie - Starman

The Beatles - Hey Jude

Elvis Presley - Are You Lonesome Tonight?

The Dubliners – The Leaving Of Liverpool

The Dubliners and the Pogues – The Irish Rover

Shane McGowan – Danny Boy

Ian Dury and the Blockheads – There Ain't Half Been Some Clever Bastards

Marvin Gaye – I Heard It Through The Grapevine

Seasick Steve – Back In The Doghouse

Gilbert O'Sullivan – Alone Again, Naturally

Altered Images – Don't Talk To Me About Love

David Bowie – Fame
Van Morrison – And The Healing Has Begun
Billy Bragg – Blake's Jerusalem
Elvis Costello – Fish 'n' Chip Paper
Ronnie Lane – The Poacher
Doll By Doll – Gypsy Blood
Marvin Gaye – Wherever I Lay My Hat
Bruce Springsteen – Trapped
Bruce Springsteen – Darkness On The Edge Of Town
The Specials – Ghost Town
Bernard Cribbins – The Hole In The Ground
Elvis Presley – All Shook Up
Van Morrison – I'm Tired, Joey Boy
Chuck Berry – Promised Land
Bob Dylan – Subterranean Homesick Blues
John Hiatt – Drive South
Creedence Clearwater Revival – Bad Moon Rising
The Jackson Five – I Found That Girl
Nicky Thomas – Have A Little Faith
Ian Dury and the Blockheads – What A Waste
Malcolm McClaren – Buffalo Gals
Tammy Wynette – Stand By Your Man
Muddy Waters – I Can't Be Satisfied
The Coral – Pass It On
Gene Pitney – Town Without Pity
Sparks – This Town Ain't Big Enough For The Both Of Us
The Carpenters – Goodbye To Love
Johnny Cash – Ring Of Fire
Tami Lynn – I'm Gonna Run Away From You
Emmylou Harris – Crescent City
The Temptations – Papa Was A Rollin' Stone
The Marcels – Blue Moon
Ricky Valance – Tell Laura I Love Her

Ella Fitzgerald – Stormy Weather
Fats Domino – Walkin' To New Orleans
Dion and the Belmonts – Teenager In Love
Bob Dylan – Shelter From The Storm
The Everly Brothers – Crying In The Rain
Frank Sinatra – My Way
Grandmaster Flash and the Furious Five – The Message
The Jackson Five – Maybe Tomorrow
Richard Hawley – Who's Gonna Shoe Your Pretty Little Feet?